Growing

Ted Mieszczanski

Part III of III

*"Mickey Mantle don't care about you.
Why should you care about him?
Nobody cares."*

from A Bronx Tale

Growing Up BX, Tevye's Story

Published by CreateSpace an Amazon Company, 2017

Printed in the United States of America.

Dedication

I dedicate this book as I must dedicate all my good works and deeds to my departed mother, Raizle Mieszczanski, and my father, Abram Mieszczanski. Whatever unworthy things I've done, those deeds are mine, and mine alone. My mother and father taught me right from wrong just as a parent should. I chose to do the rest.

I wish to also recognize the passing of a woman very dear to me, Mrs. Shifra Isbey. Sadly, Shifra, my mother's dear friend recently passed. She happily became a second mother to me and a step-grandmother to my children. Her daughters, Lusia Isbey-Harrison and Mara Isbey have always been family to me. They are my sisters.

I also dedicate this book to my dear departed father-in-law, "Duke" Bedellmus Downing and all the many Downings and Skinners who lived their lives with love, strength and compassion despite the unfair legacy of four hundred years of oppression. For all of them I say, "God is good!" but I myself cannot in conscience echo, "All the time."

I also want to dedicate this book to the living. First to my wonderful wife, Myra who shows me every single day that love is stronger than hate, and that "I" is nowhere as important as, "WE". I marvel at her generous heart. You are the best thing that ever happened to me.

See, now you have it in writing.

I dedicate this book as well to all the Downings in body and spirit whether near or far; Rachel, Aaron, Daniel, Linda, Al, Wayne, Janice, Gerald, Timaria, Trianna, Morgan, Audrey, Will, Will Jr., Siobhan, Aja, Carmelo, The William Wheeler family, Frieda, Frank, Tawnya, Darren, Kaaren, Geri and a special thank you to Lillie Mae

and Joe Watson who believed in me as a writer and as a Downing. Whoever else I may have missed, love ya!
Oh yeah, thank you Smokey Robinson for a lifetime of music!

It's BETTER THEN EVER being a Downing!
"God is good!" Okay, most of the time!

Most important of all in regard to THIS particular book is my mother-in-law, Mrs. Catherine Skinner-Downing. She was the one who kept after me to take, "Tevye's Story" off the dusty shelf and bring it back to life. "I like your first book about the two boys best!"

Thank you Miss Cat! And here it is. I dedicate this book to you!

Finally, I dedicate this story to all the children in the public schools of our great cities. You are entitled to the same decent education my wife and I both were given. Unfortunately, you have to struggle to obtain what is your right. To you I say it is not always an easy journey but it IS a worthwhile one.

Make friends with positive values, even if those friends are only your books. Choose those friends wisely. Knowledge may betray you, wisdom never will.

READ! READ! READ!

Live your own precious dreams and stop watching someone else's nightmares.

Author's note

If you picked this book up looking for Part II of Star Crossed, you will have to wait a little bit longer. This book is actually Part III, Tevye, Raizle and Leib's son's story. And so it is named, "Growing Up BX, Tevye's Story.

As you read it you will also notice that it is written in a different style and with a different, "voice" then Star Crossed." The chapters do not alternate going back and forth between different characters as they did in "Star Crossed." That is because it was written in 2003.

When I first retired from the NYC public school system I was a bit lost. That is an entirely normal thing for a new retiree. I didn't play golf, tennis, cards, shoot pool or bowl. I did take long walks all around the most interesting city in the world. It was during one such journey I realized I had to re-invent myself.

I tried a multitude of things and found that going to the gym, Tai Ji, dance classes with my wife and a regular weekly lunch date with my fellow ROMEOs filled up most of my time. But something was still missing. Over the course of my life and career in the south Bronx I'd learned a few things about how children survive and even flourish in tough environments. After all, I'd begun as a non-English speaker and had lived and worked my entire life on these same sometimes "mean" streets. As I said I love the idea of public schools. The reality of learning inside of them is tougher than one might think, but not impossible.

And so I sat down to write a fictional book that would have some necessary good survival practices embedded within it. It was a simple effort at creating a story that emphasized the importance of good friends, family, scholarship, solid ambitions, resisting negative peer pressure, anti-racism, the importance of independent thinking, valuing your dreams and trusting in wisdom as opposed to simply worshiping technology.

The real trick was to make it as palatable as possible. I did my best but as most early efforts do I filed it away in a closet (Yes, it was done on paper!) as a failed first attempt.

Later in 2017 when I finished the first part of Star Crossed (Yes, I first envisioned it at first as two books, one taking place in Europe, the second one in America) I came to realize two things. First, I was not going to write Star Crossed, Part II, Raizle and Leib's lives in America because it just hurt too much. Too many tears had already been shed writing Part one. Truth is I had several chapters of Book II mapped out in my head but then I couldn't go forward with writing it. Maybe someday it will feel better. I can't do it right now.

But curiously about then I realized I had already written another book about these same people. It was sitting up on a shelf waiting there patiently to be rediscovered. I'd written it in 2003 and it was entitled, Growing Up BX. It was my first attempt at writing.

So I hope this explains the difference in style within Growing Up Bx, Tevye's Story. While the story is a simple one I truly hope it offers a few answers to some of our children's problems. In any case I hope you all enjoy it.

As for Star Crossed, Part II, I will not say never, just not right now.

Ted Mieszczanski

Introduction

In my mind's eye I can still see him in front of me as clearly as if it were all happening today. My mother has said to me that, he, she and I, we are somehow related. Was it that he was my mother's uncle or maybe only a distant cousin? No matter, I'm told to just call him Uncle Joe, but neither one of us, he or I, believes that. That's made very clear to me as he moves around the house avoiding me as if I were a piece of small furniture.

I can see him just sitting there in the living room by the same window every single day.

What is it that he's looking for?

It can't be much because what's outside could be a painting on a wall for all the movement there is out there in the street. But still, every day he sits there, unmoving, staring and thinking.

Yes, I'm young, but even at my age I know he isn't seeing anything with his eyes. No, he's looking through a different window at another world, one in which I do not exist. He's there lost in his past living another life over again. Here, in this room, he's just waiting.

I'm just a little boy, left at home exploring the possibilities of a large empty apartment. Each day it is he and I, alone with only each other. And there he is. A big bent over bony old man sitting here with his hands clasped over one another, just waiting. Still, as I explore the rough lines and ridges of those folded hands with my small fingertips I have to wonder about the stories that are attached to the bumps and calluses.

He brought us here from out of despair in Germany right after the war, but he never says anything at all to me. All I get is an occasional pat on the head before he turns to stare out his window again.

Each day is no different. I amuse myself by playing with his scarred hands and he lets me do that. Then he ignores me to stare out of the window listening to his voices from the past.

I wish that just one time he might have told me one of his stories. It might have taught me something I needed to know, or maybe, possibly, given me some much needed comfort. But Uncle Joe was who he was, a quiet man who didn't share his life with four year olds. Apparently that is one more thing I haven't quite gotten over yet.

But that was then, and this is now! Here is some of my story, and perhaps, there is something here that may help you.

Tevye

Chapter 1

The ball's rhythmic beat on blacktop pulls me along like a junkie straight on to the courts. It isn't anything like the sound a band's drum makes. No, to me it's a lot more like the beating of a heart, my heart. Only those souls who are hoop-addicted can appreciate that sound. To us the rhythm of the rock being pounded in a playground is as enticing as the smell of French fries on a Coney Island boardwalk. We love this game!

Damn, I hope I get next! *What am I saying? I just hope I get to play today!*

I'd make the same silent wish every single day while rounding the corner of 170th Street at half speed. It was getting later on in the afternoon, about four, and I'd had to race home first to drop off the dry cleaning my mother had asked me to pick up.

Lucky for me nobody was home so in just a few minutes I was back out the apartment door, racing down the steps and headed towards one of the best places on earth, the basketball courts in the schoolyard behind huge Taft High School. Not to close, not to far, they were about three big blocks away.

Around that corner I zipped, but as the schoolyard came into sight I froze. The only ones playing inside the fence this afternoon were, "colored" kids.

Most days, if the weather was any good, there were always lots of games happening on all the five basketball courts. But there was always one going on over on the farthest court where the best ballers played. That game was often all "colored" or "black." Sometimes it was hard to know which word to use to keep people from getting mad at you.

Once in a while the best white guys from another court would mix in to that big game, but usually that game stayed "black." On the next court over you had the good white players and that game would sometimes have a few black players mixed into it. The other three courts were totally mixed up with all different kinds of colors, abilities and friendships. That's where I played with some of the guys from my block. The biggest problem for me was that my friends were all baseball players who only shot hoops to have a little fun. I was the only one who had the, "sickness". I needed to fire up a basketball every single day.

Yeah, so since I was totally and completely hooked on hoops not owning my own basketball, because my mother always told me that was a silly waste of money, I always hoped to see one of my buddies who did own a ball.

On most days I'd see someone I knew in the schoolyard with his ball and then I would get to play. But on some other days there would be no one I knew there. I knew I wasn't good enough to play on that far away court. So to me what I saw was almost the same as if there was no one there.

On that particular day I wanted to play so badly my fingers were itching, but as I saw that the only court filled was the far one I knew I had a problem. And there was also another even bigger problem. At least my mother had always acted like it was a big problem. But then when you're a kid you always have to keep in mind what your mother says, right?

"Tevye, stay with your own kind. Stay away from the goyim, the gentiles! Stay away from the Irish, stay away from the Italians, stay away from the Spanish and, most of all, stay away from the Negros, "the schvartzes!"

I didn't really know why I was supposed to stay away from all these different kinds of people; well that's not altogether true. Actually, I had a pretty fair idea about that. Sometimes when I was on the way to school there would be different groups of kids hanging around on corners just waiting for us to pass by.

Yeah, it could get bad! Sometimes when we'd go by them they'd call us names, nasty names like, "Yid, Jew Boy, or Kike. It was hard, embarrassing, even painful to hear that. I didn't have any idea what I'd done to be so hated. All of us, we'd hang our heads down low, stare at the ground and walk on a little faster. That happened even when the kids calling us names were our own size, pretty small. We'd do the same thing. Lower our heads, pretend not to hear and walk as fast as we could.

One time I asked a friend why we did that even when the kids "sounding" us out were smaller than us. His answer was simple: they had big brothers who would come and beat the crap out of us if we lifted a finger against their little monster brothers and cousins. And as it turns out he was completely right.

Sometimes those gangs would punch us just for the fun of it and then we'd have to run. They'd chase after us, hitting and cursing us from behind as we ran.

"Hey Yid, Jew Boy! You killed Christ!"

They'd howl at us like dogs barking after rabbits. But then the absolute worst things happened when they cornered us. Then they'd line us up against a building wall like we were criminals in a movie and they were the cops. I still remember the feel of those hard red bricks pushing up against my back; the wall's coldness bringing on jolts of electric fear each time one of those bullies touched me. But I also knew if I said one thing, anything at all, I was going to be hit in the face or kneed in the stomach.

Then they'd go through our pockets and steal our milk money and toys, stuff like soldiers or yo-yos. And anything they found that they didn't want got thrown on the ground and stepped on.

God forbid you were unlucky enough to have a Hebrew school yarmulke in your pocket: that entitled you to some very special attention. Then it became a double dose of, "You dirty Jews nailed Christ to the cross, you're Christ killers!"

When I heard those words icy tendrils would shoot through my lower body. I knew at that exact second someone was going to get hurt and I selfishly prayed that it wasn't going to be me. I remember my friend, Sammy, being pushed, yanked and punched three long blocks all the way to school, while we, his friends, trailed behind miserably, heads down, doing nothing, saying nothing. But you know what? The really sad thing inside was that we were still kind of glad it wasn't us getting beaten up.

At times it was hard to figure out which was worse, the icy pangs of fear, the pain of being hit or the feeling of being made to be so small. But then this one time it wasn't the same. I don't know why it wasn't, but it wasn't, and that day changed everything for me.

Chapter Two

Back in those days I loved to read even more than I do now. Maybe it's because all we had at home was a radio and that wasn't enough of the world to satisfy me. So I'd go to the library at least once a week and take out four or five books each and every time. Then one day my world experienced a terrible disaster. It was earth shaking as far as I was concerned. The library, my library, the Melrose Branch on Morris Avenue and 162nd Street, was suddenly closed.

Why, you ask? Well, so did I?

It was being closed for six months of renovations. But there was another library located my teacher said in the next neighborhood over, Highbridge. Unfortunately that was like a forbidden foreign country to us. The journey to there began when you crossed a huge boundary line, a giant two way street called the Grand Concourse.

My other problem was that this other library was not only way over on the other side of the Concourse, it was also way up on a high ridge only reachable by climbing several flights of stone steps. And, unfortunately for us, the stone steps switchback could only be approached from one direction, 169th Street. Any other way into Highbridge would take you five or six long blocks around in either direction. But even all this wasn't the whole problem. We, the kids in our neighborhood all knew Highbridge was a tough place for us. We knew that from going to our school, PS90.

Over in that neighborhood near the stone steps there was a gang of street bullies who'd pick on anyone their age or smaller if they dared to trespass down, "their" street. BUT their street was now the only way to the public library.

It wasn't fair. It wasn't right!

But as we say that's just the way the cookie crumbles.

I just wanted my books. So I decided to risk trying to sneak across those forbidden blocks crossing my fingers that "they" wouldn't be around. And that idea did kind of work for a while. If I saw their gang coming, I'd calmly cross the street as fast as I could and then try to make myself so tiny and insignificant that

I wouldn't be noticed. I'd even try to think small thoughts to make myself shrink even more!

Strange as it sounds stuff like that worked, that is until this one time when it didn't.

Foolishly that day I'd taken my little brother, David with me. I don't really remember if I thought he'd act as camouflage and that they'd take even less notice of us, or maybe I thought they weren't going to be around, so it wouldn't really matter. I got careless.

Big mistake.

My mother had told me over and over hundreds of times, "Never leave your little brother alone. Always take him with you!" But I knew she also meant don't take him on any dangerous trips into different neighborhoods.

So, right across the Grand Concourse, straight down West 169th Street we went heading towards the stone steps to climb up to a completely different neighborhood, Highbridge. I remember getting a strange look from a bunch of kids sitting on top of some car hoods across the street as we began climbing those steps to the Woodycrest Library, but I let it pass.

Hadn't I made this trip safely five or six times already?

I was feeling pretty confident. That was another big mistake. I silently repeated to myself the words I'd heard my father's say on many an occasion;

From your mouth to God's ears! Yeah, right!

So then there we were. My brother David and I were quickly moving along on the way down the steps from the library. We were busy talking about what we'd both just taken out. Each one of us had an armful of books, but getting home wasn't going to be as simple as getting up had been.

At the base of the steps four of them stepped out into our way and blocked us from going any further. First they just surrounded us. Then they quickly closed in and yanked all the books out of my hands.

Their ringleader was a tall skinny bully I knew from 90's schoolyard named Sean. He collected all my books together and then carefully, one at a time, held each book up high while reading the title out loud; The Black Stallion, King Arthur and the Knights of the Round Table, and so on. He laughed then threw each book into the gutter. The final insult was kicking them all, one by one, underneath a parked car.

I was so scared I couldn't move a muscle to save my beloved books. Then they tried to take my little brother's books too, but David refused to let them go. Finally, one of the other bullies lost his patience and yanked his books away. David didn't think about size or anything else, he jumped on the one who had grabbed his books to get them back. That thug punched at him once and I saw right away my little brother had begun crying deep sobs as he turned and ran to me. He was only in the third grade and they were in at least the seventh or eighth grades.

Suddenly, as if by signal all of them started punching at both of us. All I could do was put one arm up to try to keep from getting hit in the face and keep my other arm wrapped tight around my brother to keep him close. I could feel David's arms wrapped tightly around me as he buried himself up against me.

Maybe that icy lump of fear stuck deep in my chest mixed together with the pain I felt in my heart because something happened inside of me, and it made me feel something new. There was a terrible hot lump of anger, burning, spreading out in my chest. Rage had discovered me. But at the very same time I also felt I was being held tight in a fist of an icy coldness. I had discovered hate and I knew I'd never felt anything like it before. It drove away all the crippling fear.

So this is what it's like not to be afraid all the time, a voice within me whispered. Don't you like it? Let them be afraid of you!

It continued on seductively. At that moment I could've killed someone. I was so angry I'd begun crying hot tears, but this new coldness stopped them instantly. Only their dried up trail was left on my face.

The anger changed me. I'd never hit a person with a fist in my entire life, but now I was ready to lash out. And so I began to fight. When my closed fist punched Sean in his face he jumped back surprised. I must have hit him pretty hard, because I saw something in his eyes I'd never seen before. It was the same thing

I'd felt when Sean first looked at me. That thing in his eyes was very, very familiar.

I'd just never seen it in someone else's face.

There it was in his eyes, that miserable emotion that'd robbed me of so much comfort, my intimate companion, fear. But this time it wasn't clawing its way from up inside of me. No, now it was in the eyes of the bully standing in front of me!

He was afraid of me! I could feel it. Even if I couldn't believe it!

I started swinging punches at him, deliberate punches. That icy coldness was now in control of every part of my mind and it made me see more clearly than I'd ever seen things before.

I'd seen some fights in the streets and imitated the fighters throwing punches in my bedroom mirror more than once. Now I was moving my arms like I'd practiced. I kept my dukes up high and my elbows out. My fists were clenched so tight the knuckles stood out like sharp boney hills. A decision was already made in my mind.

I'd ignore any pain and wouldn't care how much I hurt myself, or anyone I hit. I was going to punch as hard as I could.

My nails were digging deep into my palms. And I also swore to myself I wouldn't cry no matter what!

Strangely, Sean wasn't trying to get any closer even though his fists were up too and he looked ready to fight. For a few seconds he stared straight into my eyes. Then he glanced over to the right, and then to the left. I guess he didn't like what he saw because the next thing I heard was aimed at his friends in the circle.

"Hey man, help me mess up this crazy little kike!" while turning his head from side to side.

"What's the matter Sean? He too much Jew boy for you to handle? You afraid Hymie, the Hebe is going to hit you with a salami?" mocked a voice from behind me.

The next thing I knew there was a heavy weight pushing down hard on my back. I could feel thin arms reaching around me trying to pin my arms to my sides. Another thicker arm wrapped around my neck and tightened as it tried to pull me backwards and down. A shock ran through my body as I realized somebody, maybe two somebodies, was riding my back. But whoever it was felt no different than my little brother jumping on my back for a ride. He wasn't heavy at all. I rose upwards and threw my shoulder forward and then dipped downward. Somebody fell right over me. I couldn't speak a single word, but then I had absolutely nothing to say.

"Well, well, it looks like we have Super Jew here," jeered someone to the crowd. But even as they insulted me not a single one came any closer. What they did do was form a circle around the two of us, David and me. I kept my fists up and my feet moving. Holding David by my side we circled around each other as I edged the fight up the sidewalk towards the Grand Concourse, the street that separated the Jewish neighborhood from where we had come from.

Some grown ups on the street stood by and watched, then stepped back out of the way. I don't know why no one tried to stop the fight or even said a word to help us. There were four of them and only two of us.

Maybe the people in the street were afraid too?

After every few steps one of the gang would feint in as if to fight, but something inside spoke to me.

Look right in his eyes. Don't take your eyes away from his!

Some of the same faces that haunted me every day on the way to school were now right in my face. I knew if I flinched, put my fists down or cried, I was dead.

It seemed like forever before we finally got to the Concourse. Without looking at the traffic lights David and I started quickly walking across. I thought a miracle had happened and we were going to make it, but even then it wasn't over. What the gang did then was pick up small rocks and start throwing them at us.

Now we were running through traffic. Even when a stone caught me in the leg I pretended it had missed and kept going. I kept walking even though I could feel something wet under my pants' leg. But I wouldn't stop. It was like I'd read in King Arthur. The king in those days wore red so if he was wounded the blood wouldn't show. Weakness only encouraged the enemy, like now I knew if we stopped we'd start crying and then they'd race across the street and hurt us some more. Finally, finally, we were across the eight-lane street that separated our neighborhoods. We were safe.

But deep inside I still knew I'd have to go back over there. I couldn't ever give up my library books! I also knew who'd be there waiting unless I could somehow outwit them. And no matter how many times I avoided them I also knew sooner or later they'd get me again.

I guess that's why mom said, "Stay with your own kind!"

That day she'd been right.

Chapter Three

"Here's your books!" spoke out an unfamiliar voice from behind me.

Oh no, they've followed me. It's not over yet. I'm over! This is what I'd thought at first as a new wave of cold fear gripped me. All the fight had seeped out of my body while I was running across that street holding on to my brother, David's hand. I had nothing left inside of me to fight with. As I turned around to see where'd the voice had come from I was expecting knuckles to smash into my face. With my eyes tightly shut I yelled at my brother to run home as fast as he could. And with my leg hurting me so much I knew it was impossible for me to run away. I could barely take another step without a sharp pain shooting through my bleeding calf. There was no escape this time. I knew I was about to get hurt. Panic grabbed me by the throat as I turned my arm up towards the sky to stop the fist I knew was aimed at my face.

"C'mon man, put your arm down. I ain't gonna hurt you!"

My forearm slowly slipped down and I saw a slim black kid about my own height standing in front of me. He didn't look angry at all, but my tongue was still stuck to the dry roof of my mouth.

"These books in this here bag," he questioned me again slowly. "Don't you want 'em?"

"What do you know about my books?" I stammered looking into the round face of a kid who seemed to be just about my own age.

"I know you just swung your way out of a pretty good ass-lickin' from those dam' crackers 'cross the street. And why does your little brother still look like he's runnin' for his life? I'm not gonna hurt him."

"Is he gonna be bringing trouble back here 'cause you know I'm only trying to do you a solid here! So, do you want'em, or not?" asked the brown-skinned kid standing in front of me.

He reached down into the brown paper shopping bag he was carrying and started by handing me, "I, Robot." And before another minute had passed he'd given me back all ten of the library books taken away from me, my brother's and my own; The same books that I'd last seen scattered and kicked underneath cars parked blocks away.

Pointing to, "I, Robot," my book rescuer casually dropped, "That's a pretty good series. Asimov really writes some wild stuff. You read any of his other books?"

I didn't have an answer for that. A few minutes ago a bunch of Jew-hating creeps were beating the crap out of me. Now here was this really nice black guy returning my most valuable possessions and then asking me questions about the books I loved.

Just how do I handle this?

Truth was that outside of the basketball courts I'd really never spoken more than a sentence or two to anyone who was black. I kind of assumed what everyone else, including my parents and friends had said about them was true. That was that they, black people, had their own ways that were very different from ours and, most important of all, they hated us. Now here was someone black asking me if I enjoyed one of my favorite authors as much as he did.

He had saved my books and liked them too?

Now that was very, very cool!

"Well, thanks for saving my books. I didn't even think about 'em…" I lied unconvincingly.

"Yeah, well, it's not like you really had a chance to. You were kind of busy saving your own ass," he chuckled.

"How do you know about that? And where did you get my books from?"

After a deep searching stare, he replied, "I guess what they say about white people is true for Jewish people too. You don't know me, do you? You don't even recognize me?"

I thought furiously for a very long instant.

How do I know him? Oh shit, I'm really messing up now! This guy obviously knew me and, boy, was I looking bad!

Totally embarrassed I sadly shrugged my shoulders. I had no answer to give him except that I was obviously pathetic!

"Sorry, man. Where is it I know you from?"

Maybe it's from playing softball in the park? Might be?

I thought hard still searching for some connection.

After giving me another probing stare the slim young man slowly shook his head first left and then right, and then sadly said, "Man, my uncle was right. We are invisible to y'all. Just like in the title of that book he keeps pushing me to read."

That perked up my ears!

"What book is that?"

Anything about a good book was always interesting to me. Besides I wanted to keep talking to this guy. He'd saved my life by coming up with my lost books. I would've had to pay for all of them or lost my library card. My family definitely didn't have that kind of money to spare. My library days might've been over and out right there.

And on top of all that he also liked books that I liked.

Now that had all kinds of interesting possibilities!

None of my friends cared a bit about any of the stuff I liked to read about. Actually most of them didn't even like to read much of anything but the newspaper's sports pages. But it happened that one of my most favorite subjects was spaceships and aliens Maybe it was from all that "shoot 'em up," stuff we played when we were little. I mean I loved any stories or movies about outer space. The "I, Robot," series was definitely one of my favorites and here was someone else who'd actually read and enjoyed something I'd really liked.

Wow! This guy was super interesting!

"What book was it your uncle mentioned?" I asked nervously, hoping he would slip in some information that would help me figure out where I knew my benefactor from.

'It's called, "The Invisible Man." My uncle says that all white people don't even see black people. Yeah, we're, "black" now, not "colored" anymore, exceptin' when you want us to do somethin' for you. He's always poppin' off at the mouth saying stuff like that. My mom says it's because he's just never been around enough different kinds of people to see the real truth. I kind of thought my mom's way up 'til right now. Seein' you being picked on by those shitheads… they try to do that same bullshit to me whenever they catch me alone… But maybe I was wrong and my uncle's right!"

"Man, I sit two seats back and four rows over from you in Mrs. Stein's class at 90."

"That's right Teddy, I'm in your class but you don't even recognize me?"

"Blind-ass Jew boy!" he yelled as he turned away from me and stormed off down the street.

What can I say to that?

I didn't know. I was completely embarrassed. But before I could say, "Sorry," there was a loud noise coming from another direction. It rolled upwards from down the steep hill where my block, Grant Avenue was and it made me look way down towards that street.

My voice came back.

"Wait! Hold on a minute! Watch out!" I shouted towards my book rescuer who was headed off in that same direction.

Boiling up the street from the bottom of the hill two blocks away on Grant was a crowd of my angry neighbors, and running right up in front of that wild bunch was my completely crazed father.

You have to understand that my pop hadn't lived an easy life coming to America as a refugee. More than once he'd come home bruised up from his job as a blacksmith's helper. Yeah, I know it sounds crazy that people do that, but that's the only job he could get, He shoveled horseshit for a living. "Dreck," he called it.

He would always tell my mother he'd gotten hurt working with the horses at the stable, but I knew better. I recognized the marks that fighting left. Remember, I had been punched and kicked a few times too. He'd warned me many times not to trust anyone, especially if they weren't Jewish. And after that statement he usually repeated his long list of untrustworthy peoples that spiraled on and on downward.

I remember him once saying to me in Yiddish.

"I sweat blood for every penny I make! And then those," put in any non-Jewish group you want to, "try to take it away from me!"

But on the other hand, any poor soul who came up to my Tateh and said they were hungry always got something from him. He couldn't let anyone go hungry after going hungry himself.

Life can be confusing sometimes.

"Wilson, run, run!" I yelled as I rushed past him to cut off my father and his friends "at the pass!"

"Hey Teddy… you remembered my name!" the surprised black boy smiled as he stopped to look at me for a split second. Then without another word he ran by me like a bullet shot in the opposite direction and rounded the street's corner. When I turned and followed him a few steps up to the corner and looked for him, he was gone. He'd disappeared into the crowd filling up the Grand Concourse.

"Daddy, Tateh, no, no, no!" I shouted out as I turned and ran back down the hill towards the oncoming crowd.

"He's my friend. He's not the one who did it! He didn't hit us!"

It took me a few anxious minutes to explain I wasn't hurt and that Wilson had helped, not hurt us. My father finally calmed down. When we got back into our apartment a little bit later my Tateh sat down heavily in his favorite living room chair, the fancy blue brocaded one. He called me over to him with a gentle wave of his hand. Finally, with a puzzled expression on his face he asked me a few simple questions.

"Terry why did you have to go over into that neighborhood? You know you don't belong there. What's so important that you must get into fights over it?"

"My books, Tateh," I said.

He sat quietly and thought about my answer. Then he continued on slowly switching over into Yiddish.

"You know I don't read or write the English… only a little bit in Yiddish."

That was kind of painful.

Every boy wants his father to be strong, perfect. It was an embarrassing and hurtful moment for both of us. Staring downward at the worn yellow linoleum floor I answered quietly, "Yes, Tateh."

Then with a suddenly brightening expression he asked me, "Tevye, my son, do you know the difference between a shlemiel and a shlemozel?"

"Nope!" I answered happily in English recognizing he was telling me a joke that would lift us both up to a better place.

Well, to tell the truth that wasn't completely right either. My mother had once explained the meaning of both of these words to me after angrily calling me by both names when I'd embarrassed her with some really dumb mistakes in front of her friends.

"You see," she said later in her belated apology to me, "the shlemiel is the fool who wets the toilet seat because he isn't smart enough to pick up the seat when he pees, and the shlemozel is the unfortunate poor soul who sits on the wet seat."

But I wasn't going to spoil my Tateh's joke.

Still, I must have given something away somehow because he quickly went on after a little shrug to say, "Not important Tevye, not important, because when you crossed that big street, that border, you surpassed both the shlemiel and the shlemozel to become a ganse schmuck! Ask your Mameh to explain what that one is!" he roared with laughter.

"And also by the way, next time, don't go to the library without your Mameh! You understand me?"

Yeah, he'd gotten me again!

Once again I got to walk away from my Tateh after a hug and with a big stupid grin on my face.

Chapter Four

Another day, another bowl of oatmeal, that's what people say, right? So far this day was pretty much like any other, except I was a little late getting ready for school. All of my friends, the ones who I usually walked to school with, were already all the way down the block. They were turning the corner on 167th Street to walk up the hill towards PS 90 when I got outside. I started walking down the block a little faster because I didn't like being down at the far end of my block all by myself. The reason was a simple one. A nasty punk named Miles lived down there.

Miles was this big bully who picked on all the kids who were younger than him. It wasn't just that he was so big or tough. The neighborhood was full of guys way tougher than him, real rocks. What it was, was that he was vicious. Miles just liked to hurt people because somehow, and I'm not sure why, it made him feel better. But in a way you could tell it didn't make him a happier person. Still he would do that stuff anyway. He always started off by saying mean shit that made you feel small and then followed it up with hard punches to the back and stomach.

I hated him, but he also scared me a lot. Anyway, I couldn't do anything about it besides traveling in a large group or trying to avoid him. Every single day I breathed a deep sigh of relief when I got past the courtyard of his building. But that just wasn't gonna happen today.

"Hey there, lil' Jew boy! You, the one on da' way to school t'learn how t'count ya fadda's money? C'mere! Lemme see what ya got in y'pockets?"

Again I could feel icy fingers forming down at the base of my spine and then start to spread their way outward using my trembling bones as their road map. Worse, all of a sudden I had to pee!

"C'mere ya lil' Jewish fag! Yuh lost, lil Yankel? Don't ch'ya worry bout dat! I'll take y'blind ass t'school! Even betta', youse can show me th' way t'ya school. What'sa matta' muttsy, y'don' wanna walk down th' street wit' a "goy"? Dat's whatchew

Hebe's call us, right? What's dat y'sayin'? Y'sayin' y'don't wanna be my friend?"

My mouth was now getting so dry I could feel the bumps on my tongue. I just kept trying to walk a little bit faster and a little bit faster. Then I prayed that maybe he'd lose interest in torture and maybe let me go. Now I also had to pray for luck. And if I were lucky enough I would get only a hard shove or two with maybe a few added curses thrown in. After that possibility it usually meant getting hurt and some crying.

"I'm bettin' y'can walk all da' way t'school on dat line in d'sidewalk, jus' like one a d'fag typarope walka's in d'circus! But remember now, if y'steps off d'line I'll pound y'candy ass hard, y'lil' sissy Hebe!" hissed Miles evilly right in my ear so that only I could hear his threats.

I was so scared I tried to walk that line just a little bit faster at first, and then speeded up and ran, but I was still careful to be right on that line in the cement.

And then it came suddenly without any warning.

I felt the air leaving my chest almost at the same instant that I was caught up in an inner explosion. For a second there wasn't even any pain, and it seemed like time itself had slowed. And then, boom! I felt my back burst outward with pain like a round of fireworks had gone off in it and a pinwheel of hurt was spreading. And that's when the pain came back over and over again. I realized then I was being kicked while I was lying there on the ground. When I looked up and tried to make out what was happening I couldn't see anything. I was blinded by something in my eyes.

That's when it came to me that it was a flood of hot tears pouring out of my eyes cutting me off from the world.

"Oh, lil' Yid, lil' Yid, won't y'pleeze, pleeze tie ma' shoe while y'down d'ere!" rhymed Miles aloud giving me one last punch in my back.

I picked myself up off the ground ever so slowly, sobbing quietly because I'd learned if you cried too loudly it seemed to delight Miles… and then he wanted more pain. But somehow, somehow, inside of myself, I knew this wasn't over yet. So when I bent over to pick up my book bag I kind of expected another shove or kick. But what I hadn't expected was another punch from a fist viciously hitting me in the back of my head while I was stooped over.

Luckily, I didn't fall to the ground again because that would have brought more kicks, but everything did go dark for an instant. Staggering forward a few steps I tried to catch my balance.

That's exactly when I turned and swung as hard as I could.

I must have missed him by at least two feet. I'm not really sure how what happened next actually happened, but somehow, with that swing, our roles reversed. Without a single word said between us I began chasing Miles down the street with my fists balled up to punch and my feet ready to kick. And if I could've somehow reached out and bitten him I would've gladly done that too. I hated him, but I just couldn't catch up him. He was too big and moved too fast for me to catch.

I guess Miles was finally figuring things out in his own mind because he turned his head around as he ran and said, "If I wuz youse, I'd be runnin' d'otha' way. My pals are round d'corna' here and d'en it's y'ur Hymie ass dats gonna get beat."

I was getting tired and couldn't run much longer. But that's when it happened. It was like God spread open the clouds above us and spit way down on Miles. Someone seemed to accidently step into Miles' way and down he went. I jumped on top of him in that split second. And luckily for me he had fallen forwards on his face. Because before he could roll over and push me off I'd hit him as hard as I could with my fist in his back. Once, twice and then over and over again, my fists hammered away at him with all my might. That's when I heard something I'd only dared dreamed about. I couldn't believe what my ears were hearing it sounded so sweet! And I couldn't believe what I was seeing either.

Miles was wailing like a baby!

"Don' hit me no more. Stop! Pleeze don' hit me no more. I give, I give, stop it, stop it!" he cried his voice's rising eerily into a screechy scream.

I was exhausted now and breathing in ragged gasps. I could hardly get the air out of my lungs fast enough to let new air come in. Finally, I pushed myself up off him and had to lean against a parked car to keep myself from falling down.

As I looked over to my left I noticed someone was standing there very close to me. He was holding out what looked like my book bag to me.

"You dropped this," said a very serious Wilson. "I'm getting a little tired of walking behind you and picking up your books from all over the street!"

Miles, who'd slowly picked himself up off the ground was now picking up speed running back up the street. He stopped for a second, turned around and yelled something about he'd be seeing me later. And then I also heard him say something like, "And ya' black jigaboo buddy too!"

That's when I saw Wilson's face change and go completely hard with anger. He started in Miles' direction, but without thinking about it I reached out and held his arm. Wilson seemed to struggle within himself, but he didn't move any further in the direction Miles had disappeared. Then almost magically he turned around to me, smiled and said, "Hey, my man, let's get on to school."

Walking quickly along up the block towards 90, I turned to Wilson and asked him straight out, "Why did you help me? Especially after what happened the other day?"

"How do you figure I helped you? That dumb shithead happened to bump into me while he was runnin' away from you. He wasn't lookin' out for where he was goin' too good and tripped."

"Didn't see me, too bad for his ass, right?" Wilson asked quietly making an effort to keep his eyes focused straight ahead.

"Good try, but that can't be," I answered now thinking out loud in my best Hardy Boy mode. "You just handed me my book bag. How did you manage to pick it up and just happen to be far enough down the street to "accidently" bump into Miles? You would've had to run down the other side of the street pretty fast to get in front of us. Am I right or wrong Wilson?"

Wilson's innocent expression dissolved into laughter. "You know, you're pretty slick Teddy! And I see your memory has improved too! All of a sudden you know my name! And I can see you must also read a lot of detective books. I kind of like the Hardy Boys myself, even though they never have anyone black in their books."

"But you still haven't answered me. Why'd you help me?" I persisted.

Wilson stopped walking, turned to face me and put his finger in my chest. He started off by saying, "I'm really not sure why, man! I mean I really don't know… I was just walking to school on the other side of the street when I saw that punk start hittin' on you. I was goin' to keep walkin' on my way. You know, 'stay out of it! Who gives a crap if one white boy smacks another?' I told myself, but I saw him kick you when you was on the ground. Well, man I could feel that shit across the street. Miles and his crew are always picking on people when they're all alone."

"Yeah, that punk-ass ghost always likes to stop me and ask, "Why you walkin' down my block, blackie?" Sure as shit, that's only when I'm all by myself. Can you believe that bullshit? But if I'm with my brother or my boys he don't say shit to me. He's nothing but a fake ofay bitch! I wanted to see what he'd do if he had to face you when you got steamed up! That's why I tripped his runaway yellow behind!"

"I'm pretty sure you would have seen me get my ass kicked like always!"

"Maybe so, and maybe not, that sure didn't happen today now did it?" was Wilson's easy comeback. "You know Teddy, you got a little bit of heart' in here," he said, tapping my chest. "I like that. Well, come on then, my man! You gonna have to step it up a little bit so we can get to school. On time I don't wanna be late. My moms gets upset when the teacher calls home. Pick it up a little bit, will ya! Walk faster! And when we get to school, do me a solid. Go to the Boys Room and wash your face. Nobody wants to be seen hangin' with a crybaby."

Chapter Five

The walk to school went a lot better after that. I waited downstairs for Wilson to walk by my building in the mourning. At first it was a pretty big surprise. Wilson was sure to be there in front every day. He told me that meeting me helped him to be on time. And also, we both enjoyed the jokes on the way. He told me that picking me up helped him with getting up and out, and that he didn't want to be late to school anymore. It was something about he'd promised his mom to do better with that and everything else too.

Not exactly sure about what that means?

But that was definitely cool with me too because Miles never seemed to be waiting around his building anymore when Wilson and me were walking down the block together. Sometimes Wilson would be with a couple of his friends, but mostly he came down the block by himself. He said his friends didn't really like my block. Wilson said it was because there weren't any black people living on it. But then that didn't seem to bother him too much. In fact, he's the one who told me we were getting some funny looks when we walked down the street together. At first I didn't really think that was so. But he insisted it was and he'd tell me about it when it happened. When he finally said something to me as it was happening I saw then that he was right. We were getting some pretty weird looks. But then neither of us really cared that much as long as it was only a look. I knew I had more than just looks to worry about and the staring, well, it seemed to roll right off Wilson's back. He didn't really say much more about it. He was cool like that.

Sometimes he'd ask me a little bit about this person or that one later on in the day. At first we'd only get a chance to talk about stuff during recess. We sat too far apart in class during the day to talk to each other. I guess that was really a good thing because our yaps would definitely have gotten us into a whole lot more trouble.

"That lady, the really old one, who's always hanging out the first floor window of the yellow brick building on your block," he said to me one day at recess. "Is she wearing an ugly mask or does she just hate black folks?"

I had to laugh at that one. Wilson had a funny way of summing things up. She actually was a kinda funny looking old lady whose husband had died a long time ago. Her children had all grown up and moved far away to Long Island. Now they hardly ever came around to the Bronx to see her. So I guess she seemed kinda alone and lonely. As for her funny appearance, for some strange reason her lower lip hung down almost touching her chin. And when she spoke she would spray spit with almost every single sound she made. She was kinda old and I guess she probably didn't even realize she was doing it. So when she was talking you had to keep your distance and be ready to jump out of the way.

Her name was Sadie and for some reason of her own my Mameh really, really liked her. My Mameh even told me to call her "Tanta" Sadie, that's Aunt Sadie in Yiddish, even though we were not at all related. Just my luck I figured.

So every day, no matter whatever time I passed her window in the afternoon, she would always ask me, "Sonny boy, would you go to the store for me?" She always called me, "sonny boy" or, "boychik" even though she knew my name very well.

I think she liked to use that old lady thing to hide the fact she was still a pretty sharp cookie. In her own way she was always watching us and sometimes, I think, even testing us. It was kind of like a, "are you a mensch" test. You know, like to find out what kinda human being you were.

Maybe it was just my imagination, but I don't think so.

The kids on the block used to rhyme her name. "Sadie, Sadie, old lady," and then they'd try their best to run away whenever they saw her coming our way from far down the block. That's because she was always asking us to carry her shopping bags or run some errand here or there.

Sadie also always had this strange sad look on her face. That didn't help much either. Maybe she'd had a bad life or maybe something terrible might of happened to her. But then one of the fellas said that look was only something old people got when they got really ancient.

Anyway, I was under strict orders from my Mameh, my mom, to not only go to the store for Tanta Sadie, but to stop playing whatever game I was playing and carry her bag to her house no matter what!

What a drag, and no fair either! Why did it always have to be me?

That little "job" caused lots of situations for me, like for example, when we were "choosin' up" sides for stickball in the gutter. Someone might say, "Don't pick, Teddy! He's gonna stop the game every time an old lady walks down the street with a shoppin' bag!" But somehow I managed to get picked anyway.

I wasn't a two-sewer guy when it came to hitting, but I could nail a Spaldeen with a broomstick pretty good!

Truth is nobody really cared about someone having to leave the stickball game, unless it was a serious for-real game, because everybodies' mom would be yelling for somebody to go to the store all the time. It was just another strange part of the game, like, "Time out!" for a car coming down the street.

Like I said, being sent to the store was just a fact of life. We all had to do it. But it was mostly because we played our stickball games in front of our buildings that it was so obvious to me. On the other hand, Tanta Sadie was a pretty good sport about our games. After she'd finished complaining, "Don't break my windows, boychik!" she would draw down her window shade and let us play our game. A lot of the other people on our street would keep screaming at us until we either moved or just quit playing. Sometimes they'd keep our balls when they got stuck on their fire escapes or went in their open windows. But that wasn't what Tanta Sadie was about. I think she just wanted us to acknowledge she was there and that we had asked her in her own way for permission.

Sadie was also the unofficial block's "watcher." She looked over each and every person who walked down Grant Avenue, no exceptions made for sex, age or beauty. She also made full reports to our parents about every single bad thing we said or did on that block. I once got the beating of my life because of one of those reports, but that's a whole different story for another time.

But my most favorite thing about Tanta Sadie was that she disliked Miles and his family even more than I did. She called them, "Hazaarim." I think that meant they lived like a bunch of pigs.

Well. I guess if the shoe fits, then you should wear it!

I remember thinking that to myself after hearing her describing his family's daily rudeness to everyone who lived on our block.

I was busy telling Wilson all these details one day sitting at lunch. It was the very first time we'd sat together. You see at 90 everyone had to sit in their assigned seat at the same table with your official class. We were never allowed to move around from one table to another, or even move to another seat without the teacher's permission. That rule was in place so that when we were ready to stand, line-up and go we were already in size places. At least that was how it went on cold days. On other warmer days we usually caught a break, that's if we weren't on punishment, and went outside and played some punch ball.

In the outside yard when the whistle first blew we had to "freeze" like you do in freeze tag. That meant you had to stop whatever you were doing right away. And on the second whistle, we'd run like crazy to line-up.

Usually, when we were eating I sat between some of my classmates at the "taller" end of the table. But that day when I looked over to my left, I guess I saw something I hadn't noticed before. Wilson was the very last one sitting at the very end of the long table all by himself. It didn't surprise me much that he was at the end because he was one of the tallest guys in the class. But he wasn't the tallest, Big Steve was. Still he seemed alone.

What did surprise me was that he wasn't talking to anyone at all. He sat there chewing and kind of looking off out into space. Wilson later told me he liked to take lunchtime to think about the adventures he was reading about and then kind of put himself inside of them.

Anyhow, I just got this feeling I wanted to talk to Wilson. So I raised my hand. My teacher, Mrs. Stein, gave me the "go ahead" signal, a small ladylike wave towards the bathroom. That meant to just go ahead, but I kept waving my hand. Sensing a sudden emergency, she walked over and bent down to let me whisper my embarrassing situation in her ear. I always loved that part. Lady teachers always smelled so good. I think I fell in love with almost every single one of mine after just one or two whiffs of their perfume.

"What's the matter, Teddy? Is there a problem?"

"Excuse me, Mrs. Stein. Would it be okay if I change my seat to sit next to Wilson's?"

Mrs. Stein gave me a slightly puzzled look. She looked over towards where Wilson was sitting apart by himself. He was sitting there quietly munching away on his sandwich and staring off into space. He did look a little strange. But I think that also started some wheels turning in the teacher's head.

"Well, I don't know. You know I don't like to change things around like that. Then everyone starts asking for things and the next thing you know..." said my teacher obviously uncomfortable with the idea of changing our routines.

"Please Mrs. Stein, I promise we'll be quiet," I pleaded giving her my most soulful expression. It was the best one in a very large repertoire.

"Well, all right then, but I don't want you to think you can make this a habit!" she finished speaking in a hushed voice while turning and hurrying back to her fellow teachers' table, anxious to continue hearing the latest gossip.

I got up and slipped into the empty spot next to Wilson at the far end of the table. For a second he didn't even realize I was there. Then with a skeptical look he asked, "Where did you come from?"

"My momma's stomach, why'd you ask?"

Good comeback. He had to laugh at that one.

Cracking a smile Wilson continued, "Well, this is the first time anybody in the class wanted to sit next to me."

That wasn't funny.

"Well, I didn't know that, but I have to admit I didn't know you that well until you helped me out on the way back from the library."

"So, what about Gracie over there?" Wilson said, tilting his head in the direction of the only other black kid in the class.

"Are you waiting for her to save your ass also before you can be her friend?" His voice had begun to rise.

Damn, I was feeling really small inside.

Wilson was right. But I guess he felt like he'd made his point because in the next second he laughed and whispered to me.

"Man, Gracie is a stone fox, but she's so stuck up she wouldn't tell time to either one us!"

I knew then that in Wilson's own way he had forgiven me for something important. I hadn't done the right thing before and I promised myself that wasn't going to happen again. I swore I was going to try to see everybody around me, especially all the people who weren't like me. I didn't like the way I'd just felt. It was pretty much as bad as that cold fear I'd felt when Miles and his friends bothered me.

I'm going to do better.

"Wilson, what were you thinking about before I came over?"

That strange look on his face was still sending me some weird vibes.

"You kinda looked like you was off on another planet."

"How did you know that? I was. I really, really was! How'd you guess that?"

"Have you ever read any of the Foundation books, by Isaac Asimov? That's some great sci-fi. Man, do I love that stuff!"

"Tell me about it," I was interested at once. "Is it as cool as "I, Robot?"

I'd read, "I, Robot."

"A ton crazier than that, this sci-fi stuff just gets better and better. Hey man, what kind of sandwich you got there? Smells good? Want to trade a half for half a peanut butter and jelly?"

I looked over at his sandwich suspiciously. I know this might sounds strange but I'd never tasted peanut butter before, even though I'd seen it and smelt it hundreds of times.

We don't even have it in our house, but I do like peanuts though, and it does smell kind of interesting.

"Okay, trade," I said, passing over half of a chicken salami with mustard on rye.

"Now tell me some more about that funny looking old lady on your block. Why's she always lookin' so sad?" asked Wilson, happily munching away.

"Whah? Wha' didja' say," I mumbled my mouth full of deliciously sticky stuff. "Well, I ca.. ha.. Tanta Sadie…"

We sat there talking, laughing and enjoying something new. Wilson had tasted regular salami before, but not my favorite, kosher chicken salami.

Boy, did he seem to love that spicy stuff!

And me, I kept tasting and later re-tasting the peanut butter that seemed like it was gonna to be stuck forever on the roof of my mouth.

Funniest thing though happened when we were walking home later that day. Who do you think we meet? Yeah, no one else but Tanta Sadie, who's turning to walk home at the corner. She was on the way back from shopping at Olinsky's, the appetizing store on 167th Street. Of course she had her usual full shopping bag, as always.

That old lady was a good eater!

And I could see right away she was about to ask me to carry her shopping bag home for her. But before she could get her first word out Wilson stepped out in front of me and quietly asked, "Tanta Sadie, can I carry your bag home for you?"

At first she didn't seem to know what to say. I could see in her eyes that she was asking herself, "Who is this dark skinned stranger?" Really, she seemed mystified until she caught sight of me and realized we were that same pair that walked past her window on the way to school every morning.

She lifted her bag and passed it over to Wilson's waiting hand.

"Don't shake up my milk, boychik! I don't want cream!"

She turned around with a smile and shuffled away down the sidewalk. After a few steps she walked back and took each of our hands in hers. Then she started laughing. Tante Sadie was a kinda pretty lady when she smiled. I could see from the happy lines in her face that once upon a time she must have laughed a lot.

"What a lucky lady I am today," she said walking between the two of us. "Two handsome boychiks want to walk with me, one tall and one taller. Who knows, maybe later I could get a date!"

Later on that night in my bed I finally understood why my Mameh liked Sadie so much. She was funny and pretty when she smiled.

I have to make her smile more! Tomorrow I'll stop by on the way home from school and tell her a joke before I go upstairs! What, it can't hurt?

Chapter Six

I made a bad mistake today.

Usually me and my friends from the block go to the movies on Saturdays. It doesn't matter what's playing, because it's always a double feature with at least one or two cartoons. Sometimes my Mameh just gives me the money, that's a quarter, for the show and then adds another dime for popcorn, but other times she can be tough. That's when I'd get one of my friends to come to my house and beg for me.

"Teddy's mommy, can Teddy please come to the movies with us? All us are goin' and we really want Teddy to come too!"

They'd plead pitifully for me. And we always made sure it was little Arnold out in front doing the begging.

He was a beggar extraordinaire, a beggar's, beggar.

Arnold was the smallest one on the block with the cutest, saddest face and usually did all of our major begging. The mothers in the neighborhood all loved him because of that chubby little baby face, but he didn't come cheap. The cost was usually a giant handful of fresh popcorn out of your bag or half of your soda. Sometimes he'd drink the whole thing if you weren't looking out. Then he'd laugh and give you the same old line.

"I had to drink the whole thing. My half was on the bottom!"

But then Arnold was, "The can't miss kid" and because he was expensive I used him only when I knew I couldn't pull off the movies on my own.

After a few minutes of Arnold, the ultimate weapon, and a promise to finish my homework AND clean my dirt ring out of the bathtub, I'd get my quarter. Then we would race out the door and down the three flights of steps skipping them two at a time. The movies were always great.

But sometimes going to the flicks could be a little dangerous. That's because there were always the giant assholes hanging around that you didn't want to see either inside or outside our favorite theatre, the Luxor on 170th Street.

Bad weather Saturdays were the absolute most dangerous because you knew all the thugs were around and you couldn't even go to the bathroom alone. If you got caught in there by yourself the very best thing that could happen is that you got robbed. But the kids on our block pretty much knew the game. We mostly traveled as a group wherever we went. So usually there were never any big problems besides being called some names.

Like I said, we always went together and we always left the same way. I also liked the extra company because some of those movies scared the complete crap out of me.

I remember the first "Wolfman" movie. After I saw Lon Chaney change into a werewolf under the full moon my trips home from Rabbi Rabinowitz's Hebrew School in the dark were never the same. To get home from his house I had to walk about five blocks in the dark. I'd walk quickly down College Avenue dodging between the shadowy streetlamps suspiciously watching every single doorway and in particular cellar openings. I was waiting for that single moment when the Wolfman would jump out and completely bite my head off.

Believe it or not, I would start praying. The prayer for bread, the prayer for wine, it didn't matter. This strategy strange as it might seem made sense to me because I figured I now had Almighty God on my side. After all, I was on the way home from Hebrew school.

I guess the scariest part of my trip home had to be when I raced as fast as I could through the dark shadows between the streetlights. Then I'd walk more slowly once I got into the brightly lit parts. My heart would lift every time the streetlight brightened and then drop into my stomach as I stepped back into the murky shadows.

When I finally got to the front door of my building I would start running, jumping two and three steps at a time to get up to the third floor as fast as I could. I just knew Dracula was silently stalking me from the landing right below me. Finally, I would tear out the key to 3K hidden on a shoestring under my shirt and shove it in the lock.

"Please God, don't let me fumble this key!" was my ever present prayer mumbled out loud so God couldn't say I'd never asked for his help, just in case things didn't work out. There were a few times I thought I heard steps coming up the staircase behind me. Or maybe it was the sharp sound of the front door of the building slamming shut below. But even beyond those scary moments the absolutely most terrifying experience of all was to feel a whiff of cold air kiss the back of my neck.

Was the creature so close its icy breath was touching me?

Then with the speed of an eye blink I'd slammed the door shut, flipping the lock with the most practiced of turns.

"Whew," I remember taking a deep breath, "I barely made it this time … again!"

But I loved the movies so much, too much in fact! I'd sit back in the dark and get lost inside every single story. It hardly even mattered what the movie was about, I was hooked on the whole experience. I felt I just had to go every single Saturday.

But when Saturday finally arrived that particular week, the movie theatre that my friends and I usually went to, the Luxor was playing something even more boring to them than usual. I guess it was something really mushy because all my friends flat out said, "Heck no!" Since there was no give there at all I suggested we all go to the Earl, another theatre about six or seven blocks away in different neighborhood. The show there, an all cowboy triple feature, was exactly what I loved, but my friends didn't want to go there either. It was too far, and blah, blah, blah! That had happened before and I'd ended up going by myself.

No big deal, done that before too.

The movie was great, as usual. Three westerns with people riding fast horses, chasing each other around, good people in white hats dueling villains in black hats. I got out of the theatre very late because of the extra feature and cartoons. But now it was getting dark and I had to make a choice.

Should I take the longer route around through the streets that were familiar and safe or take a shortcut through a bus tunnel under the Concourse that cut two long blocks off of my trip home?

Of course you know my answer to that question. There would hardly be a book to read if I JUST DID WHAT I WAS SUPPOSED TO!

Yeah, I chose the tunnel.

Come on, it's just like coming home from Hebrew school. There's no real Wolfman. Just walk fast and you'll be home in a few minutes. Think positively, Teddy! Act like Mrs. Stein always says to do.

I had a bad feeling as soon as I entered the shadowy tunnel, but the cars whizzing by with their headlights on kind of comforted me. They were real, the monsters in my mind weren't.

Someone will stop and help me if they see a monster jumping me.

That's what I kept repeating to myself over and over.

I forgot to pray…

But then I felt my spirits suddenly start to rise! I looked up ahead of me and saw the light at the end of the tunnel. That's exactly when a rough fist grabbed my shoulder.

The Wolfman had found me.

"Well, well, well, look who we gots here," snarled a familiar voice that made my heart fill with a cold dread.

It was Miles.

When I turned around I quickly knew it was going to be much worse than I first thought. There were others with Miles. That meant I was going to be either hurt really bad or be totally humiliated. Today there wasn't going to be any running away or fighting back. My legs began to tremble violently. I was scared, very, very scared.

"Where's dat spade friend of yers at t'day? Wha's his name again? Wilson? Like in Woodrow Wilson? Hey Freddy, did youse know we had a prezdent who wuz related to a jig?"

Miles laughed, but never loosened his grip on me. Then he turned around to smile happily at his boys. He was still looking at them and laughing out loud when he viciously slammed me back up against the concrete wall of the tunnel.

In a far distant place in my mind I was oddly thinking how much Miles sounded like the donkey boy in Pinocchio, braying loudly and stupid. That's what my brain heard, but all I could see was fuzzy darkness. I suppose that was because my head had just bounced off a cement wall. Tears were pushing upwards into my eyes and I wasn't sure if it was the dull pain that'd brought them or the fear of what was coming next.

But then did it really matter?

"So now y'thinkin' youse a tough guy, hey, Jew boy?" he whispered in my ear burying his fist into my chest with a powerful short chopping punch. "Ah'm guessin' we bout t'fin' out jus' how tough y'really is, ya' lil' bitch!"

Then he punched me again in the side of my face while I was slumped over from the first shot.

"Step up! Step right up, all a yez! Who wan's a piece of this durty lil' sheeny? Sean, how's bout you? I hear Teddy Bear here kicked y'ass wit' all y'boys watchin'. I hear ev'n his lil' brother whale'd on ya'? Want a turn at d'dance?"

I looked up and there was the smaller monster I'd had trouble with coming home from the library. A grim sneer crossed over his mouth, but he hadn't made a move towards me… yet.

I could barely breathe off the sharp pain in the center of my chest. A greater pain came from knowing that there wasn't going to be any rescue today. I covered up my face with my two hands and waited for what I knew would be coming.

Miles had to let go of my jacket for a second as Sean stepped past him to take his turn. My old tormentor pulled his fist back getting ready to take a shot at the part of my head uncovered by my raised elbow. But then he stopped and quickly stepped backward.

"Jeez, Miles, look at his fukin' head! He's bleedin' like a stu'k pig. You busted his freakin' head wide open. I ain't touchin' 'im. If I get mockie blood on my clothes my moms will f'sure kill me!" Sean mumbled backing further away from me.

"Well, I don' give a flyin' fu'k! Dis kike piece'a crap hit me while his nigga' pal held my arms back from behind! So ah'm gonna use his Yid blood to spit shine my shoes," Miles yelled back angrily at Sean. And with that he spun around back towards me aiming a knee at my stomach.

In that instant I knew I had to run. If only my brain was working right!

I felt like if I asked my feet to move, they might not obey me. But I'd made a choice. I was still shaking like a leaf, still blinded by my tears but couldn't wait any longer for the next punch or kick to land.

Somehow, I knew then that I was running. I could feel my feet pumping away as fast as they could and suddenly, strange as can be, there was no more pain, only fear.

There was lots and lots of that.

"Get 'im, grab his Hymie ass, that little mudafucka!"

The voices behind me howled like angry wolves. I didn't feel my head pounding or my chest aching anymore. The blood dripping into my eyes didn't matter. I just ran as fast as I damn well could. In fact, I barely felt the ground touching my feet as I seemed to be flying towards the quickly growing light at the end of the tunnel.

I was weightless in a way I'd never experienced before. It was like I was running in a dream! Now if I could just make it out of the tunnel I would be safe. Someone would see me, and they would help me.

But dreams come to an end. And then so did this one. I fell down. I don't know why I fell down, I just did. I would love to say I picked myself up, got away and everything worked out fine, but that wouldn't be the truth.

The truth was an explosion of burning pain in my face. It was far worse than the head slam I'd gotten a few minutes ago. Then what happened became clear to me. I had slid heavily face first into the same broken sidewalk that had tripped me. I lay there face down for a second just feeling the new pain spread out like a sheet of dry newspaper being set on fire. Then I remembered why it was that I had to get up.

But I couldn't move. Something was holding me down?

It was in that moment I realized that none of it mattered anymore. Mostly because I heard myself screaming. My hands felt like they too were on fire. An instant later I felt the connection between my knees and forearms as they lit up in flames too. After that, there was only screaming as the pain came on, one wave after another.

"Holy Jesus, Mary and Joseph, he's cover'd in blood!" One of my tormenters yelled as they emerged from the tunnel and saw me. The entire gang turned as one and ran.

Me, I just turned in the direction of my block holding my bleeding hands out while screaming from the pain and walked. And that's exactly how I stepped out of the shadow of the tunnel. Right alongside of me I heard a car come to a screeching stop, doors opening, slamming and a woman shouting, "Mel, give me your handkerchief. Get a blanket from the trunk. That boy is covered in blood!"

I don't remember a lot after that. I woke up in my own bed bandaged up like one of those mummy monsters I was so afraid of.

My face, my hands and even my split head were all stitched and bandaged. I missed a few days of school, maybe a week. I don't remember.

Then my Mameh told me I had to go back to school even with some of my smaller bandages still on my face and hands. Everyone there kept asking me what had happened. I just told them I had tripped when I was running for the bus.

I didn't want to tell my Tateh the truth. I knew he'd have tried to kill someone and I didn't want that. I also knew they didn't really believe me but now there were really more scrapes left over than anything else. Except for one last thing, I had fractured my nose. It now had a large broken bump that would never go away. I would have to carry this brutal souvenir for the rest of my life, all thanks to those punks.

The worst part of it all was seeing Miles walking across the street after that.

He smiled at me.

Everything had been put right again in his world because he knew I was afraid of him.

Yeah, monsters do exist.

Chapter Seven

My mother had walked me back to school a little late on the first day I was ready to go back. I remember it was about ten in the morning on a bright sunny day. I still had some bandages on my nose and around my hands. It wasn't a very pretty sight to see.

Looking at my face in the bathroom mirror that morning had been frightening. What stared back at me was still barely recognizable between the swelling and the bandages.

Half a mummy…

I remember thinking while grimacing through the pain of brushing my teeth. And I still remember the very moment I walked into the classroom and the way it suddenly fell quiet. The teacher, Mrs. Stein, who was apparently expecting me, made some obligatory remarks to the class about, "learning to get along with one another," "being a good friend," and, of course, her favorite, "fighting doesn't solve anything." Then she spoke to my mother for a moment while I shuffled uncomfortably towards my seat.

I was walking slowly down the long row towards my desk in the back when I was stopped for an instant by a little girl, Hannah, who sat in the middle of the row. She reached out and took my hand. It was such a gift of kindness, like she really cared about what had happened to me.

My face and hands were really hurting a lot, and there wasn't any more medicine that could help that. But I don't think I even felt the pain for that second when Hannah touched my hand. That showed me there were still some people who cared for somebody else's pain. It was almost worth the beating.

Nah, it wasn't…

At lunch later it seemed everyone already knew the story of what had happened to me, everyone that is except Wilson.

"What the hell happened to you? Who did it? Why didn't you tell me…" demanded Wilson angrily swinging his arms in the air.

"Tell you? Tell you what? Why? What could you have done for me? Share my ass kicking?" I interrupted him trying to be funny. But I knew I couldn't hide my real feelings from Wilson.

Eventually, I had to say something. He was getting to know me better than anyone but my Mameh. And I didn't want him drawing the attention of Miles and his boys anymore than he already had.

Wilson whispered angrily to me as we sat side by side in the quiet lunchroom, "You better just tell me. You know I'm gonna find out sooner or later anyway, so you might as well just tell me now!"

I knew he was right and the truth was I was hurting bad inside. Yeah, I wanted to tell someone, so I let it all come out. I didn't even tell my mother and father the whole truth, but telling Wilson was different. He'd become like a part of me. He was my best friend.

Before I knew what was happening tears were rolling down my face as I spilled my guts about everything. And Wilson listened to it all without interrupting me even once. He just took it all in while chewing on his sandwich and looking straight into my eyes. Then he handed over his hanky so I could wipe my face.

Finally, he told me what I already knew, "You know this shit ain't over. He's not ever gonna leave you alone 'til you make him."

What could I say? That I was scared to death of Miles and his gang? What could I do? I didn't really know how to fight with my fists. If I fought him face-to–face after school I would probably just get beat up some more, and then embarrassed too. How was that going to help me?

Wilson must've been reading my mind because he whispered, "You're coming with me after school!"

Most afternoons, if I didn't have to go to Hebrew school, I'd play punch ball with the kids on the block. I didn't have anything special to do that afternoon, so I thought it would be okay to go with Wilson.

"Okay, where we goin'?"

"We're gonna play some ball round my way. It's time for you to play something else besides punch ball. We're gonna shoot some hoops. You have, "hooped" before? You know, "balled," "hooped," played basketball before, right?"

"Oh yeah, yeah, sure, of course, I have. Last year I was one of the best players in my class."

Telling lies is getting easier and easier!

That's what I thought to myself. Truth was I loved basketball, but I was only okay at it, except I was still growing taller and had okay co-ordination. So sometimes I surprised myself pleasantly when I played.

"Cool, cool, good deal, my man," replied Wilson enthusiastically. "And when we get to the park I want you to call me, "Sweets". That's what all my round-the block buddies call me. It's "Sweets" because when I was a little kid I always had some kind of candy stuffed up in my jaw. I chewed up so much candy my family just started calling me, "Sweets."

"You're gonna need a nickname too. Your name, Teddy is cool with me, and I dig it and all, but everyone in the park has a street handle. So, you know you got to be on time too. We need to get you a name you can be down with, before the guys give you a handle you hate, like Jewy or Paleface. Hey, wait a minute now! Paleface is not all that bad!' chuckled Wilson.

"Well, cool, okay," I said, "if you really think it's gonna help. I guess I'm good with it."

But the trouble was I just couldn't think of a good name, especially something as cool sounding as, "Sweets." In fact, I couldn't think of anything that sounded even a little bit cool. My mind went blank every time I tried to think of something that sounded extra streety or dangerous. I guess it was mostly because I wasn't cool or dangerous.

I was just a big Jewish doofus, scared of my own shadow and a lot of other shadows too.

Well, we left school and headed back towards my house, but this time we passed right by it and kept on walking. Wilson and I were laughing and making jokes about stuff that had happened in school that day. At first the sidewalk was choked up with dozens of us walking home. There were lots and lots of kids in our neighborhood and heading home at three o'clock was like being part of a big parade. But as we walked further along people were quickly disappearing into the old six story apartment buildings that towered on either side of Grant Avenue. As far as you could see down the street there were tall buildings that lined both sides from corner to corner. It was kind of strange that you had to look either straight up, or way, way down the block to see the sky. Everything around us was made of brick or cement. Also kind of strange was how now the only kids left walking down the sidewalk were black and Hispanic.

Uh, oh! A warning flag popped up my brain.

I'm walking down the wrong streets now. This isn't my neighborhood anymore!

Straight in front of me there stood a giant school building that took up a whole city block. It also had a huge schoolyard attached in back of it. It was William Howard Taft High School, and it wasn't a place I usually went to for two very good reasons. One, it was in a tough neighborhood and, two, I wasn't a high school kid yet.

Me and my friends usually played all our games in the street in front of our houses. After all it was, "our" block. We played stickball, punch ball and even some football in between the moving traffic. Sometimes if we could get enough people together we'd go up to PS 90's schoolyard and play against the guys who lived around there. But those guys mostly didn't want us around because we interfered with their usual teams' sides.

Taft High School was a place we didn't even think about going to. Besides which, we knew Miles and his gang hung around in that yard. That was their school, the one some of them went to. That's when they went to school. You know we didn't want any part of them.

I slowed down as we crossed 170th Street walking towards the schoolyard's gate. I guess Wilson saw I was scared because he grabbed my jacket's sleeve and pulled me on straight through the opening gate.

"Hey man," I said under my breath. "Look over there on the corner court. It's him."

"It's who?" Wilson asked.

"Look over there, there, on the first court in the left corner. It's Miles and those other guys who got me. Let's get outta here right now, man, while we still got the chance," I urged Wilson.

Outwardly, I was trying to maintain some shred of calmness, but on the inside fear was taking me over again.

At first Wilson's eyes widened a little bit looking at the court Miles was shooting baskets on. Then they narrowed into angry slits.

"It's too late to turn around now Teddy. Just follow me close. We're gonna walk right past them to that main court over there," said Wilson in a low firm voice. "I know some of those guys playing there. Come on now!"

I didn't move a single muscle.

"Look, it's either walk with me now or run from them forever," Wilson continued looking at me expectantly.

When I saw Miles shooting baskets I felt the old terror returning. That familiar icy hand grabbed my spine and I couldn't take another step. I was frozen.

I have to go! I have to run away or they'll hurt me again. Run, run, run away! JUST RUN AWAY! Don't even think about stepping towards those monsters. Just run!

"C'mon Teddy, man! Let's shoot some hoop!"

Wilson calling out to me brought me back into the moment. My friend was still pulling me, tugging my jacket sleeve onto the blacktopped basketball courts.

This is it. Miles, that dog's behind, doesn't see me yet. I can still get away! There's still time!

I tried to convince myself to run! I really did! But there was something in Wilson's voice that made me trust him. I let myself get led through the gate and then through a second inner fence that led onto the courts. Now I was walking on the first basketball court, the one that Miles and his crew were playing on. I tried my best not to look at them as I walked quickly across the backside of the court they were shooting baskets on. I walked along faster following the back of the metal fence staying about as far away from them as possible. And I kept praying I could get past them without them noticing me. That didn't happen. Sean, one of the boys who had chased me the day I had fallen saw me.

"Hey Miles, Guess what? Look who's here to pay ya' a little visit? It's the little Jew boy track star come all this way to visit witch ya'! Well maybe then what we got here is true love? Everywhere ya' go, Miles, Little Jew Riding Hood ov'r there is right behin' ya'!" he hooted, his hands cupped around his mouth to make sure everyone in the schoolyard could hear his insults echoing through the air.

Miles turned slowly around and stared right at me. I could see his face turning a brick red as his boys taunted him from their positions near the backboard. He instantly turned back around to face them and swore that they'd better shut their big pieholes or else!

Then Miles turned back around again and trotted quickly over to me. It was simple to see that he was going to cut me off from Wilson who had just kept right on walking straight ahead. Wilson hadn't even slowed down or hesitated for a second. He never looked back at me, not even once. I was all alone. Miles smiled and leaned forward until his ugly red face was just a few inches away from my own.

"Tel' me, butthole, when did ya' ev'r get my permission fo' yer Jewish ass t'cum in t'dis schoolyard? Our schoolyahd, Jew boy, not yers, nev'r yers, nev'r, ev'r yers!" he spit out into my face making his last point with a thick-fingered jab deep into my chest. His saliva was now spraying out in all directions all over my face.

"I can see y'hav'n't learn't y'lesson yet. That's fo'shit-sure! Hey fella's, watch!"

And with that he reached upward to grab my face. To me still bandaged up that was scarier than a punch.

What was he gonna do with his fingers? Was he goin' for my eyes?

I quickly raised my arm to ward off his hand with my elbow, but he just pushed it aside. Before I realized what was going on he had grabbed hold of the bandages that were plastered across my broken nose and ripped them away. The instant pain shocked me and forced me to jump back against the fence holding my face in my hands.

"There y'go ag'in! Prayin' in public, where's ya' respect for God?"

Miles mocked me while jumping forward and yanking my hands away from my burning face.

"By th' by, where did Black Beauty trot off to? I gots somethin' f'his black ass too!"

"My, my, but you're one deformed ugly asshole," joined in Sean, my other tormentor, approaching me from my blind side.

"But we can help you out, amigo," he said as Miles and his gang closed up in a tight circle around me. "Ya' see, mockie, I decided a career in plastic surgery is the one fo' me. It's gonna be my life's work. Ain't that right fellas?" cackled Sean. "And you, Moses, Noah, Abraham or whatev'r th' fuck y'Hebe name is, are gonna be my very first nose job!"

There was nowhere to run to, nowhere to hide inside this circle of hate.

My Mameh was right! I hadn't learned my lesson and stayed with my own kind!

I was about to get beaten to a pulp again. And there was nothing but fear and desperate tears behind my closed eyelids.

"Don't touch'im, muthafuckas!"

My eyes were shut so tight I thought my ears weren't working right.

Who is that?

"Sumthin' wrong with your ears, whitey! I said, don't-fuck-in'-touch-im!"

I felt a giant hand pressing down on my shoulder. I mean a really big strong hand. And from my sad experience I could tell it was a whole lot bigger hand than Miles'.

I opened my eyes slowly and there he stood right next to me. A truly large tall black man was standing there, exactly between me, Miles and Sean. He was speaking slowly and carefully in a deep baritone voice.

"Now, if you do decide you have the stones to touch'im, I'm gonna have to do some touchin' too! In fact, I'm gonna have to put my foot so deep up in your skinny asses your mommas' bellies are gonna be hurtin'. You fella's diggin' what I'm sayin'! There ain't gonna be no accidents happenin' here today! Y'all are hearin' me, correctly?"

"Hell yeah, there ain't got no beef witch you, big man!" said Miles. "But why ya gotta stan'up f'the Jew boy? D'is the schoolyard bro'. Everybody hea'h got t'stan'up on d'ere own, and fo' d'ere own."

"Where's all d'oth'r Jew boys at? Why ain't they here wit'im? Why you gotta be in this? Whose d'is Hymie t'you?" Miles whined inching backwards trying to save some face by talking big.

"That shit ain't none a'your business, man, zip, none a your business a'tall! All you need to know is that Teddy's with me. It's just that plain and simple," repeated the powerfully built speaker looking casually at his clean nails while holding a basketball buried under his other big arm.

"But, but he's nuttin' but a Yid, a goddamned mockie!" Sean jumped in angry and frustrated.

"And you both nothing more than a pair of ofay pimples on my black ass! Now you wanna go, or you gonna get in the wind? Pick one, throw down or git? Whatcha gonna do?"

Silently, the pair turned around and walked away. Sure they looked back over their shoulders with angry glares a few times, and those looks had some evil promise, but not one more word came out their mouths as they left the schoolyard.

I was saved. I wasn't sure how it had all happened, but I was grateful, very grateful. I turned around to my rescuer ready to say thank you about a hundred times but no words came out of my open mouth.

That was something new right there.

And that was exactly when Wilson stepped out from behind my very large sized hero.

"Teddy, meet my big brother, Stan."

Chapter Eight

"Hey, what's shakin' lil' dude?" asked Stan with a gentle smile. That smile made him look a ton less threatening than he seemed only a few minutes earlier.

"My brother 'Sweets' been bending my ear a whole bunch about the stuff you guys been up to lately. He tells me, you both in the same class at school. That right? You must really be into books too, because he sure likes 'em!"

"Y'know, you two are straight up with me, two egg heads, yeah, scholars!" he laughed, pleased with the conversation. "You gents just keep right on pushin', and good things are gonna be happenin' for you, you hear me? Oh yeah, and any other problems you have with those punkass-gangsta' wannabe's you jus' lemme know 'bout that!"

I was so overcome with relief all I could do was keep nodding my head up and down, yeah, yeah, and yeah to everything he was saying. And all the time he was talking I just kept mumbling, "Thanks man," over and over again.

Wilson came up from wherever he'd been behind me, put his arm around my shoulder and whispered close to my ear, "See, Teddy, I told you I had it all under control!"

Then he ran over and snatched the basketball out of his big brother's hands. He took three long rhythmic dribbles towards the basket getting ready to layup the ball. But one of the taller guys standing near the basket slid over a step to block his lane to the hoop. Then the big man raised his arm up and jumped trying to block Wilson's shot. It didn't seem like there was any way in the world that a ball could get through those long arms stretched straight up towards the sky. But Wilson somehow brought his knees up and easily corkscrewed his body around while still in mid air. Then, as he continued rising upward, he deftly switched the ball to his opposite hand, his left, and with a smooth reverse spin laid the ball in the basket.

Nobody said a thing, not a single word was uttered. They all acted as if Wilson's acrobatic shot was nothing much out of the ordinary, yeah, business as usual. In fact, they kept playing on as if nothing at all special had happened. The players' rebounding and shooting never skipped a single beat. Watching Wilson's magical move made my mouth drop so far open that my chin was sitting on my chest from the shock of what I'd just witnessed. Wilson's move had defeated gravity! He'd made the hardest shot I'd ever seen!

Amazing, on this court nobody even cared!

The very same guy from my class who read, "I, Robot" with me was now flying around this basketball court like a comic book super hero and nobody, but me, seemed to think it was anything special.

"Teddy, are you gonna play ball or did you come here just to watch?" Stan asked. "Sweets called and told me to meet you guys here after school, and he told me his friend had some game. This is the place, baby! Time to show us what you got, my man!"

I moved over right next to Wilson who was standing under the basket waiting to snare another loose rebound and whispered, "I think I'm going to be heading home now."

"Why Teddy, why? What's up? Not another problem is there? Come on now! Let's play a little ball and then we can roll on over to my house for some eats!"

"Wilson, man, uh, I mean Sweets, man. I can't play with you guys on this court," I confessed, a little embarrassed to even be standing on court number one.

Wow! I'm standing on the court the best players in the schoolyard play on! And they're askin' me to play?

I was in awe of how good these guys were up close.

"What are you talking about? What d'you mean, 'I can't play?' Why the hell not?" Wilson demanded. "You hurt or somethin'?"

"Nah, nah, I'm okay, fine, but I'm also not that great a basketball player either. Okay, maybe, just maybe I might have exaggerated a little bit about how good I am. I mean I'm okay and all, but I don't think I'm good enough to play with you and your friends. By the way, how come you never told me how good you are?" I asked him accusingly. "That was a killer move you just made. It was much better than anything I could ever do. In fact, what you did was beautiful?"

Wilson looked at me as if he was trying to decide if I was making fun of him or something. I didn't know how to answer that look. Then he grabbed a rebound, dribbled out beyond the foul line, turned and shot another graceful jumper from where we were standing.

"Hey, Teddy, man, don't make this b.s. bigger than it is. Basketball is just somethin' a bunch of the dudes on my block love to do. Some of us play ball, some of us don't. Some do other stuff. We're all different. Just like you and your friends are different. You the only one of them I see here. I've been playing ball behind Stan since I started walkin'."

"If you think I'm good you need to come back around here on the weekend and watch Stan or my dad and his friends play with the other older guys. They can really hoop it up. And I'm thinkin' Stan might try to go pro pretty soon. At least that's what he says he's working on. Hey, you want to see something real special? Watch this!"

Wilson turned and called out to Stan who was standing just inside the foul line. Pointing his forefinger towards the sky Wilson called out loudly, "Alley...."

"Oop!" came the answer out of Stan's mouth as he shot from being bent in the slightest crouch to a fully extended leap with both his powerful arms flying upwards towards the rim. In the next instant he'd snatched the ball right out of the air above the metal rim with two hands and dunked it through the hoop in one lightening move. Stan then delicately hung up there, swinging on the vibrating rim for an instant to emphasize his stylish dunk and finally, lightly dropped to the ground. He turned around and gave us a wink and sort of a half bow. Then he ran off to chase after whoever had rebounded the ball.

Turning to Wilson I realized that I was having trouble controlling my babbling mouth.

"Holy shi... I mean, "Whoa!" I've never seen anyone jump that high! How did he do that? Can you do that? Can I do that? Could you teach me to do that? How did...?"

I probably would have kept on asking questions, but Stan's voice suddenly boomed from behind me again.

"Are you ladies gonna play ball t'day or you gonna yakkity-yak-yak all day?"

Tossing me the ball Stan continued, "Here lil' fella, you take the pill back out behind the line and let's run one!"

Catching the ball in both hands I first stepped over to Wilson raising the ball to cover my mouth and whispered to him.

"Quick, tell me. What's 'the pill'?" I asked out of the corner of my mouth while stepping back behind the foul line.

"The ball, stupid, the basketball in your hands. It's called the "pill" or the "rock." Gimme that thing! Come on, pass me the "rock" and let's get it on," called out Wilson extra loud trying to take some attention away from me. "Our outs, Teddy, baby! Pull it out, your potata' out behind the line! We're playing straight up, no takin' it back! Make it, you take it!"

I figured it out soon enough.

All I actually remember about the rest of the afternoon is a haze of running, jumping, shooting and, best of all, laughing a lot. Before long the bandages on my fingers and palms, even the last one left on my face, had gotten dirty and sweaty. When they lost their stickiness they dropped off onto the court's blacktop and then were just kicked over to the side so nobody would slip on them.

I didn't need 'em anymore. Whatever they were protecting was now covered in a layer of dirt anyway. It took me only a little while before I started to feel the rhythm of the game and then all the pain was forgotten.

Gone, gone, gone!

The games that day were more fun than they'd ever been for me. Maybe it was because everything was happening a lot faster than it did when I played with my friends.

But then another weird thing started happening. In my mind, I started to see patterns of what I thought guys were going to do a split second before they actually did them. When I first got the ball all I did was pass it quickly to someone else on my team. I was afraid to mess up and look stupid so I just kept passing the "pill." But then I took a chance. I thought I saw something happening, a hint of body language spoke to me. So I bounce passed the ball towards an empty spot. In the next instant a hand and a body flashed through that spot meeting my pass and then without breaking stride smoothly laying up the ball for an easy score.

"Great pass, Teddy," called out Wilson. "Right on the money, baby!"

And that's how the afternoon went on.

Boy, I'm having fun! I already love basketball, but I didn't know hooping could be like this!

Every once in a while, I made another good pass and I got another compliment. They called it, "Gettin' your props!" Honestly, I felt more like I was a puppy filling up on doggie treats.

"Good pass, Teddy," "Nice play, Teddy" and even one, "Money shot! 'T"!"

Whoof! Whoof!

It was then that the most incredible thing of all happened.

It's something I will remember forever and ever!

I was standing to one side of the basket out over by the foul line and was pretty much alone. There was no one guarding me for that split second. I took a quick pass from Wilson and then suddenly broke in towards the basket for what I thought was going to be an easy lay up. All I needed was two quick dribbles and I would loft the ball in easily off the metal backboard.

But a quicker body flew out from alongside me and blocked my path to the basket. Something inside my mind reached back to before the game and I could see Wilson blocked in the very same way by the tall guy with the very long arms. There he was in my mind, knees lifting, body turning and pumping the ball down to his chest and then upward. Without thinking about could I do it, I tried to do the same thing. Then exactly as I had seen Wilson do it earlier, I switched the ball from my right hand to my left and spun it upwards towards the backboard. And, unbelievably, it went right in.

Everything on the court stopped and got real quiet. I figured I must've done something wrong and someone had made a "call" on the play.

But in the next instant Stan's voice boomed out, "Dammmn, Sweets! Teddy just made your move! I don't know how he got it down so fast, but he damn sure made your exact move little brother!"

One of the other guys from the sideline jumped right in behind him, "Yeah, yeah, Sweetman, my man Chunky White over heah, looked like the A-train rollin' uptown just blowin' to the basket, and then he just up and changed th' tracks. Yup, yup, brotherman, it's like my man over here switched over to the A-train Uptown Express! Whooh! whooh!"

Even I had to laugh at that funky description of me. We all started laughing, trying to top that rip, slapping palms and giving each other some skin. It was a very cool moment. But the best part of all for me though was, for a change everyone was not laughing at me. They were all with me.

Just before it started getting dark, when we were finally walking out of the schoolyard, Wilson smiled at me. "Not too shabby at all for a first day at the schoolyard. You even got yourself a nickname, and a pretty cool handle at that …A TRAIN!"

YEAH! Listen up world, I am now known as the "A train"! Now how cool is that?

Chapter Nine

"Next stop, my house, "A Train!" laughed Wilson a sly smile covering his face. "My moms been wanting to meet you for a while now. You know I've been tellin' her 'bout you, and by the way, she makes some great chocolate chip cookies."

"Your mom wants to meet me? Really, she said that? But why? Why would she want to meet me?"

I couldn't think of any reason in the world why any grown up besides my own mom would want to talk to me.

"Tell me again? Why'd you say your mom wants to meet me?"

"Actually Sherlock Holmes, I didn't say, but since you're so nosy I'll tell you anyway," was Wilson's reply. "See, it's like this. I told my mom I'd finally made a friend in my class. Understand, I've been in that school for almost a month and haven't made any new friends. Can you believe that mess? But mom, she just keeps on sayin' to me, "It's a 'good' school, honey and could you please, pretty please, try to do your best?"

"Besides, I also told her we like a lot of the same stuff, like telling jokes, snappin' on each other, reading and stuff like that. So then she says she'd like to meet you! That's about it in a nutshell, squirrel boy! Now, you got some kinda problem with that?"

"Did you tell her about Miles and the other stuff," I asked.

"Now why would I do something stupid like that? That wouldn't be too smart, would it? Then she'd be all uptight and wantin' to be all up in my business. Nope, I left all that other stuff out. I kept it real. I only told her how cool we were in school. She's lovin' that part to death! She keeps tellin' me, "Told you so, Sweetie! Told you so!"

When I thought about it for a minute it all kind of made sense. But then again I thought back to what my Mameh asks me over and over again.

"Where are you going? What are you doing? Who are you going with?" And, of course she would always add on the whipped cream and cherry on top, "Why are you looking for trouble? Stay with your own kind!"

I didn't need to think about what she'd say if she knew I was walking around in a 'bad' neighborhood and hanging out with "schvartzes?" And then what she'd say if she knew I was going to hang out in one of, "their" houses. And my father, my Tateh, I couldn't even think about him? He'd probably be flying back to Vilna without an airplane if he found out where I was.

What to do? What to do?

I'd have to be crazy to disobey my parents. I got the shakes just thinking about how terrible my punishments would be!

Yeah, definitely more than one!

"Okay, no problem, Wilson, I'll go. But I can't stay too long!" I answered, easily tossing away all my Mameh's common sense advice.

So down the street we were walking. It was Wilson, me and Big Stan. The sky was still the dimmest shade of blue when we turned the corner on to College Avenue, a street of small private homes with tiny green yards in front.

This was all so different from the long blocks of six story apartment buildings I was used to walking up and down on. We stopped halfway down the block in front of a neat light blue wooden house edged with pretty white trim. You could tell it was an old house because the tree in the yard was huge! The one maple tree in front stretched up so high it's branches hung way over the third floor attic window. The house looked a lot like something you saw on TV. It wouldn't have surprised me at all if Lassie ran out the door to meet us. But it looked great to me. Even more important then all that was the aroma wafting its way out to us through the open front door.

"Mmmm, that's one delicious smell! What is it?" I asked hopefully. My jaws were suddenly aching after only one little whiff of some heavenly baking.

"Smells good, right Teddy? Those are the cookies I was telling told you about," smiled Wilson. "My mom can really burn when it's time to get down in the kitchen!"

"Last one in gives up his last cookie!" yelled both brothers, who were already leaping porch steps two at a time. They'd left me standing there in their dust.

No fair guys, I'm supposed to be the guest!

"Boys!" called a voice from far back in the house. "Don't you sit down at that kitchen table until you wash your hands. You hear me? And make sure you use that soap! No fakin'! Are you listenin' to me?"

"Yes Ma!" Wilson and Stan both yelled at the same time pushing their way into a small bathroom off the front.

"She has to be the cleanest woman on the entire planet Earth," grumbled Stan, but I could tell he wasn't really angry at all. In fact, he seemed pretty happy to just be home, washing up. My wet fingers contrasted with their darker ones as we all stuck our hands under the running water trying to be the first one scrubbed up, dried and out the door.

"Don't worry about being last Teddy, we're only playing with you," Stan said blocking off Wilson's scrambling escape with his broad butt. It filled up most of the doorway.

"Yeah, right, Bigfoot's behind!" laughed Wilson as he burst past Stan's hip and raced down the hallway towards the dining room.

"Sorry bout that teeny fib! See ya' later, Train!" called out Stan as he too spun around and chased Wilson down the hallway.

I, of course, arrived third into a room filled with two laughing brothers and a smiling mom.

"This is Teddy, mommy. He's the one I was tellin' you about. You know, the boy from school and the library."

Wilson's mom was a pretty dark skinned lady with the kind of smile that made you feel warm inside before she even spoke to you.

"Hi, Teddy," she said. "Do you like chocolate chip cookies? This batch only just came out of the oven a minute ago. Now why don't you sit right down over here by me. I've been hearing a whole lot about you from mister over there. It's always Teddy, said this, and Teddy, said that around here!"

That was a little embarrassing for Wilson and me, but I was still happy to sit down in front of that plate full of warm cookies. I looked over in Wilson's direction, but he was acting like he hadn't heard anything his mother had said.

But I knew he had! Those words from his mom were pretty nice. Someone actually liked my company and said so!

It was about then that I realized, I'd also been telling my own mom about Wilson. I had to smile to myself. We were becoming good friends and that gave me a warm feeling inside. And the delicious smell of those fresh-baked chocolate chip cookies was giving me another warm feeling inside.

"Yes, ma'am. I really, uh, really do like chocolate chip cookies," came stumbling out.

Dummy, what a loser! You can't do better than that? Say something smart, or polite. Just don't just sit there grinning like an idiot with your mouth hanging open!

"Uh, it's really nice to finally meet you ma'am. Wilson has told me so much about you," I lied trying to keep a straight face.

Wilson was looking at me, wide eyed and open mouthed, exactly like I'd lost my complete mind.

His mother continued on happily, "I was hoping Willy would bring you by. I wanted to ask you something. By the way, where did you get all those scratches on your face? Did you get into a fight with a cat?"

"No ma'am, I just had a little accident. I fell down while I was running in gym class."

"That's not the truth mom! Teddy's fibbin' his behind off!" jumped in Wilson. "That cracker, Miles, you know the mean one I told you 'bout, made him fall a few days ago, and this afternoon they were gonna beat his ass up again when we were in the schoolyard, but Stan scared them off."

I threw Wilson an angry look.

So much for keeping his mom out of my business!

"Willy, baby, I asked you not to say such things in our home. Now please don't call white people, "crackers." You know I've told you about that before! It's not helpful to insult people, son," insisted Wilson's mom. "The Lord doesn't separate his sheep by the colors of their wool!"

Whoa, I was impressed with that one! That made a lot of sense to me.

I made a mental note to save that example for Hebrew school when they told us how we were the Chosen People and were better than everyone else because we were Jewish!

"Always remember that we among all others are 'God's Chosen People,' thundered the teacher!"

It was incredibly easy to remember what the teacher said because he always made me sit in the front of the room by his desk. I played around too much in the back so I had a permanent seat right up front.

Whenever the Hebrew school teacher became excited listening to himself, he would occasionally spray us with spit as well as wisdom. And of course if you had the nerve to ask the wrong question like for example, "Where did all the other people come from that Adam and Eve's children married?" there was usually a sad pitying look accompanied with a few Yiddish words for the idiot child. It made it all that much more memorable!

Sitting there in Wilson's mom's kitchen, I was feeling pretty happy. I had a warm cookie in one hand and a cold glass of milk in the other. It's kind of strange how a day could be so filled up with so many different kinds of feelings.

Today, I've already been scared out of my mind, had a great time playing basketball with people I thought I'd never speak to, and now was having the best cookie I ever tasted.

But hey, it all seemed to be working out! Life was balancing out pretty well.

"Wilson, sugar, can I ask you something?" His mom continued sweetly after checking on her oven. "What did you learn today at school, honey?"

"Uh, nothing much mom," he answered absentmindedly while making a stupid face at me.

He leaned over the table towards me and whispered, "My mom asks me that question every single day when I get home. It's like our own little thing. We sit, talk and eat these great cookies! Not a bad deal, huh?"

I nodded my head in agreement unable to speak through a mouth stuffed full of chocolate chips. It sounded a lot like what my mom did with me, except for us it wasn't an everyday thing. She worked most days, and also, my mom used slices of homemade sponge cake, not cookies. But I had this itchy feeling inside that something here was not going exactly right.

"Willy, baby, was your regular teacher, Mrs. Stein there? She wasn't sick or anything was she?" His mom continued gently.

"No, Ma. She was there. She's fine."

"Good, I like her. Well then, were you listening to her carefully? Were you paying good attention? What about you, Teddy? Were you minding what the teacher was sayin'?"

"Yes, ma," interrupted Wilson before I could get a word out. "I was paying attention. Teddy was too. You know we're in the same class. Why do you keep askin' the same question, Mom? Hey, Mom! Why are you pulling the cookie plate away Mom? Hey, hey, Mom?"

It was true. There went the plate of fresh baked cookies! Just as Wilson and I were both reaching for a second cookie she had pulled the plate away out of our reach. Wilson's mom now had a stern squint in her eye as she looked us over carefully and said.

"Well now then boys, if your teacher was there, you say she wasn't absent, and you were both there, and you were both payin' attention then you both should have learned somethin', not NOTHIN'! And in this house, boy, nothin' begets nothin', and that especially includes these cookies!"

Bam! She'd caught us in her trap fair and square!

Now I recognized the odd feeling I had just a minute ago. I'd been here before. It was the old mother set-up trap and we had fallen right into it.

Man, caught just like rookies!

But I immediately knew the reason I hadn't recognized it at first. It was because my sixth sense, my Mameh sense, had been clouded by the scent of fresh cookies. Now we had to prove we had learned lots of stuff or give up the goods, those cookies! I knew the deal. We were being trained like puppies to learn our lessons and bark on command.

Still, those were awfully good cookies!

"I learned how to subtract mixed fractions and borrow from whole numbers."

"And I learned all about the three branches of the federal government," I added loudly, eyeing the far distant cookie plate.

"And photosynthesis, yeah, photosynthesis, I know all about that. C'mon Ma, give us a break? Come on!" Wilson was doing his best puppy imitation.

Arf, arf!

"All right, all right then," she laughed as she pushed the cookie plate back across the table in our direction. "But the next time I ask you what you learned in school, I'd better get an answer that makes some kind of sense. Remember, I don't send you to school to learn, 'nothin'!' I send you for 'SOMETHIN'!' And you better be ready to tell me what that somethin' is!"

"Yes, ma'am." we both repeated sheepishly looking downward together. Then we caught each other's eye and started laughing. We all knew this was just Wilson's mom's way to remind us about why we were going to school. And just when the quiet sound of cookie munching had taken over the kitchen a brand new sound shattered the room's calm. It was a gruff voice loudly invading what had been a quiet room only seconds before.

"Why'n Hell is a lil' honky sittin' in my chair?" echoed off the walls of the brightly lit dining room.

Chapter Ten

I must have jumped a foot straight up out of that chair. It felt like my tuchus, my behind had touched a red hot stove.

Everyone in the room turned around to stare at the doorway where the deep baritone voice had come from. Standing there was a hulking giant, a huge bear of a man. He was easily way over six feet tall and so broad he had no trouble filling the doorway. Wilson, Stan and their mom all stared for an instant at the giant with their mouths hanging wide open. And then, almost as one person they burst out laughing and laughing!

"My man, Uncle Fred, that was really a good one, baby! Yeah, Unk, way to play the dozens! You shocked the mess outta us and look! Looks like you scared Teddy half to death! Honky, that's rich, Unk! You are a funny, funny dude!" giggled Stan wrapping his large fingers around another equally large chocolate chip cookie.

"Freddy!" Wilson's mom chided. "I just don't know what's come over you lately? What exactly is wrong with you? Why can't you act your age and show even a little bit of the good sense the Lord blessed you with? Teddy is Willy's guest in our home! You know the Lord expects hospitality, not hostility! I'm so sorry, sugar," she continued turning back to me.

"My brother Fred just doesn't want to use the intelligence God gifted him with. Please forgive us for his poor manners!" She finished up by tossing an emphatic glare in her brother's direction.

"Yeah, sure, sure thing, no problem," I answered a little bit bewildered. "But can you tell me, just exactly what *is* a honky?"

"You a honky, boy! You are! You're a honky!"

Wilson exploded now doubled over laughing again so hard he was holding on to both the table and his stomach. Both he and Stan were so far out of control, cookie crumbs were spraying outwards from their mouths all across the kitchen table down on to the linoleum floor. Then Stan coughed so hard milk suddenly exploded downward out of his nose. And with that last display of flying chocolate chips and milk Wilson rolled down on to the dining room floor clutching his stomach and gasping out loud for his next breath.

"Stop it! Please stop it! I don't think I can breathe?" choked Stan as he pushed himself away from the table holding on for support to the back of his chair. Then he suddenly clutched his stomach with both hands and bolted for the door to the backyard.

"Please God, let me stop laughing! I can't take anymore of this, please, please make it stop!" Stan's echo called from outside.

I was still puzzled. Just what was a, 'Honky'? And if it was something bad, why did everyone think it was so damned funny?

"Is that another curse word for a Jewish person?" I inquired uneasily.

"You tellin' me you Jewish, boy?" asked Uncle Fred slowly raising his eyes up from my feet to meet mine. It was like he was seeing me for the first time.

"Yeah, I mean, yes sir, I am. Is that a problem for you?" I asked nervously. "Am I right? Is that what a "Honky," really is?"

"Nope, nope, not at'all!" roared Uncle Fred slapping his thigh with delight again and again. Slowing down he continued.

"Fo' yo' info'mation, young buck, a honky is just an ignor'nt shit kickin' white man. You don' appear to be ignor'nt at'all, and ya' definitly not a white man, anyhow. You a Jew! And all a Jew is… is just a very mixed up colored anyhow ya' cuts it!"

This Uncle Fred is a very strange man, but still kind of interesting...

I decided to play along and ask a few more questions.

Maybe I will learn something special here.

"So then, what you're telling me is that I'm not really white? I'm a Negro like you?" I asked hesitantly.

This was all news to me. I didn't think my Mameh and Tateh would ever believe they were, "schvartzes" either.

All the Jewish people I know believe they are as white as brand new snow. What makes you right, Uncle Fred and them wrong? I'm going to ask him that question!

So I asked him, "Just look at my arm! Anyone here can see I'm white, definitely pure white! What makes you think I'm not white?"

"Well now, lil' fella," Uncle Fred began speaking again. "There are a lot of good reasons why you not white, but I'll give ya' just a couple for starters." His eyes were gleaming as he continued slowly on. "First of all, I want you and Willy to come over here 'neath this heah window. Now, roll up y'sleeves and les' give a good look-see. Who's darker?"

I looked carefully at my arm and then at Willy's, oops, Wilson's.

Maybe it's the light.

No, that wasn't it. There was still some late afternoon light.

Maybe it was my eyes?

No, they were okay.

He was right.

We weren't the same color. My skin was just a tiny bit lighter than Wilson's. Wilson wasn't even as dark skinned as his brother Stan. But my skin wasn't that light either. My arm was almost as dark as Wilson's! Now I was confused. Wilson's face, on the other hand, got a thoughtful look. But he didn't seem to be as confused as me.

"Got nothin' t'say to me now, do y'boy?"

Uncle Fred went on. "Did Sweetie ev'r tell you where we from down home? No, well then, I'll tell ya'. We're from Leeds, Alabama. Now I'm askin' y'ta jus' listen. I'm gonna be tellin' ya' bout somethin' I seen happ'n in that lil' country town when I was a youngsta' jes' like you."

"Y'knows what a general store is, don'cha? It's the kind of store sells y'everythin' y'needs to live if y'livin' in the country a 'ways from a big town."

"Well, the family owns this here genre'l store was Jewish, name a Shapira. Decent 'nuff folks in they own ways 'ceptin' at times they might talk down t'people a smidgin'. They even called us, "nigras," from time t'time, jus' like some of them Civil War lovin' white crackers down there do."

"Well then, one day I'm at the store buyin' my ma a sack a suga'. Some of the local Kluxers and Jew Man Shapira gets into a little dust up, y'know, an argament over sum'thin'. It wasn't nuthin' important cause I don' even rememb'r the why of it. What

I do rememb'r is th' white man gets real angry and calls the Jew man a 'nigra'. Mr. Shapira gets real mad too, all red in th' face angry, y'understand? He stands up to the ofays and sez he's as white as they mommas."

"That one honky's back froze straight up. He spins all round and tells Shapira, cold as ice, 'Nigras and Jews ain't but one and the same as a dumbass mule, ya' turns one inside out, ya' gets ya'self th' other!"

"Then he turns and walks away but 'fore he sets a foot outside th' door, he heels all th' way around and tells ol' man Shapira, "I'll be round to see 'bout ya' later."

"That night the Shapira's store burns down to' th' ground. Lucky they ain't livin' round back where they use' ta no more. In front a th' store they's a burnin' cross standin' there as plain as day. When old man Shapira comes round in the mornin' he nev'r sez a word. Just turns around, gets in his car and goes back home. Next day, th' Shapiras packs up and they's gone."

"What I learn't that night is simple. Jews might look white to each othe'r, but they only light skinned nigras to those Klan folks! Down home, man, we always knew y'all Jews ain't black, but that day we learn't that y'all sure as shit ain't white neither! Y'all are jes' souls lost betwixt different worlds, just like we Africans livin' in th' U. S. of A."

"Well, now Teddy, whatcha' thinkin' bout them there apples, my curious lil' Jewish brother?"

I was even more confused now, and a little more upset. I didn't have a clue to most of what Uncle Fred was talking about. But I knew how I felt. I was uncomfortable, except for one small thing. Uncle Fred had used the word, 'brother' when he spoke to me. And he was looking at me kind of sad, like he meant it. I decided to think more about everything he said later on, but for the meantime I would just follow the warm feeling of kindness I was feeling in that room.

I looked from one face to the next going around the table. Everyone had fallen silent during Uncle Fred's story. Now they all looked kind of sad and embarrassed for me, and maybe for themselves too. Wilson's mom had an angry look on her face.

"You know that wasn't necessary Fred. He's only a boy, and a guest in our home. Willy invited him here to meet the family and there you go laying four hundred years of slavery on him. Then confusing him with all that color foolishness! That's not neighborly, Fred, or Christian either! You know Momma would make you go get a switch for what you just did! You need to apologize to Teddy. What you did wasn't right Fred!"

Uncle Fred looked perplexed. He seemed to be struggling with himself. When his face finally cleared up he said. "Hey there lil' Jew Man, I'm sorry. Sharon is one hunnert per-cent correct. I shouldn'a call'd ya' a honky. That wasn't fair. I guess I was jes' lookin' for a cheap laugh. She's right though! That was foul, not at'all Christian of me. Can y'find it in y'heart t'please fo'give me, lil brother?"

It's not like I was angry, hurt or anything serious like that. I liked everyone there, including Uncle Fred. It was only that I didn't know exactly what to make of all of it. Except for one thing, that part I didn't have to think about at all.

"No problem at all, sir. Any uncle of Wilson's is okay with me! Could you please pass the cookies down this way? Thank you!"

I could tell Wilson was happy with my answer because there was only one cookie left on that big plate and instead of snatching it for himself he was pushing the plate over my way!"

"Can I have a cookie too, please?" asked a musical voice from behind me.

When I turned around I was looking into the deepest brown eyes I'd ever seen. I tried to say something, anything, but I felt like my empty mouth was crammed full of oatmeal. I just held out the plate with the last cookie and tried to close my wide-open trap.

Chapter Eleven

The pretty eyes belonged to a younger version of Wilson's mom.

"Teddy, this is my niece, Myra, Fred's daughter and she'll be staying with us for a while. She's one reason why I wanted to talk to you. You think you could introduce her to some of the girls in your class? I'm going to register her tomorrow at PS 90. Maybe she'll be in your class with Willy? We'd all like that! I'm going to ask the principal since Myra doesn't know anyone else there. What d'you think?"

"I sure hope so," blurted out of my mouth.

Myra just covered her mouth and smiled as I embarrassed myself. I looked down at the checkered tablecloth afraid to say anything else.

Thank God, Wilson jumping in to help me out!

"Well… I guess it's getting to be about that time," he said loudly. "I think I'll be walking Teddy back up the block a little ways before it gets too dark," he continued pulling me out of my chair by my arm and steering me towards the front door.

At the door he whispered, "Let's go Romeo before Myra decides to use your tongue to mop up the floor. It's already hanging halfway down there."

I stammered a goodbye fumbling my way out the front door. Uncle Fred stopped me there and pulled me in for a hug.

"My man, lil' curious Teddy, keep on pushin' on them books, boy. Go afta' that knowl'dge my pint size Hebrew broth'r. Y'come on back hea' anytime!"

It was quiet as we walked along back up 169th Street towards Grant Avenue. I guess we were thinking over what had happened today. Wilson stopped and asked me a question.

"Teddy, have you ever had a girlfriend?"

It wasn't a hard question to answer. A simple, "yes" or, "no" would've been fine, but that wasn't me. It only took me a second to answer the question with my own question.

"How do you know when you have a girlfriend or a girl who is just a friend?" I answered and asked.

Wilson looked at me like I was a lawyer from another planet.

"Well, I guess it's when both of you kind of have a special feeling for each other and you tell each other about it. Then comes handholding and dates. There's other stuff also, but I don't want to spoil the surprises for you!"

Wilson said all this with a dead serious expression so I was thinking this must be the real deal he was telling me.

"Nope, Wilson, then I guess I never had a real girlfriend. The daughter of a friend of my mom's did once show me how to dance in her kitchen. Then I took her to a Saturday night dance at the Y. But we ended up not even dancing. That's about as close as I ever got to a girlfriend. You got a girlfriend?"

I was hoping he would tell me, "no". But Wilson wasn't laughing at me like he had in the kitchen when I didn't know what a honky was. He just put his arm around my shoulders and said, "Don't let this get out cause I have to protect my rep. I've never had one either. Now Stan, he has a whole bunch of stone foxes chasin' him and he tells me everything!"

"Wow!" I couldn't help but cry out. "You mean he tells you the truth, everything! That is so cool, so stone cold cool. C'mon, c'mon now, tell me some of the good stuff?"

It was pretty obvious a guy like Stan, a big handsome basketball star would have lots and lots of girlfriends. Visions of all kinds of dating mysteries being revealed floated around my brain dazzling me.

I've struck the freakin' mother lode here! Yeah, baby!

"Sure thing Train, you know I got you! But tell you the truth Stan is holding out on me with some stuff. He says I need to get a little older before he's gonna share everything, but hey, whatever he does share, you got it!"

I slung my arm over Wilson's shoulder as we started walking. He did the same and we walked on a few more steps. I stopped there and turned. I knew I wanted to say something I was feeling inside, but it was hard getting it out. I decided to just spill it.

"Man, I never had a friend that shared stuff with me like you do. I never had a friend that stood up for me like you do. You're my best friend."

Wilson didn't say a word, nothing. I thought maybe I'd said too much and put him on the spot. He probably didn't even want to give me an answer.

I'm so stupid. I screwed up! Now I'm going to lose my friend!

I tried to say something to take away the pressure he must be feeling. But before I could get a word out Wilson turned towards me and put his right hand out, palm straight up.

"Best friends then. Slap me five, on the light skinned side!" he repeated as I brought my palm down on his. He then turned both our hands in a half circle griping them into a closed fist and bumped it first against his heart and then against mine. Letting go he turned and walked quickly back towards his neighborhood. He never looked back. I stood there my heart feeling full of something. I wasn't sure exactly what it was but I knew it made me feel special. I turned towards my block and ran down the street hoping I could get to my corner before it got any darker.

There's still that damn'd Wolfman for me to worry about.

Chapter Twelve

Next morning I was ready for the walk to school extra early. My oatmeal was still burning hot when I gulped down my first big spoonful. Usually I cooled it off by pouring a little cold milk from the full glass my mother made me drink before I could get out the door. Truth is today I was in a hurry, and my burning throat didn't matter. I only knew I had to get downstairs early, real early. I needed to be there in case Wilson decided to break our routine and not wait for me.

But no, there they were right on time. I could see Wilson, his mom, Uncle Fred and, of course, Myra walking slowly my way enjoying the sunny side of the block. I tried out my coolest, "Hi!" along with my most casual nod falling in step with my friend. Of course, I was really trying to catch Myra's eye, but somehow she never seemed to be looking my way.

Shot down so soon?

When lunchtime finally came I saw Myra on the other side of the schoolyard jumping rope with some of the other girls from another class. I'd kind of hoped she'd be in our class, but I guess it wasn't meant to be. Now I knew I needed to think of something else if I wanted to get to know her.

Meanwhile the guys in my class were choosing up our regular punch ball game. I was okay at punch ball, nothing special. The rules were the same as baseball but only you had to punch a rubber Spaldeen instead of using a stickball bat. Funny thing, Wilson wasn't any good at punch ball either. In fact, he was telling me he'd never played punch ball before he came to PS 90, so it wasn't much of a shock when both of us got picked last.

That was something else we had in common.

I didn't care much about being picked last when we chose up sides except for one thing. People laughed at you. Sometimes it was because you weren't that good a player but mostly it showed you weren't that popular a kid.

Being picked last always hurt.

For me, whatever the reason, being picked last was always a possibility. Sometimes I'd just skip the game altogether. It was easier than being a reject. I'd say stuff like, "I don't feel like playing punch ball today. I'd rather shoot some hoops!" and walk away like I meant it. But that wasn't true. Sometimes I'd feel that way, most times I didn't. Once in a while I got the feeling other people would rather hoop it up too, but they were afraid it would put them on the outs with the in-crowd who ran everything in the schoolyard.

There was a single iron hoop hanging at the far end of the schoolyard, but its rim was bent and tilted against the backboard. What made things even worse was that the only basketball the teachers ever brought outside was egg shaped and bounced funny. You had to love the game to keep shooting with equipment like that! That's probably why Wilson and me were alone at the far end of the yard hoisting up shots with the Humpty Dumpty ball and talking about, "Foundation", a great Isaac Asimov science fiction novel about Earth in the future. We'd already decided we were going to the library after school to take out everything else we could find by Asimov.

I was chasing down a long rebound that was taking some strange bounces when I heard something loud and turned around. A surprise was waiting there for me. It seemed like every boy in the schoolyard was walking towards me. The punch ball game had stopped and both teams were coming towards me. I couldn't figure out what was going on even when a kid from our class yelled out something that sounded like my name. He was walking next to Big Steve.

A cold shiver ran through me because Big Steve was bad news. He was the class bully, the school bully really. Big Steve was a lot bigger than the rest us and at least a head taller. It probably had something to do with him being left back two or three times. No one knew the truth because no one had been here as long as him.

Steve was a little on the slow side in class and with a large helping of meanness thrown in, he was a completed butthole. Oh, and by the way, he also had it in for everyone who wasn't "exactly" like him. Now that was pretty much the entire world but for some reason of his own he had a particular dislike for Jewish kids. Now that easily had to be the weirdest thing of all about him because Steve was Jewish!

One of Big Steve's most favorite things was punching people in their backs on the twisting school staircases. That was pretty easy for him because Mrs. Stein, the teacher was usually walking all the way up front and his victims were all the way in the back. Sometimes he'd even hit the girls he didn't like, or then again maybe it was because he did like them. Who knew how that twisted brain operated? He was scary.

Unfortunately, his choice of prey on the staircase usually came down to either me or this other tall boy in front of him on the class line. We were his closest victims, his favorite punching bags. He didn't do it every single day, but he did seem to get some special pleasure from being able to surprise his victim. Even on days he didn't hit us he liked to whisper little things like, "Gotcha!" and then laugh at our shocked expression. Then he'd follow up by whispering in your ear what would happen to you after school if you told.

"Steve I told you so! I told you so!" flashed me back from my Big Steve nightmare to my Big Steve for real minute. Yeah, it was that little brown nosing weasel Robby yelling gleefully as he got closer. Robby was skipping back and forth in front of the crowd like a trained monkey on a long string.

"Whadayamean, 'I told you so?" I asked him puzzled and a little on edge by now.

"It's you, Howdy Doofus!" snarled Big Steve pointing straight at me.

I didn't say anything back to him. Usually looking down and keeping your trap shut would spare you from getting smacked, but only after a little public humiliation. Being singled out like this was nerve rattling. I wracked my brain trying to figure out what was going on.

What did I do to put myself in this tough spot?

I thought hard to myself, but couldn't come up with anything except, G.P, general persecution!

I sighed and decided to wait, and hope for the best.

"It's your shirt, stupid! Robby sez he got the same shirt your wearin' right now at home. Only he sez it's the top of his pj's. Robby sez you came to school wearin' your pajamas. That makes you a double dumbass greenhorn!" sneered Big Steve pushing his thick finger into my chest and shoving backwards.

"Oh no, no, nope, this is a regular shirt, Steve. My mother just bought it for me at Alexander's," I answered weakly, my knees starting to give way.

Of course I knew it wasn't true.

That same morning my Mameh couldn't find a clean shirt for me because she'd come home later than usual from working overtime. She was tired and it was too late to wash one out for me like she usually did most evenings. She said to just wear the pajama top for one day and that nobody would ever notice.

Boy, was she ever wrong about that one!

"This is a real shirt. It's just old, man! They must've made his pajamas out of the same material. That's why he has them confused. But anybody could make that mistake," I lamely trailed off offering Robby a way out to save me. "Anyone could make that mistake," I repeated desperately using my eyes to plead with Robby. But Robby just smiled back at me smugly, enjoying this.

"You callin' me stupid, greenhorn?" growled the small mountain towering in front of me. "You know, I'm getting tired of you Jews all actin' like y'betta than me, like everyone not raisin' their hands for every single question the teacha asks is an idiot! Maybe you're the idiot for wearin' your pajamas to school! Maybe your mama is the idiot cause she dresses ya' funny!"

"And just maybe you should blame Y'MAMA for droppin' you on your pointy head instead of pickin' on kids who're afraid of you," said a loud voice from right behind the huge bully.

"WHO FREAKIN' SAID THAT?" bellowed Big Steve spinning around like a bank's heavy revolving door. "Who's azz is gonna get kicked across this yard after I finish wipin' the floor with this little schmuck!" the enraged teen monster bellowed.

The crowd parted like the Red Sea before Moses and there was not so tall, not so dark but still very slender Wilson.

"Oh yeah, yeah, lemme see what I got here?" crowed Big Steve. "Now I gets it. Now I see what's up here! Here comes Spot, little Dick's, guard dog! Where's Jane, Spotty? You know what, little Jewish Dickhead? I got somethin' here for you and for Spotty over there too! You'd betta run Spot! Yes, see Spot run! Run Spot run, run, run, run if you know what's good for ya'! What's this now? Spot ain't runnin'? I can see Spot and Dick need some of this special, pow, pow, pow!" he said pounding his fists together.

"Yo, you over there, Chocolate Boy, listen up! I'm gonna meet your Oreo azz across th' street at three. Hey, and, you, Jew Boy, and you too, Spotty, don't you make me come lookin' for youse guys! Y'hear me loud 'n clear, faggots!"

And with that last ugly shout he turned and stomped away with little Robby trailing like a cork in his wake. The rest of the crowd had become frozen into an icy silence during Big Steve's vicious outburst.

Before I could get a word out of my mouth the line-up whistle blew and everyone except Wilson and I ran to their class line-up spots.

"What th' hell are we gonna do?" I asked, finally remembering to exhale. I was totally and completely terrified at the thought of being massacred at three o'clock. I didn't know how to fistfight, not even a lick and said so.

"Train, what makes you think Garbage Mouth over there knows any more about throwin' down than you do?" asked Wilson with a sneer. "All that dog's dick does is smack people when they're not lookin'! Just let go and get mad, man! You're not half-bad when you bug out a little," he laughed, turning away and jogging towards line-up. My mind was left a total blank. I was so numb I couldn't feel my legs, and I don't remember how I got upstairs to our classroom.

But I do remember wondering if there was a Hebrew school prayer, a brucha, for surviving a fight after school.

Chapter Thirteen

I was ready to cry. And I would have if anyone had been close enough to say, "Boo!"

Once we were in the classroom everyone kept turning around in their seats to stare. Some looked, others smirked. Some people shook their heads from side to side and mouthed, "uh, oh!" Some were even crueler. They pointed their fingers at me from behind the teacher's back and pretended to laugh right in my face. Well, so much for false friends. But it didn't bother me as much as the kids who looked back at me mirroring the same terror in their eyes that I felt inside. I was left sitting alone on my hard wooden seat dying to run up to the teacher's desk and beg her to please, please call my mother.

MAMEH, PLEASE, PLEASE, COME AND GET ME! PLEASE!

My toes felt like sweaty ice cubes and I swear I was beginning to feel lightheaded.

Right now! Go up there and tell the teacher!

My inner voice was shrieking gibberish. That part of me was hiding all balled up in a little attic room, a lost faraway someplace in my head. But another part of me refused to listen to the screaming voice. I wouldn't do it. I just sat there at my desk shaking away on the inside.

I turned myself around and glanced over to the other side of the room where Wilson was sitting. He was getting a lot of the same looks I was getting.

How could he not after sounding off on Big Steve like he had?

But with Wilson it didn't seem like it was making any big difference. He didn't look upset at all, at least not on the outside. Wilson was sitting there writing in his workbook like it was just any other day in school.

Man, he is cool or what?

Seeing him like that helped me. Sensing my eyes were on him he sent a big wink my way. Still, even with that message the beads of cold sweat wouldn't stop rolling down my back.

Hang on, hang on in there, baby, just stay tough! Maybe Big Steve will hit us a few times and let us go!

That was my prayer to Him. I prayed it over and over again.

That's the way it usually went. If you didn't fight back it was one hard punch, some name-calling and the whole thing was over and out. It was too bad Steve didn't know Wilson's big brother, Stan. If he did we sure as hell wouldn't be in this mess.

And to think that all this was happening just because I wore a pajama shirt to school.

Life just isn't fair sometimes!

That afternoon I watched the moon faced clock hanging over the front blackboard like a hawk. It was clicking off minutes like it had somewhere important to go.

Why did it seem like it was moving so much faster this afternoon?

When I looked down to my desk I noticed something different right away. Sitting in the crease that was made to hold your pencil was a long salty pretzel stick.

I really like those. But where had this one come from?

Looking over to my left I saw that the girl I usually walked upstairs next to on line was smiling sympathetically at me. She leaned over towards my desk and whispered, "Don't be scared. Steve is only a big bully. He lives on my block. If you hit him back he cries. When I was little I hit him back and made him cry! I know you like these long stick pretzels so I saved you one. It's going to be all right. Just do your best. Hit him and then run away real fast. Steve's as slow as a turtle!"

I nodded gratefully, especially for the pretzel.

Pretty good for a last meal.

The last part of what she'd said made a lot of sense. After all, I had run away many times before.

Why stand and fight when you knew you were going to lose? Hit Steve back? She must be nuts! That was plain crazy! I might as well tease an unchained wild dog!

All of these different ideas were banging around in my head. But then I thought about two things that did make a big difference to me. If I ran away I would hear those same hated words shouted behind me. The ones I had suffered with before!

Yellow Jew, punk, kike, bastard!

I was tired of hearing that kind of stuff. My father had fought the Nazis in the war before I was born.

He told me he was always afraid in battle. Being afraid, he said, was normal. Everyone was afraid. But not letting your fear rule you was what measured a person's courage. He also told me to use common sense and run from a fight whenever possible, but then that sometimes it would not be possible. Then it was time to fight. I knew this time running was not going to be possible.

The second reason I was going to have to fight at three was I knew Wilson wasn't going to run. I was sure of it in my heart. He was my best friend. I knew he would never run away and leave me by myself. So I decided no matter what happened to me, I wouldn't run away this time.

The bell rang. It was five to three and everyone jumped up to pack up their books and get on the dismissal line. Big Steve looked over at me again pounding his fist into his palm a few extra times. There was also a nasty leer splitting his face into two apple shaped red halves. I was hoping he wasn't watching me too closely because he would have seen me shaking right down into my shoes.

We marched down the wide hallway until we entered the "down" stairwell. Wilson and I were now only a few people away from the back end of the line. Big Steve was in his usual spot, dead last. It looked to me like he was covering the rear a little more carefully today in case somebody decided to do a "Houdini." You know, do a disappearing act. We started our five-floor journey downstairs with the sound of Mrs. Stein's loud, "Class, forward!" Down we went one floor at a time, turning around quickly on the switchback's landings halfway between each floor.

But before we took the first step down past the fourth floor landing, Wilson grabs my arm and jerks me around the frosted glass to run around to the reverse staircase also going down. Our teacher at the front of the line never even noticed our escape. We were gone. There were just too many kids to keep track of. Our, "Houdini" had been pulled off in a split second so Big Steve had been caught completely off guard. He was so surprised that he forgot where he was and yelled out loudly, "Hey, where d'hell are you two dipshits goin'! You're both dead, y'two chick'n shits!"

Whew!

"Thank you God!" I said out loud gratefully glancing upwards towards Heaven while scrambling quickly down the steps behind Wilson. I was giddy with happiness.

It's sure lucky for us that Wilson smartened up! And now, whew! we're gonna run out of one of the school's many dozens of exits before our class even makes it downstairs.

Strangely, once we were zipping down the steps Wilson started slowing up. We'd slowed down now to the point where we could clearly see our class going down the steps on the other side of the wire reinforced frosted glass. Usually when that happened I loved to make faces at my friends through the glass separating the two sides of the staircase. That was fun! But stopping to make those funny faces today was suicidal!

What was Wilson thinking slowing us down to look through the glass?

Today the only one interested in looking at us was Big Steve. And he wasn't making any happy faces. I kept trying my best to hurry Wilson up, but he wasn't having any of it. In fact, he was making sure we came down at the exact same slow pace the class was going until, guess what? We all arrived together on the ground floor.

Then Wilson stopped, turned and waited until almost the entire class slowly walked right by us, except for Steve. Big Steve stopped all right. He eyeballed us for a few seconds, and then walked on to the outside exit. He stopped there blocking the doorway and called back over his shoulder, "I'll be waitin' for youse guys cross th' street. Don't make me come lookin' for yer yella' belly azzes!"

For a full three seconds there was only silence. Wilson reached over and pushed my arm. Then he said, "Wait a minute." He didn't have to ask me twice because there was no way I wanted to go out the door with Big Steve waiting.

Finally, I asked him why we were waiting when we should be running. He smiled at me.

Wilson leaned his back up against the iron and wood banister and continued, “My pops taught me there’s a time to run and a time to fight, and I’m not running from that punk-ass’d ofay shit kicker today.”

“But wait a minute Wilson, I’m the one he made fun of, me, remember Mr. Pajama Shirt!” I pleaded hoping for a change of heart. “And I have no problem whatsoever running away from him!”

“Nope, Teddy. You need to stop lookin’ at stuff like it’s only about you! You’re the only one thinkin’ this is about you, but it ain’t! Big Steve’s mouth is always shootin’ off blowin’ shit around. He’s always got some B.S. to mouth off about.”

“This ain’t just about you anymore, it’s about us, me and Myra too! The other day in the lunchroom that cracker threw a chicken bone at me and told me he was gonna send over some damn watermelon. That B.S. ain’t flyin’ with me t’day! I should’ve fucked him up right then, but I remember’d what my mom asked me. “No more fightin’ in school”. So I let it pass... again. And to be honest, I was a little scared of that big white dick, you know being in a new school and all, and yeah, all right, because mostly, I was all by myself too. But today’s different, right? T’day I got me some back up, right? You do got my back, right, Train?” Wilson looked at me searchingly.

“Are you fuckin’ crazy, man? Have you lost your complete freakin’ mind?” I yelled back at him. “Here I am telling you I can’t fight, not even a single lick and, “let’s get the hell out of here,” and you’re asking me do I have your back? You can’t be serious man? Let’s just call your brother Stan and let him straighten Big Steve out while we both are still alive and in one single piece!”

My voice had been rising slowly, but surely, until I suddenly realized I was now yelling.

“Teddy, man, be cool, man... Stan ain’t the answer this time. Sometimes you got to be a man and to take care of your own business, do your own work…” answered Wilson calmly.

"Do you remember why the Robot was unbeatable in every Asimov book?"

Again, I looked at him like he'd really, really lost his mind.

"Willy, man, this is real life, not an, "I, Robot" book. Quit day dreamin' for one goddamn minute! You are not a robot or any kind of comic book hero. You're just a kid about to get beaten up by a much bigger, meaner kid. … And all you have for back up is me, a scared little schmendrick who can't fight his way out of a wet paper bag! Now, let's go find another exit on the other side of this building and get the fuck outta' here!"

I might as well have been a page of the Daily News being blown around in the gutter on a windy day for all the attention I was getting!

Wilson kept right on talking at me like he hadn't heard a single word I said.

"What made the Robot a winner is that somehow he had a human heart. He never gave up when even the metal he was made of did. He always gave his best and that's what really matters."

"Yeah, I get it! You're not the best with your hands, brother, but you do got a ton a heart. I saw it the first day when you fought for your little brother and your library books. Then you showed it to me again the day you turned around and fought that prick, Miles on your block."

"There's two things I'm for sure, one hundred percent of today," finished Wilson. "One, we both got heart and Big Steve don't. And two, we're gonna win this fight and he's gonna lose."

"Now let's go outside and kick Jumbo's muthafukin' ass! You down with me, or what?"

I didn't know what to say to that!

Wilson is totally, fuckin' nuts! He's a madman! Should I listen to him?

I could hear the voices of my Mameh and Tateh telling me to walk away, no run away, as fast as my feet could carry me. But then in my head I kind of also heard my father's voice whispering to me.

You can't always run.

That's when the thunderbolt struck me!

Why didn't I see it before? It was so simple.

I'd never been in a fight with a friend fighting right at my side. At least it'd always felt that way.

Maybe this time things will be different?

And there was one other thing. If I ran I knew I would lose Wilson's friendship forever. I didn't want that.

So there it was. It was now settled in my mind. We were both going out to fight Big Steve. That was my decision alone and our decision together, God help us!

"Okay, Wilson," I sighed. "Let's go across the street."

"Last thing, Train, you can call me Willy. All my family does."

Chapter Fourteen

We crossed over the one-way street to the corner where Max's candy store was. All the after three o'clock fights started in front of Max's. It was tradition. A crowd of kids was already there waiting for the show to begin.

It was always the same thing. Every time there was gonna be a fight after school a crowd would show up as if by the snap of a finger. It was something like what I'd read about when sharks feed. As soon as they smell blood in the water they'd come to get fed. Same thing here. The buzz about the fight had been burning up the school's bathrooms and hallways since lunchtime and the kids in front of Max's meant feeding time had officially arrived. Even worse, it seemed like every one of them was trying to stand in the same exact place. And that spot was right behind our big boned executioner, Big Steve.

The first thing I noticed crossing the street were my friends from the block standing off over to one side. Their unhappy faces said they were already at the scene of a very bad accident. With a glance I could read their minds. Their expressions clearly asked, "Why on earth wasn't this poor schmuck running for his life?"

Believe me, it's not like I didn't want to.

Somehow I was walking, but my legs felt like "Jello" being controlled by some unknown puppet master. Each one of my steps was uneven and a little bit jerky, but I still managed to hurry up and keep in step with Wilson's measured stride. The buzz in the street continued getting louder until I could barely separate the car sounds from the people's voices. Then, as if on command a hush fell over the crowd as Wilson stepped onto the sidewalk.

Wilson was now face to face with Big Steve. Only six feet of empty space separated them. I was standing alongside Wilson's right hand wondering if anyone was looking at me because if they were, they would have seen I was shaking. They might also have noticed as I did that Wilson's hands were all balled up into tight fists and he wasn't shaking at all. It actually calmed me down to see that one of us was still in control of his body's functions. In fact, I stood up just a little bit straighter. Then from some unknown place inside myself I gathered up the nerve to lift my eyes and look straight at Big Steve.

You know, I don't think Steve appreciated that because he jumped right back at me.

"Yo' y'eyeballin' me pajama-boy? Now ya thinkin' y'gonna try t'punk me too, Jew boy?" he snarled viciously. "Ya' thinkin' you d'man all of sudd'n just because you got lil' smokey ov'r here t'fight y'battles? Y'betta' think again, stoopid! Say "pretty-please, Big Steve!" Maybe I'll be nice and give both a youse a runnin' headstart!"

And with that he threw his head back like a crazy hyena and howled a mean laugh that usually meant someone had gotten punched in the back of their heads. Laughing even harder he half-turned to make sure his audience was enjoying the show.

That's when he made his second mistake.

His first one was just starting with Willy to begin with, but to be fair who knew what was coming? Big Steve staggered backwards, first one, then two shaky long steps. I guess it was because he had been sucker-punched in the side of his head with a heavy roundhouse.

I stood there frozen by what I'd just saw. Willy had waited patiently until Big Steve turned his head back around to his boys and then with lightning speed he'd taken a running giant step and slammed Big Steve. He jumped back to me and quickly whispered out of the corner of his mouth, "Get behind him while he's lookin' at me! Get his attention so he can't bear hug me! I got the rest!"

I nodded numbly mostly because I couldn't get a peep much less a word to come out of my mouth. It was frozen shut. All I could get out as I stumbled to the right was a mouse-like squeak. Then a bunch of stuff started happening real fast.

I'd never been in a real street fight. Wrestling with my brother in bed or play fighting with my friends was as far as my experience went. We all liked to act tough and get in each other's faces. Sometimes we even leaned into each other and bumped heads and chests.

"Whatchyagonnado? WhatchYOUgonnado?" would go back and forth a few times, but we all knew it wouldn't go any further. Your true friends always stepped in and stopped it before things got serious. This time with Big Steve was gonna be different.

When Big Steve got hit with that surprise roundhouse punch he'd fallen backwards, but he never went down. That was scary all by itself. Willy had hit him as hard as he could!

I saw it plain as day!

Big Steve touched his face with both of his hands to see if there was any blood flowing. He definitely had a hard coconut because there wasn't even a drop there. He did have a slightly confused look on his face for two or three seconds until he finally figured out what had happened. Once he realized he had been sucker-punched and by who, I could see his complexion changing.

Was his head replaced by a giant red tomato?

Boy, was he angry. Actually enraged said it a lot better.

With no other warning Big Steve exploded towards Willy like a mad bull elephant.

"You skinny black muthafucka'! I'm gonna break your freakin' back!" He bellowed at the top of his lungs. "I'm gonna beat th' livin' shit outta ya'! C'mere!"

Willy danced backward instantly moving out of his path. His fists were up and weaving, cobra heads ready to strike again. And had his face changed! It had a fearful look of concentration tattooed on it. Man, was I amazed because he almost, no, he did look like a whole different person! And whoever was there had none of the fear in him that I felt in my guts.

I know he has to be scared!

He'd told me himself he didn't want to mess with Big Steve because Steve was a scary cat. But then again I remembered what my father had said about handling your fears.

I guess Willy's dad must've told him the same thing.

I was still standing in the same spot where Willy had left me. The crowd pushed in on me from behind. But there I stood stone still frozen with fear. I couldn't make myself move. That's when Willy's eyes met mine. I knew he could see, even feel my fear, but that's not what I saw when I looked back. I saw Wilson's determination, and yeah, some fear too, but even more important then that I saw his trust. Wilson knew I was scared and ready to piss myself but I saw he believed I wouldn't let him down.

The next thing I knew I was flying through the air screaming something, I don't even know what, but it was at the top of my lungs. All I know is I landed on top of Big Steve's back yelling something, punching at him and finally wrapping both of my arms around his head.

Maybe I covered his nose and he couldn't breathe? Maybe it was his eyes and he couldn't see? I'm not sure…

Maybe it was only my weight on his back or him being surprised but whatever it was, it turned him away from Willy.

Now I was his problem, and he was mine!

Big Steve began spinning around in circles trying to buck me off like a wild mustang trying to get rid of its rider.

The crowd had been stunned into silence by the scream that accompanied my leap onto Big Steve. But it didn't take them long to recover. They roared back breaking out into whoops and catcalls as Big Steve spun around and around yelling out, "Get 'im off me! Get 'im off me!"

They were merciless. "Get 'im off me! Get 'im off me!" they mimicked until it grew becoming a chant. I guess that must've been funny right up until he got his two hands on me. I was trying my best to keep my hold on his head but he was way too strong for me. One of his hands caught on to my belt and then I knew it was over. The crowd knew it too. I could hear a collective, "Ooooh!" come from them as I was lifted up high in the air by a pair of huge hands.

Finally, I felt myself being thrown. I know this might sound strange, but as I sailed through the air I had a slow motion moment. I wasn't really afraid of Big Steve anymore.

Yeah, I knew I was going to get hurt when I landed, but I was still happy in a weird way.

I hadn't run.

I'd sure wanted to but I didn't. Instead I'd stayed and I'd helped my friend.

Chapter Fifteen

Where am I? I can't feel anything?

My eyes blinked. I hadn't even realized they were closed, but now I saw only clear blue. I was hoping it was the sky. At that moment it wouldn't have surprised me if it were the ocean. And it was also strangely quiet. I mean I couldn't hear a thing, no birds, no cars, no nothing besides the voice in my head.

Where was I?

Wherever it was, was someplace very blue and very quiet.

Then a switch flipped and many mixed together sounds came flooding in.

"Jay-sus, I think he's hurt real bad! He ain't movin' or makin' a sound."

"Boy, did ja' see how far he flew before he landed? Big Steve is a freakin' beast!"

"Well, maybe now his stupid ass will learn a lesson. Rumblin' with Big Steve ain't too smart," bounced back a voice with a wicked chuckle. "Dumb schmuck could a' just bashed his head up against a brick wall and screamed "yippee" if all he wanted was to be brain dead! Wait up a minute! Yeah… yeah, I think his eyes are opening! He ain't dead after all!"

"This here's one lucky lil' Yiddle! He's lucky he landed flat on top of this car's hood or his brains would a' been mashed p'tatas on th' sidewalk, maybe even be croaked!" chirped in little Robby's familiar high pitched whine.

Croaked…dead?

That word woke me up in a hurry. And it brought back a bunch of other things too. Suddenly, the numbness in my body was being replaced by a burning sensation spreading like a liquid through my back and shoulders. In only a few seconds I was feeling like I had fallen asleep on a kitchen stove's lit burners. My body was on fire. Hands were lifting me under my arms and legs. Then my body was propped up into a sitting position on the sidewalk. Through my clothes the rough cement tore into me and a hard rubber tire and hubcap pushed back hard up against my back.

"Don't move'im anymore. He might be hurt bad. Just let him sit there for a minute and catch his breath. Man, did you ever see anyone fly through the air and bounce off a car hood like that?"

"You okay? You okay? How many fingers do you see?"

I kept hearing different voices asking questions. Then I heard something even stranger. It sounded like my own voice answering that I was okay even though I wasn't sure if I was or wasn't. I could only hope it was the truth.

What the hell had happened to me? Had I been hit by a car? Maybe I had tripped running across the street and hit my head hard?

But no, something was still missing. I could feel it. It was then I heard the whispering inside my head.

Run! Run while you still can!

An insistent voice was commanding me.

RUN!

That's when it all came flooding back to me. Using the palms of my hands I pushed off the ground trying to get up. At the same time, I needed to push away both the pain and the hands trying to hold me down.

"Stay down, stoopid! You're hurt!"

But now I remembered everything.

There was a fight going on. I could hear the sounds of it all around me. Suddenly the memory came back to me.

I'd been in it. It was get up quickly, or else…

I was standing up, but jammed tightly in front of me was a wall of people. They were a shoulder-to-shoulder crowd packed tightly together with their backs turned to me and they were watching something going on in the middle of the street.

Lowering my elbow, I squeezed into the mob using hands and arms to force cracks in that human wall. There was pushing and a lot of shoving before I finally got up to the front. But what I saw when I got there hurt me much more than any of my pain.

The fight had slowly but surely shifted out into the middle of the intersection. Traffic was stopped in all four directions and blowing horns made it seem even crazier than it was. The crowd had quickly grown from a few dozen school kids to a large mob surrounding the fighters. Like a living thing the big crowd had moved around to keep Wilson and Big Steve at its center. As they battled and moved the ringside crowd shifted right along with them.

But now I could see that Wilson was no longer dancing around like he was in a real boxing ring. There was no more sliding in and out or bobbing and weaving. The room needed for that kind of fight was gone. At the instant I broke through Willy was picking himself off the ground and charging straight at Big Steve. Big Steve easily caught him around the shoulders and gathered him up in a tight bear hug. Then he squeezed Willy hard with all his might once and then twice all the while grunting like an angry bear. Everyone there could hear all the breath being pushed out of Wilson's mouth and then seeing his body go limp.

Finally, Big Steve half threw, half punched Willy to the ground. That last body shot was accompanied by a nasty smirk. Then he turned around and strolled away from Wilson who was laid out flat on the ground. Big Steve was dusting off his hands as if he had just handled something dirty.

Maybe the fight should have ended right then and there, but it didn't. At almost the same instant he'd hit the ground Willy gathered himself up and re-launched his body once again at Big Steve's back!

This madman was someone I didn't even know!

Wilson's, I think they were Wilson's, eyes were now huge dark pools of burning rage. His face was contorted in a soundless scream and in only two quick steps he was going at Big Steve at full speed again! Big Steve must have sensed something because he turned around in mid-step just in time to snatch Willy right out of the air.

But not before Wilson swung and rocked him with another lightning right and left punch to the forehead. Staggered, but still trying to act like both punches were only fleabites he held Willy up high in the air for a split second before he threw him to the ground even harder than the last time.

"Stay the fu'k down, azzhole! I'm warnin' y'for th' last time, dammit! You'd betta' stay down this time or I'll body-slam y'azz so hard all y'friends will be spendin' th' afte'noon pickin' up chocolate chips! Stay th' fu'k down, muthafucka!" cussed Big Steve out of breath and maybe a little too loudly.

But Wilson wouldn't stay down. He just wouldn't do it. Maybe, he couldn't do it.

Please stay down Willy! You're covered in blood and dirt! Just please stay down and this will end. Please, please Willy, please just let go of this thing and give up!

But he wouldn't do it. It seemed as if he was bouncing off the sidewalk like a hard rebound off a backboard, again and again. Then he'd get up and go straight back after Big Steve. Here he came once again. Big Steve didn't even have time to half turn this time. He was still facing directly at Wilson when he came charging.

"Whadafu'k is wrong with you? Don' y'even know when your azz is whipped? Y'lost the fight, blackie! Go th' fu'k home! Get th' hell outta here or I'll knock your skinny azz right back inta' yesta'day!" screeched Big Steve desperately, his voice now rising into an almost girlish scream.

But Willy kept on coming. If he'd heard any of the words Big Steve said it didn't matter. He just kept right on going at his target, Big Steve.

And here I was again, not knowing what to do. I thought my part in this was over, ended. Even though only a few seconds had passed I knew I had to make another decision, and it had to be now. I felt paralyzed, trapped in a fearful place in my head, but there wasn't any more time to think.

My heart took over. It screamed, 'Right now!"

So I did it. I charged straight at Big Steve from his right side. Luckily for me he was concentrating only on one "crazy man," Wilson. He never even saw me coming at him from my direction. I just tackled him around the waist like I saw the football players in the park do. Then I held on with all my might as tightly as I could. It didn't even occur to me to punch Big Steve because I really didn't know how to even do that. I only knew I had to hold on and that if I let go it would end up being much worse for both of us.

Almost immediately I could feel Steve's big fingers pulling on my hands, trying to break my grip. But I'd joined both my hands together into one fist and I refused to let go. Then all of a sudden something else must've happened. It was probably "Superman"" Wilson attacking because Big Steve stopped grabbing at my hands and started hammering me in the back, but using only one fist. I guess he was using the other one to fight off Willy.

Strangely enough, I had felt Big Steve's punch in the back before and I knew I could take a couple of those. But I was still trying desperately to duck my head. I knew it would be deadly if one of those hams connected. But it was no use. He nailed me with a big one! A huge fist caught me hard in the back of my neck and that was it. I could feel my fingers losing their grip, no matter how hard I tried to hold on.

Next thing I knew I was face down on the ground… again. It should've been over then but somehow as I fell my arms had wrapped themselves around one of Big Steve's legs. He swung a kick at me with his other foot, but luckily it missed. It came to me he must still be busy with Willy! Still I knew if I let go of that big leg of his he could easily move himself around and then try to stomp me. It wasn't about winning a fight anymore. Now it was about trying to survive! That was giving me the strength I needed to hold on. I knew I couldn't let go of that leg no matter what!

In that next instant I heard what General Custer must have been praying for during his last seconds on earth. Someone had arrived to save us, and it was a voice I knew.

"SHOW'S OVER, BABY! THAT'S IT FOLKS! This shit's over unless it's you and me gonna rumble! WE ARE OVER AND OUT!"

"**The next one who throws a punch gets my foot dead up they ass!**

"Let go of the polar bear, Sweets!" the same but lowered voice said.

Suddenly I felt a weird sensation besides happiness. I was being jerked up into the air by the seat of my pants. The yank was so powerful it stood me upright on to my feet.

So now there I was, standing straight up, grinning from ear-to-ear looking upwards for a face to face with my rescuer. I even snuck a look down first to check and see if I had peed myself out of sheer relief.

Yes! There he was! It was six foot five Stan the Man standing right there, Stan, Wilson's big brother. And I do mean his big, very large, strong brother. He'd lifted me up off the ground with only one hand. I knew that he had to be real strong because under his other arm, fists still swinging away, was a spitting mad Willy.

"Hey little man, you good?" he asked me almost apologetically. "You're gonna have to give me a few minutes because "Sugar Ray Knucklehead" over here is still busy actin' the fool! I'm gonna need both hands to hold on to him. You do understand, right, Teddy? Are you sure you're all right lil' fella?"

I numbly nodded, "Yes", and then stood there unsure of what I was supposed to do next. I looked around, up and down, and guess what? I had peed myself, but only just a teensy little bit.

But guess what else? Right there on the ground sitting on his big fat ass rubbing his face with two hands was no one else but, you guessed it, Big Steve. His face was all covered with bruises, lumps and even some blood.

"Hey man, yeah you, big boy! Raise yourself up off of your fatass'd rump! Get up off th' ground!" growled Stan with a sideways menacing glare.

I was kind of scared myself looking at Stan glowering down at busted up Big Steve. Stan had to be at least six foot five, all chiseled muscle and showing some bad attitude at this exact minute. I guess Big Steve saw what I saw because he wasn't making much of an effort to get up.

"I said, you'd best get your ass up off th' ground while I still got Tony the Tiger here all wrapped up! No one here's gonna hurt you… not yet. But my advice is you'd be wise to get yourself up and outta here before I decide to let this one go! At least that's what I'd do, if I was you!" Then as strange as it might seem, Stan started laughing real loud.

Big Steve nervously stood up. As he did he started taking small backward steps while whining to anyone who'd listen in a high-pitched voice, "Y'know that wasn't ev'n a fair fight. Ev'rybody could see dat! It was two 'gainst one! I nev'r had a chance! No fair, man! T'ain't right!

Suddenly, Stan pretended to let the still swinging Wilson go, while at the same time laughing louder.

"So what you're sayin' Big boy is I should just let my little brother Willy here go right now, and that's cool by you? I mean, you tellin' me all you want outta this is a fair fight, right?"

Meanwhile an enraged Wilson, still swinging, lunged at Big Steve while wordlessly trying to throw a flying kick at the same time. Big Steve leaped backwards like a snarling pitbull had lunged at him. Terror was written all over his face.

"Nah, Nah, Nah, don' let 'im go! Don' let 'im go! He's nuts! Complet'ly crazy! Please, don' let 'im go!" Big Steve cried out his palms held out upwards in a plea for understanding.

Stan continued laughing at Big Steve's frightened expression and said, "Look here, this here fight is done, over. But if I hear anythin' 'bout you or any of your boys botherin' my guys, Willy or Teddy again, I'm coming straight here for behinds, your dumb ass goes first and then all them too! Ya' dig what I'm puttin' down here? You know you don' wanna see my face around here no more! Capiche?"

"Y'right, man, y'right! You got it! Don' worry! There ain't gonna be any more probl'ms of any kind! Right Wilson? Right Teddy? Everythin' is gonna be straight up 'tween us! Right fellas?"

Big Steve kept right on babbling away as he backed slowly out through the parting crowd and then all the way down the rest of the street. He made sure he turned his head back around every five or six steps to make sure Willy hadn't broken loose and was coming after him. And then he turned the corner of 166th and was gone.

After Stan saw Big Steve turn the corner he bent down towards me, put his arm around my shoulders and whispered,

"What d'you think, Train? Can I put Willy down now or is he gonna take off after that cracker?"

I just nodded, "Yes" even though I hadn't the slightest idea of what Wilson would do. This was a whole different Willy than the one I was used to.

Stan continued on, "I'm guessin' you didn't know this before, but Willy is as crazy as a wet rooster when it comes to fightin'. Nobody in our entire family will mess with him because he loses it as soon as he gets hit. Either he wins or he gets knocked out."

"Sometimes we just have to tie him up, and drop him in his bed," he chuckled. "I'm tellin' you the boy has never lost a fight with his eyes open! He's lost teeth, hair, shoes and glasses, but he don't ever lose fights. With him it's always to the death. That's why I raced over here when Myra ran home and told me he was at it again."

"See, this school is a brand new chance for him. Willy's real smart, but he's got some anger bunched up inside and needs a quieter place. That's why we moved 'round here, quieter school and all. Now, we can't have him beatin' up some stupid big kid in a new place who doesn't know what he's getting into! It's too bad really, because things have been goin' mostly a whole lot better for Willy lately. Now this crazy b.s. had to start up again."

I was stunned. I had no idea Willy was dangerous.

What a F-ing great friend to have!

The chicken shit part of my brain exulted.

Once the word gets around we'll be safe from everybody from now on! No one will want to mess with Wilson. He's a psycho, and I, me, am the psycho's best buddy!

Who would have thought things could get so good from such a lousy beginning?

I looked from the now buzzing crowd to Stan who was whispering softly in Wilson's ear and then said to him, "I don't think Willy is going to have any more fighting problems at this school."

Stan tilted his head and asked earnestly, "You really think so, Teddy?"

"Definitely, without any doubt!" I answered.

I looked over to see if Wilson had returned to being the nice person I called my best friend, but he was still struggling to break free from out of his brother's tight grip.

Well, maybe I can talk to Willy later about how nuts he is?

"Time to go, little man. Get your books, pick up Willy's stuff too, will ya, and let's split!"

The crowd slowly parted for us and we got in the wind.

At least I'm pretty sure that's how sane Willy would have put it.

Chapter Sixteen

Whoa now! I'm a celebrity! That's right, me, Mr. Pajama Shirt!

Everybody in school looks at me differently now. If I'd known getting beat up by Big Steve would've made such a huge difference in my social life I would've picked a fight with him a lot sooner! Now I'm getting pats on the back all the way to school and get this, being picked first or second to play punch ball at lunchtime. And stuff like wearing that pajama shirt to school or rubber boots on a sunny day, yeah I had to do that one too, are never mentioned. Even my Mameh is happier with me now. I never told her about the fight with Big Steve because I really don't think she'd understand about me having to stand up for myself.

Why didn't you just walk away?

But I think she sees I'm not as nervous about school as I was before. I even run out the door in the morning with a big smile on my face now. I also know she's a lot more comfortable with Wilson than she used to be.

I remember the first time I brought him upstairs to see my comic book collection. He just loves Superman, and me I'm deep into Batman. We're always arguing about who would win in the ultimate one-on-one super battle. Wilson thought Superman's powers made him "invulnerable" to everything, but I always point out a super hero as cool as Batman would have some Kryptonite dust saved up someplace in his all-purpose utility belt.

You know, just in case!

So then one day after school Willy comes up to my apartment for a comic book visit.

You can never tell when a good trade might happen!

He was there in my room sitting on the edge of my bed when the apartment door suddenly opens up. In walks my Mameh both arms full of grocery bags. From where she's standing in the hallway she can see right into my room after she closes the door. She looks up, sees Willy and stands as still as frozen ice. Mameh doesn't say a single word. But then she doesn't have to. I see a strained expression hardening in her face. Jumping out of the chair where I was sitting out of her view I called out a hasty introduction.

"Ma, you know my good friend Wilson. Remember, I told you about him. He's in my class at school," I finish up lamely looking at her hopefully.

"Hello Miss Teddy's mom," Willy calls out politely.

Mameh replies with only a cold nod and then walks straight into the next room, the kitchen with her head down. You didn't have to be a genius to see something was wrong, so I left Wilson with Superman and quickly followed her.

"Mameh, what is it? What's wrong?" I ask.

"You shouldn't have!" She reproaches me angrily turning her face away from me.

"I shouldn't have what?" I reply innocently but feeling the beginning of a knot in my stomach.

Mameh turns back around her face now blazing angrily and looks me directly in the eye. Then in a fierce hushed tone she explodes, "You shouldn't have brought a "schvartze" into our home!"

I have to admit now I was confused. It was not like my parents had never used the word "schvartze" before, they had. But I had always taken it to mean a Negro person and nothing more. I thought it was kind of like someone calling me a Jew or someone else an Italian.

It was what it was.

Now I wasn't so completely dumb or innocent I didn't know some words could mean bad things as well as good. It was how you said them that mattered. And right now I knew that the way my mother was using that word that it was not good. But her intense anger attached to the word, "shvartze" was new and frightening to me.

"Mameh, you are always telling me in America we're all free and equal. I've heard you and Tateh say that to your friends over and over. All of a sudden you're telling me something different. Now I can't bring my friend in the house because he's not the same color as we are?"

"Teveleh, you don't understand," pleaded my mother using her pet name, my Yiddish name for me. "Those people steal! That boy is probably taking things from your room right now! Was he in my bedroom? You tell me? Did you leave him alone while you went to the bathroom? Haven't I always, always told you over and over, "Don't bring any strangers upstairs!"

I was stunned, embarrassed, frozen! This was my sweet generous mother saying ugly things I'd never heard from her lips. To make things worse, she seemed to be working herself up into some kind of a frenzied nervous attack. I decided I wouldn't yell back at her although that's what I wanted to do. I was going to remain calm even though I also could feel both embarrassment and anger in hot flashes.

"Mameh, you're always telling me how some of the ladies at your job, some of the ones who are not Jewish, are so nice to you. Remember how you say you all share things and help each other? How you teach each other new stitches and help each other to finish up your work? You're always telling me that they are "gut shikses"! Am I right, or am I wrong!"

"What are you talking? That's a completely different story! That's not the same thing! Are you stupid, or what? Those ladies, we all work and sweat together! In the shop the boss already treats everyone like, like, "dreck". If we don't get along together our jobs will be even more miserable than now."

"But you do get along with the black and Spanish ladies at your shop, right?" I persisted adding on an innocent look for good measure.

"What do you know about what you're talking! Those women, they're altogether different! Gladys and Ruby work very hard! They work so hard for their families... until their fingers bleed! They don't steal! They wouldn't take...not even a bobby pin," she continued vehemently until I gently broke in.

"Well then," I said, "just suppose Wilson's mother is one of the ladies who does piece work with the schmattes in your shop?"

She looked at me like I had lost my mind then quickly asked in a suspicious voice, "Then tell me, momzer. What's her name? Who is she?"

I answered hopefully, "I only said, "suppose," not that it was so! But would that make a difference to you?"

After a pause she replied slowly through gritted teeth, "Yes, that would make a difference to me. But he's not really one of their sons, is he?"

I instantly replied, "No, he's not. But he is my best friend, my buddy, and I'm asking that you trust me and give him a chance? Wilson is not a thief. Actually, his family is great and they treat me great!"

"Wait a minute here! You wait just a minute mister! What are you telling to me? What kind of business is this? "They treat me great!" What are you telling me? That you have been visiting, "shvartzes" in their houses and I know nothing about this?"

With a rising wail she continued to question me, "When have you been to his house? You never asked me for permission for that! What's going on here? Ganevfasheh kopf, don't think I'm not going to tell your father how you lied to us, and he, he's going to kill you! And another thing, and believe me when I say this, I'm going to tell him as soon as he walks in the door!"

"Wait Mameh," I begged, "just wait a minute, please! You know you always let me stop at my other friends' houses after school. I mean I never, ever had to ask you for any permission before? Why is this time different? Second, I stopped at Willy's house just to do some homework and play some basketball. What's wrong with that? You have to admit I've been doing much better in school lately and a lot of that is because Wilson and me have been studying together. Now, what do you say to that? And also, when I go to Willy's house I always get lots of smiles and chocolate chip cookies!"

That had all come out pretty fast!

Much faster then I had intended!

So fast I hadn't realized my voice was rising to the level of a train whistle. Now I was completely done, maybe in more ways than one! I saw my mother standing there mouth open looking at me stunned, speechless.

So then, what the heck!

I jumped in and finished what I had to say.

"And they don't treat me like I'm gonna steal stuff from their house. In fact, their furniture looks better than ours and they don't seem too worried about me stealing."

Too much, now I was really finished!

I realized I'd said way, way too much! There I stood my frustration making me tremble like a single leaf in a storm.

I regretted that last part of what I'd said as soon as it flew out of my mouth. I knew I had gone too far. My mother was a kind and generous person but she was also quick with a smack if she thought I deserved it. I could see now that she was struggling with her emotions through her hands. They were both rising to the occasion.

Uh, oh!

After what seemed like forever, but could only have been a few seconds she sighed deeply. Shrugging her shoulders Mameh said haltingly, "We'll see, we'll see. Maybe you're right, maybe, possibly? At least, for your sake I hope you are."

"Meanwhile we're forgetting our hospitality. Why don't you bring your friend Wilson into the kitchen for some fresh sponge cake and a glass of milk? I baked early this morning, but first I need you to promise me two things."

"Eyns, first, you must tell me when you're going to your friend, Wilson's house after school and, tsvey, second, please, please, try not to bring your friends here unless your Tateh or I are here. Okay, tateleh? Do we have an agreement?"

And with that she came over and gave me a big hug. Then she leaned up on her tiptoes and kissed me on the cheek. "Okay then, Teveleh?" she asked one more time.

"Okay Mameh!" I nodded gratefully. I was truly happy I hadn't had to run away from an angry broom. That much had been a very close call. Anyhow, Wilson loved the sponge cake so much he happily munched his way through three big slices.

"Yeah, son, this cake is on the money, really delicious!" He mumbled aloud with a large smile on his face and his cheeks completely stuffed with cake. "Can I get a slice for my mom too? I know she's going to love this! Teddy, you know how my mom is, she loves to bake too!"

"But of course! Of course, young man!" came back my mother's deeply delighted reply reaching for another dish and some tin foil.

My Mameh was so flattered by Wilson's appetite that she cut out a big slice for my father and then wrapped up the half of the cake still left on one of her very best china plates. Of course that was also only after Willy had been so polite and funny that my mom was shushing me whenever I tried to get a word into their conversation.

"Shah! Shah, Tevye! Be polite! You see we have a guest! Can't you see Wilson's saying something important to me!"

That's when Willy really started to impress my mom by throwing around all the Yiddish words I'd taught him at school. My mother's eyes grew large as he pointed out things all over the house, and named them! Finally, Wilson proudly pointed to his eyes and said, "Eigen." My mother bounced up and down in her chair like a giddy little girl clapping her hands with glee.

I have to admit Wilson was putting on a pretty good show, but the very best part of it all was when he pointed at me and said, "shmendrick". My mom began laughing so hard she had to hold on to her sides. Then she reached all the way around Wilson's shoulder and pulled him in closer to her.

"Now Wilson, I want you to hear me carefully! I'm going to teach you three new words," she said tears of laughter still rolling down her cheeks. "Eyns, is that what you said was so very funny it made me want to, "plotz." That means I am bursting from laughter. You know our rabbi always tells us, 'laughter is the best medicine!" And Wilson, you are so funny that I'm feeling much better now! The other two words are "zisser" and "kinder". Those two together means you are both my sweet, sweet children!"

Then she grabbed both of us in a big hug and gave we two another squeeze and kiss. It was amazing! Bad feelings had turned into good ones in only a few minutes! Wilson had scored another big win but this time his opponent had been a heck of a lot tougher than Big Steve.

Chapter Seventeen

"Mameh, can I please go to church with Wilson's family this Sunday? Please? Can I?" I asked in an almost innocent voice. This particular voice, sweet as honey, was almost always a sure thing for all the little stuff. Like I said before, it usually got me the quarter for the movies. But this was a way bigger request then the movies and I knew it. It was also clear to me that using the "honey voice" was my only choice. I knew that what I was asking for was like exploding a bomb in my house. Not a little bitty firebomb like the many they had used to burn down entire German cities in World War Two, no, this one would be more like the A-bomb, the single one that erased Hiroshima, the Japanese city.

I sat at the kitchen table hopefully, not moving even a solitary muscle. Sitting there staring at my mother's motionless back for what seemed like forever was not easy. Nothing was happening. There wasn't a sound, or a movement coming from Mameh.

This was a terrible sign. I was forced to consider my other options. Like there was pretending nothing had ever been said and quietly sneaking out of the room.

You know, just tiptoe out quickly while there was still a chance of escape!

I nixed that because in my house it was suicidal to be caught running away. That was admitting your guilt and opening yourself up for the bigger punishments. Staying and fighting it out or maybe even crying and begging for mercy were the other choices left to me. But again, showing weakness just got you more punishment.

Besides, a spoon thrown to the back of the head hurt a lot. At least if you were facing the pitcher you had a chance to dodge. Then you could try to make a break for it before the next windup.

It had now been at least a full two or three minutes that had passed and Mameh still hadn't moved since the word "church" left my lips. A new alarm level, "Code word, Uh-Oh!" was blaring away in my head. Finally, knowing I had to do something, anything at all to break the quiet in the kitchen, I made the chair leg scrape the linoleum as I stood up. Casually I mumbled, "Ma? What do you thin…?"

That sure did it!

"NOOOOO…!" echoed out her scream through the apartment. She didn't just say it loud. She turned and howled it with all her might. I knew then I had totally misjudged my ability to convince her. The only thing filling the small kitchen now was an unknown source of pent up rage.

"But why?" I countered knowing emotionally I was cooked, not badly burnt, but incinerated. I also knew I didn't have many tricks left in my "gimme" bag. Our battle to the end was now joined and I had to use any weapons left carefully if I were to have any chance at all of winning. So I loaded up carefully and tried again.

"But Mommy you didn't even give me a good reason why I can't? Why can't I go? It's just like a visit to a friend's house!" I continued to lie easily. "You know it's just for fun and it'll be very interesting! Come on, let me go, please?"

This was a tougher nut than usual, but I had begged my way to a win before. I also knew time and erosion was on my side, even though this looked like the Mount Everest of 'No's!" A flash hit me suddenly that this might be more about my Mameh's painful history, her own hurtful past, than only about my silly request.

My mother could be strange at times. Imagine if you can someone who would stop and angrily spit on the sidewalk when she passed a church. The larger the church the angrier she would get. When I was three or four she'd sit me down and list the terrible things done to our family in the name of the cross, some of them she witnessed when she was only a little girl. Honestly, I got the feeling the things she left out were even more terrible than the ones she cried about. I also knew in Mameh's mind she somehow blamed the church for the murder of her whole family during the Holocaust. On her good days she'd say they, the Christians, the "goyim", stood by and did nothing to help them. On her bad days the pain of her loss drove her to moodiness and unending tears. Either way she did not like the church. But that was still not the real reason she didn't want me to go. The real reason I thought, and I want you first to know she was not crazy …

Was that she really feared if I even went into a church, somehow, in some way, it would end up with me converting into a Christian!

That's why, in a weird nutshell, I didn't think I could win this argument, but I was still determined to try. I really wanted to go with Wilson to his church.

You might ask why going with Wilson to church was so important I had to try to defy the Mameh I loved so much?

Well, first, Wilson's family had invited me and I really liked them. And then to tell you the truth I was really curious about what went on inside there. So I'd stubbornly decided that I was going to keep on trying!

I decided I would be the water and Mameh would be the stone. And you know how that turns out.

I just didn't know if I had the time to wear her out.

"Why can't I go?" I demanded again.

"You can't go!" thundered my Mameh.

"But Wilson's mother invited me!" I whined on pitifully.

"That's very, very nice of her, but I don't care! Let her take her own son to her own church," was her sarcastic come back.

"His whole family thinks I'm coming! They expect me!" I pleaded and whined once again.

"Expect? Expect? Tell them you also have a family to "expect" with, and, "thank you", but, "No, thank you!" quickly flew back another sarcastic shot.

"But I really, really want to go!" I said theatrically.

"But I really, really, really don't want you to go! What's wrong with you? You don't go to schul, except to be Bar Mitzvahed, but you'll go to a church! Here's another idea for you! Why don't you run straight to that brick wall over there and bang your head against it! Then shout out, "Hurray!" until you start thinking a little bit better. That's right, "Hack dein kopf ein vant une shrei, "Bravo!" Because you've lost all your common sense! And, I might also add mister, YOU'RE STILL NOT GOING!"

Her answers hammered me like scoring one counter punch after another.

"But I do go to shul with Tateh," I whined weakly trying hard to add the slightest touch of righteousness to my losing cause.

"Hah! Tateh goes to shul only twice a year, and that's double what you go, mister. And you, you went only once this year, and that was to your own Bar Mitzvah!" she roared back at me.

That one hurt. But it was true. My Bar Mitzvah had been a small affair for a tiny family of four. And I hadn't been back to shul since. That was almost a kayo, a knockout punch. I was losing this argument badly. A lightning bolt suddenly struck me, a parting gift from the gods of debate. My last straw had arrived and I was grabbing on to it!

"Mameh, I think it would help me in school very much if you let me go! It could be very educational." I slammed my trump cards on the table hopefully.

"Educational? Shmeducational? What could you possibly learn about in that, that place?" was her suspicious response. "It's a church you want to visit, not a library!"

"The Bible, of course, and its history too! You know, learn about how other people see God and see the world! That's like what you learn about in COLLEGE!" I thundered using the magical "Open Sesame" card in a viscous slam. I could feel her defensive wall crumbling. She was beginning to give in.

Mameh said nothing at first in response to my thunderbolt, but she did give me this dubious look. College was the magical key! Mameh wanted that magical place for us more than anything else in the world and she was prepared to make any sacrifice for it that she had to!

Aha! I could see she was thinking it over carefully. It was beginning to look like it was almost over…

Somehow, someway, I had stumbled onto the weakest chink in her armor. Now I was positive I was on the road to victory. Without showing any emotion outwardly I began to celebrate on the inside gleefully!

"Gott in Himmel! You can ask God in the sky anything you want when you see Him, you should only live to be 200 years old! But don't ask me about this anymore! That's it! That's all! I don't want to hear anymore!"

That's what my mother finally cried out throwing her hands up in the air and walking away. "That's enough, enough, I don't want to here no more! I'll let your father decide. But just remember I said, "No!" But no more speaking, nothing! You talk to your father when he gets home! He'll decide."

Victory is mine. She's caved in. I thought I lost, but I won!

Mameh and I both knew my father would agree to almost anything if he thought it would make us happy. She was walking away brushing her hands off to emphasize she was through, so he was all mine. I just knew I had won.

There I sat, enjoying that thought when my father walked quietly in from outside totally unaware of what was waiting for him. In the next minute his whole world changed to upside down, and not for the better. From seemingly out of nowhere my Mameh magically reappeared. And before I could get out a single word my mother was spitting fire at him.

"There he is, your son, Tevye, your precious seed, the apple of your eye! Do you know what this ungrateful one wants to do now?" she roared as if she had never said a single word to me. "Do you know what this, this, "momzer" is asking to do now? Do you know? Do you? Do you? Can you even guess? Try! I want you to try? Try harder! In a million years you could never imagine the narrischkeit, the foolishness this nebbish wants!"

I had to give my Tateh some credit for nerve. Although he could see he'd clearly stepped into a world of trouble, through no fault of his own, he gamely tried to answer back with a little humor.

"Maybe if you told me what he wants to do, I could yell at him also. Remember two heads are smarter than one, and two mouths are louder also!"

Good comeback, Dad! Way to hang in there.

Clearly, he was a brave man.

Mama speared Tateh with a single piercing glare.

"So now, Mr. Comedian, Mr. Tummler, Mr. Milton Berle, I see now where he gets his smart mouth from," Mama spat contemptuously at him from the side of her mouth.

Appearing now to be even angrier than before Mameh continued to dig her sharp tongue even deeper into him.

"You, Mister Big Mouth, you always have something smart to say. Well, what are you going to say now Mister Smart Mouth, Mr. America, Mr. Abraham Lincoln? Your son wants to be a "goy," a "shaygetz!" What do you say to that, Mr. George Washington?"

"And listen to this, President Eisenhower, he doesn't want to be just any, "goy." This one, he wants to be a shvartza goy and go to a shvartza church with Negroes!"

With sarcasm dripping like sweet poisonous syrup from her lips she continued on, "And this is all your fault, YOUR FAULT MISTER! Do you hear me! DO-YOU-HEAR-ME-YOU, YOU-YUTZ? That's because you, Mr. U.S. of A, DON'T GO TO SCHUL! If you went to schul like all the other real Yiddisher menschen, he would want to go there too! AND THAT'S WHY HE'S LOST HIS MIND!"

Switching gears and swinging around like a trolley Mameh continued now shouting aloud to herself, "Why? Tell me why am I killing myself? I work every single day, morning to night to pay for Hebrew school. I wanted Tevye to be a tsadik, a learned man like my sainted father, like my brothers, God have pity over their poor souls! Instead of a Rov I get a gentile, but no, not just any "sheygetz"! No, I'm the luckiest one, the luckiest one in the whole wide world! I will get a schvartze sheygetz! Gott en Himmel! Gott en Himmel! Vayz meir!"

And with her last appeal to God exhausted, falling on divine deaf ears she stormed out of the room slamming the door so hard my eardrums cried out for mercy. But it didn't end there either. I could easily hear her yelling to no one and at everyone, "You're not going! No, not ever, never, never, never! Do you hear me! Over my "geharghed" dead, cold body will you go! DO YOU HEAR ME, YOU PUTZ? OVER MY MURDERED DEAD BODY YOU WON'T GO!"

Who didn't hear her?

The walls in these old tenement buildings were very thick. It was usually very hard to hear even normal noises through the thick plaster walls. But our neighbors above, below and to the sides lost no time banging on the walls with brooms and pots to protest the early evening racket!

My father who had said nothing at all after what he thought was only a joking remark turned around and stared at me thoughtfully.

"You know, I thought you loved, even a little, your old Tateh? I mean, couldn't you have tried just a little more harder to keep me away from all this tsuris, this grief," he commented dryly.

"I'm sorry Papa, but I really didn't think it was going to be this bad. I don't know what happened? I thought I had it all settled with Mameh before you walked in. Then you come in and she goes crazy!" I mumbled mostly to myself while looking at the floor to avoid his gaze.

Suddenly, there was another loud crash and what sounded like new angry shouting inside of the kitchen.

"Did you hear that Pop? What was that? Do you think Mameh is all right?" I asked nervously. "Do you think we should go in there and make sure she's okay?"

For an instant Tateh looked concerned, but then he listened carefully to something Mameh was shouting in the next room. He turned back around to me with a half smile covering his face.

"I think, no," he said. "I'm pretty sure, no. Your Mameh is a little bit, a bissel verklempt. I'm certain I heard your Mameh just say,we are both yutzes and we should, "Gay cocken afen yam!" I gave him a blank look.

Why would she be talking about the ocean?

He burst out laughing and explained, "Whatever you said to her before, it made her crazy, a meshuggeneh! Your Mameh never, ever uses bad words, never! At least almost never," he corrected himself. "But I'm pretty sure she just said that you, you're an idiot, a yutz and that me, I'm a putz and we both need to go take a shit in the ocean!"

Now you know I had to laugh at that one.

"She's real mad, huh, Pop?" I laughed uneasily thinking I may have stepped out a little bit too far on this one. The thought of dodging a swinging strap in the middle of the night suddenly jumped into my mind.

"Yuh, she is Tevye. She is! But truly, I have seen her worse. There was the time she grabbed a scissors and began stabbing the eyes out of Adolf Eichmann's picture in the Daily News! Now that was frightening! I had to fight with her. As smart a woman as your Mameh is, sometimes I don't think she really understands her tsuris, her troubles. She's so angry. You need to give her a little more time and let me talk to her about this thing."

After I explained everything that was said back and forth to him I asked him, "Tateh, do you think it's so terrible that I want to visit Wilson's church? If you do I promise I won't go!"

"No, Teveleh, it's not a terrible thing at all to want to see new things and share them with a friend. Yet, you must understand your mother's pain. She has been suffering for many years and she needs to place blame somewhere. She has chosen to fight the one she loves the most. She's picked God as her enemy. And that is the most difficult choice she could have ever made because it is so hard for anyone else to help her. She's by herself. It doesn't really matter to her if it is God in a schul or God in a church. She blames Him for her brothers, sisters, parents, grandparents and cousins, all murdered."

"Mameh was the baby of her family and misses them all so much. Your Mameh must find her own path back to Him. Didn't you ever notice how she dislikes going to shul?"

"I thought she didn't care, that it was only for us, the men in the family," I stammered.

"You know your Mameh's family always loved God. Her grandfathers and father were holy men, teachers, rabbis and tzadikim. She always tells me she believes you have that holy part of them inside of you."

"Does that mean I will have to be a rabbi one day?" I asked a little fearfully.

"Only if you wish it to be so my son," he replied tenderly. "My own family were only everyday people so you can surely choose to be whatever you wish. But I am very sure of one thing. You love God just as deeply as your mother loves Him deep within her soul, So, if you want to visit God in another one of his houses it should not be a problem."

"Tateh, could you explain all this to Mama like you did for me?" I begged. "You make it sound so easy to understand, so true!"

"I'll try my best, Tevye. But just don't expect the sea to open wide immediately. My middle name is Moishe, Moses to the Americans, but I am not the original!" He finished with a smile.

Another crash came booming from the next room. This time instead of being frightened I walked over to my big burly father and hugged him. It hadn't been such a long time since he had wrapped his arms around me. But as always, it felt as good as ever.

Chapter Eighteen

The next day on the way to school I told Wilson about the argument I'd had with my mom. But he didn't say anything just then. We'd now gotten into the habit of leaving for school a few minutes earlier every day. That way we figured we could use our new found fame to play punch ball for fifteen minutes before the line-up whistle blew. When the whistle blew the entire schoolyard had to stop instantly. It didn't matter what you were doing. You just froze. But we always made sure we were doing something real stupid. That way we could laugh at each other while we were frozen in the dumbest poses. It was like a take-off on "Freeze Tag" and a great way to start the day.

The sound of the second whistle brought us racing like trained penguins to form a perfectly straight line. The class that did this best won points towards a class prize. We all took that prize very seriously. It was usually a round tin can of long pretzel sticks, my favorites, and a colorful banner to show off through the class door window. More important it gave your class a chance to look down on everyone else's. But before that whistle blew we had time to play whatever we wanted to.

Today it was sunny and cool. Wilson turned to me and said, "Let's skip the game today and rap for a minute." That's when he asked me for all the details about what my mother had said the night before, especially the part about her cussin' in Yiddish. That's the part that seemed to actually impress him.

Go figure?

"That crack about shittin' in the ocean is beautiful! I love it. I'm definitely gonna use it when I play the dozens with Stan," he chuckled. "That's funny as hell. Come on Teddy, tell me again how you say it?"

"Hey, man, I don't want your mom blaming me for teaching you how to curse in Yiddish," I complained giving him a playful shoulder shove.

"You're kiddin' me, right?" Wilson laughed out loud. "My mom thinks that stuff is hilarious! Those Yiddish ranks got a beat that just makes you want to laugh till you cry! Come on now!

Every time I bring home a new word from you my moms is all over me to teach it to her right away. Hey man, she even makes me practice that stuff with her over and over again. Then she lays it on the Jewish ladies on her job. She says they love it when she drops some Yiddish on them."

"Everybody in our house is now a "bubalah" or they tellin' "bubbamisahs." Even my dad and uncle are dropping Yiddish sounds all over the house. No, joke, they say it helps on their jobs too. It may sound kind of crazy, but my mom says Yiddish is kind a soulful, you know like when Black folks talk personal junk to each other. Yeah, Yiddish definitely got some heart. I kinda enjoy listening to it myself."

"Like for instance sometimes I just can't help myself! Check this out, I can't stop saying, "Oy vey!" It's like a sickness! You just can't stop saying it! Last night we started 'Oy veyin' each other at the house. We were killin' it all night and just couldn't stop laughin'!"

I looked at Wilson like he had lost all his marbles. But before I could get a word out of my mouth he looked at me giggling.

"You got to know this mess is all your fault!"

This 'mess' all started in the yard yesterday when we began ranking on the names of our classmates. As we said each name we would point to the person wherever they were in the schoolyard and then hold our hands over our foreheads and exclaim mournfully, "Oy vey!"

"Irving, oy vey!"

"Pricilla, oy vey!"

"Candy, oy vey!"

"Principal DiLorenzo, oh Noooo!"

We kept it up until we were laughing so hard we had to lay out on the benches we were sitting on.

The whistle blew so we got up and all ran at full speed to our line up spots. It was amazing how those lines came together so fast. I slipped into my size place right in front of Big Steve,

"Hey Teddy. What's up PJ-man?" asked Big Steve.

"Nuttin' much, Steve," I answered still grinning away from the memory of the 'Oy vey!' marathon.

"Wanna play on my team at lunch?" asked Big Steve with an eager look lighting up his face.

"Sure thing," I answered casually, almost too casually.

"Ask Willy for me too, will ya, 'kay?"

"Right, I gotcha, Steve," I mumbled no longer even bothering to look at him. Things had gotten a lot better with him and for a lot of the other kids who used to be bullied by Big Steve. Wilson and I had these to the floor heavy reps now. But I knew what was up. It was really all about Wilson's brother, Stan, not me. People kept telling me that Stan was really, really tough. He was like the ultimate football lineman and power forward. Even the MC's like the Fordham Baldies and the Reapers didn't mess with Stan. Stan was feared and respected as a man with a very dangerous rep.

Funny thing to me he seemed like the nicest guy in the whole world. All I knew was he'd saved my ass twice and he was cool with me.

Later at lunch I told Wilson what my father had said.

"I think I can go to church with you on Sunday," I announced. "My dad says he's gonna work it out with my mom."

"Cool, cool, that's better than good because Sunday is "Bring a Friend Day." That means if I bring you, my Sunday school teacher will take us both out to White Castle for burgers after the service."

I had to smile at that picture. "That's a lot better deal than I ever got at Hebrew school. Come to think of it, the best I ever did there was a piece of hard candy. Tell me the truth now. What is church like anyway? Is it fun, cause synagogue ain't any fun at all. And I'm not joking either. Schul is pretty serious stuff all the time! But I'd have to say the worst part of the whole thing is we are always praying in a language I don't even get. That makes it very, very boring. Is church anything like that? Because if it is, maybe I'll skip it"

Wilson thought over what I'd said for a minute and then answered carefully, "It can be boring sometimes if the pastor is dull. Ours isn't. But most of the time it's kind of interesting because pastor teaches you about stuff that happened in the Bible and then connects it to what's up today."

"Is it all in English?" I asked hopefully.

"Of course it's in English stupid! How else could we understand him," snapped back Willy laughing out loud. "And we sing a lot too. That's one of my favorite parts. You're gonna flip out when you hear my moms sing. And our choir is smokin' hot, hot, hot!! They're so hot we have to keep all the windows open when they start to work it on out. You diggin' me?"

"We kind of sing in schul a little," I returned weakly. "We're just not hot, hot, hot!"

"Stop it, stupid!" Willy said giving me a curious glance. "No singing? Really? Truly?" he asked disbelievingly.

But the thought of singing in church perked me up a little. I liked listening to music a lot. I especially loved listening to my little transistor radio late at night in my room. I even liked listening to my Tateh's favorite kinds of music. Every Sunday on his day off my father would turn on the Yiddish radio station. They would have Jewish singers on all day long. I liked listening to them because they all seem to sing from someplace straight in the deepest part of their heart. There was a lot of feeling in the air.

To me the very best ones were the ones who sang in Yiddish, not Hebrew, because then I could understand them. When they sang in Hebrew I could only pick out a word here or there. That's the main reason schul was boring to me. It was all done in Hebrew. Sometimes they would have a special singer, a cantor. He was always a man, never ever a woman, but someone with an even more beautiful voice who would sing from the holy scrolls, the torah. With that image in my mind I repeated myself to Wilson again.

"Hold on a minute! Yeah, yeah, we do sing in synagogue!" I said loudly again thinking about the cantor's soulful songs. "But what kind of songs do they sing in church? Are they sad songs or happy ones? Do you think I will like it?"

Wilson kept giving me that same look over and over.

You know the one that says, "Man, are you crazy? What's

wrong with you?

"Listen Train, you're going to love it, trust me?" he assured me one last time. "It's the best part of the service. Everybody at church loves singing along with the choir. The buildin' shakes! Besides, I told you my mom is in the choir and she used to work it on out professionally. They still play her stuff on the radio in, you know, background music. Do you like dance music?"

Now I knew I had to go to church. Willy's mom was the nicest, prettiest person who had ever given me a chocolate chip cookie. And she could sing too? I was definitely going to church!

Wilson went on, "And after church, you can come over to our house for Sunday dinner. That's after the White Castle of course! We're having Virginia ham! Mmm.., boy, that's my forever favorite."

"Better hold on to your horses right there, Ranger! I can't eat ham! It's traif!" I interrupted.

Wilson turned back to me and asked uncertainly, "Traif? What the hell does, 'traif' mean?"

"Traif means it's unclean, not kosher. And I'm not supposed to eat any of that stuff." I answered slowly!

"Oh, wait a minute now! Oh sure, sure, yeah, yeah, yeah, I get it!" Wilson answered hurriedly. "Yeah sure, of course I know what you mean now. My cousin Leon is a Muslim. He's always telling me pork is unclean also, and he won't eat it either."

"Traif," huh! You know what? To each his own my dad always says. But it's still cool! That means there's more ham for the rest of us. How do you feel about chicken, collard greens and corn bread? Are they 'traif' too?"

"Nope, they sound good," I answered hopefully not knowing for sure. Truth was only my Tateh kept kosher in our house now, my mom didn't anymore. Tateh said eating "traif" was one of Mameh's ways at getting back at God. So chicken and cornbread was sounding pretty good to me. In fact, they sounded delicious!

"They are good! Better than that, they're mouthwatering delicious! Okay, now that we're talking about things we like to eat, do you think your mom might have any more of that homemade sponge cake layin' around if we just happen to stop at your house later?"

"Yeah," I sighed, "as a matter of fact she baked last night and left it on the table for tonight's dessert."

I had to laugh looking at his suddenly hungry face waiting for my answer.

"Well, all right then," giggled Wilson. And then he stopped and smoothly danced a few slick moves down the middle of the sidewalk while falsettoing a few lines from a song on the radio.

"Please Mr. Postman, stop and see.
Is there a letter, a letter for me?"

"What's that step you're doing there called?" I asked curiously watching him slide effortlessly to the left. Then he slipped back to the right with his hand coolly tucked in his waistband.

"That's called, 'The Slop' baby! It's brand new! Check this move out! It's tight, right and we will be eatin' chicken!" And with that he spun completely around and moved backwards, balanced on only one foot with his hands now on his hips.

"Watch me! Watch me now!" Willy sang out loud. "Hey! Hey! Hey! y'all! James Brown, that's my main man, the Godfather!"

Hypnotized by the smoothness of his moves, I blurted, "Can you teach me to do that?"

"Sure, sure, no problem, bud. We can start with a little dancin' right after Sunday dinner. My brother and cousin Myra are really good dancers. They teach everyone in the family the latest moves. But you gonna have to add a little more soul to your roll, put a little glide in your stride and if you comin' to my house you WILL definitely be eatin' chicken on this Sunday!" Willy laughed. "I mean I know you got the heart, but question is, do you have the soul to be real? That's the real deal?"

Not sure of exactly what he just meant I groped for a cool answer.

"Everybody has a soul, Willy," I answered trying to be impressive with my worldly knowledge. "What kind of dumb assed question is that?"

"No, stupid," he tapped me in my chest playfully. "Soul like the kind in soul music!"

"Well, what exactly are you talkin' about? What's the dif?"

"Hmmm," he said out loud a thoughtful look coming to his face. "Soul is like, like a message from the heart that plays out in how our people live their lives."

"Oh, you mean kind of like the music you hear inside yourself when there is no music playing on the outside?" I asked.

"Yeah, yeah, that's kind of it. You got it! It's like your heartbeat vibratin' into the stuff you do every day. You see it all the time in how people talk, walk and dance, Yeah, my man, you can see it in that and in other stuff too! Like the styles you wear and the kind of food you eat too. Soul's in everythin' my man, everything, but you got to feel it!"

"So then do you think I have soul?" I hesitated looking hopeful.

"Do you have soul? Teddy, you askin' me do you have soul? Most definitely, yes, you sure do! Think about it bro? You got all kinds of soul, but it just may not be exactly our kind of soul. What you do got tons of, my man, is the Jewish kind, you got Jewish soul!"

"Jewish soul?" I asked myself wonderingly. "I've got Jewish soul?"

Now here was something new and amazing to wrap my brain around!

Willy went on persuasively, "Yep, that's why I think I find Jewish people so cool. Your kind of soul and ours are like apples and oranges, a little bit different, but both still fruity and both delicious!"

I took that in for a minute while we went on walking silently down the street. Then I turned to face him and looked him straight in the eye.

"Wilson, are you jivin' me? Do you really think it's possible that maybe everybody has some kind of soul? Tell me the truth, what do you really think? Don't give me any more of your second hand bullshit."

Willy didn't hesitate, even for a second.

"You know, now that I think about it, I'm sure they all do, but sometimes people like to squash theirs. Like they don't want it to mix up their lives. Maybe they're afraid to feel things, or maybe they are just too busy to really enjoy it. Hey, but not us, man! You and me, we're good to the bone. We got it!"

I thought about that. I wondered about how much I enjoyed my father's favorite Yiddish music on the weekend. Those singers and musicians definitely had soul. I could feel the answer inside myself. They did have soul. Their music always moved me.

It all made sense to me now.

"I'm with you Willy. I must have soul."

Wilson hugged me and laughed, "That's why I love your Jew boy ass, man! Now don't worry about learning a dance step. Everybody who got soul can dance!"

And with that he shifted his weight so he was bent half over and did another cool sliding step. So I jumped in and tried to follow.

"All right then, James Brown, break it down like the Godfatha! Get down with your funky bad self and work it on out!

Chapter Nineteen

"I can go," I heard myself saying the next day.

"Whadya' say? Y'gonna have t'speak a whole lot louda cause when I'm on, shootin' it like I am t'day, I can't hear nuttin'," chuckled Wilson sounding pure Bx.

"Swish, nutt'n' but net!" he sang out as one jumper after another dropped straight through the chain link cords attached to the basket's hoop. I watched in awe as he rolled arcing basketballs up off his long fingertips one, two, three, four... one behind the other.

There we stood in the schoolyard just after four o'clock taking turns rebounding, passing and hoisting up jumpers.

Wow, practice does make perfect, well at least better!

We'd been shooting around for about forty-five minutes before we headed over towards the new library on Selwyn to do some homework together. Willy had introduced me to another of his favorite science fiction writers, Isaac Asimov. I was in the middle of reading this fantastic science fiction novel called, *Foundation*. It was about a huge manmade planet in a far off future and how men from it had ruled a galactic empire.

Yeah, it seemed pretty cool to imagine living in the future.

Maybe it was that way because the present world around us was kind of tough.

Asimov seemed to be saying different times, different worlds, but same people, same problems. Hmmm...

The book was so good my mom actually had to yell at me right through the shut bedroom door last night.

"Gay schlufin, kleyne momzer! Put out those lights so your little brother can sleep! Where's your respect for others!"

But it was still such great stuff to read and so hard to put down that I'd read under the covers using a flashlight.

Back on the court again it was shot, bang, good! One more shot, bang, basket again. And over and over again, Wilson fired away. BANG! nothing but net.

"It's so gooood! I tol' you I was on t'day, A Train! I'm re-e-a-lly feelin' it t'day! Make it rain again! Make it rain! Dollar bills, dollar bills fallin' down, money, baby, MONE-E-EY!"

Willy screeched wildly dancing around and around while spinning backwards against the clock with both his arms outstretched to the sky in a "V" for victory sign.

I smiled to myself watching his moment.

Man, oh man, Willy really can shoot a basketball. And when he was "on" it was always lights out for the other team.

Like he always said to me, "A Train, I'm a b-a-a-a-d man with a b-a-a-a-d jump shot!"

"Now, Train, what was it you were trying to tell me as you so humbly witnessed the majesty of my Super "J" lightin' up this little corner of the known universe? What be up then, pa'dner?" Wilson burbled on as he slapped me five and we sat down on a nearby wooden bench.

First I cleared my throat because I was feeling myself shaking from excitement, "Didn't you hear what I just told you? I can go! You know, to church with you on Sunday! Remember you asked me?" I reminded him. I was a little exasperated by the fact that he wasn't as excited by my announcement as I was.

Wilson looked right at me, smiled, then stood up and heaved the ball at the basket standing all by itself more than thirty feet away.

Bam!

Once again I couldn't believe it! Swish, straight in.

Okay, maybe it was straight in off the backboard…

Then Willy wheels around eyes bright and happy.

"I knew your momma would come around! She's great! Besides, anyone who bakes like she does has got to be cool! You're coming this Sunday, right! See, I'd already told my mom you was coming. Ha, ha, yeah, I'm goin' to be lookin' real good on, "Bring Your Friend Day"! Yeah, baby, yeah!"

"Uh, but Wilson, there's more, just one more little thing really," I mumbled looking down at my scuffed Cons. "You gotta come to…"

"Come to what? Come to dinner at your house? No problem, my man. Your mom can seriously burn! Just tell me when? This Friday, Saturday, you name it, I'm there! You got it, no problem! Now, pass me the pill, my brotha'. I'm hot, boy, hot, hot, hot!"

"No, not to dinner, man, to schul, to synagogue on this Saturday, or I can't go with you on Sunday!" I blurted out.

"You're gonna have to go to shul with me to make this thing work!"

Willy stared at me like I was completely nuts. Then he took a step closer so he could stare straight into my eyes.

Tilting his head slightly to one side he slowly continued, "So what're you sayin'? Are you invitin' me to synagogue with you or not?"

"Well, yeah sure, my pop said the only way my mom would let me go to church with you on Sunday is if you go with us to synagogue the day before. I guess she just wants me to get a good booster shot of Jewishness so I don't all of a sudden convert and become a Christian the next day," I explained with a weak smile.

"C'mon man, what do you say? You can come back to dinner Saturday night too. And if you come I'll ask my mom to make something special, something real good, like latkes!" I finished up hoping for the best.

Wilson continued looking at me intently. Finally, he said, "What's this "latkes?" Is it as tasty as sponge cake?" He finished looking at me hopefully.

"Latkes are potato pancakes," I replied eagerly. "And believe me, it's as close to heaven as Jewish kids can get on our planet Earth!"

I must've had a convincing look on my face because he just shook his head back and forth.

"Your momma is something else, my man. Yeah, she's as slick as they come." His voice was oozing with admiration.

"Why do you say that?" I asked innocently dribbling the ball from left to right and back.

"Well," he continued, "didn't you say your dad and you don't go to shul but a few times a year?" I nodded.

"All right then, I guess you're both going to be there again this Saturday cause I'm gonna be there too, right along with you. What do I have to wear?"

I was a little bit in shock even though this is what I thought I wanted. Shul was definitely not one of my favorite places. I mean even though I understood Yiddish, everything in shul was done in Hebrew. So, I was usually completely lost and frustrated. Now I was a little bit surprised when Wilson said he wanted to go.

I was pretty sure he wouldn't and I was pretty sure I didn't!

"You mean you're okay with going to shul? You do know it's kind of dull sometimes," I tried to explain, a bit of a nervous stammer hindering me. "That's mostly because they pray and sing in Hebrew. I mean, if you don't really want to go I'll understand. It's cool."

A moment passed and Willy didn't say anything. In fact, neither one of us said a thing. At last, he turned to me and asked, "What's up with you, bro? You ashamed to take me with you?"

I felt a cold shiver go through me.

"Willy," I could barely hear my own voice, "you're my best friend. Why would I be ashamed of you?"

"Maybe because I'm not exactly like the rest of your friends. In case you haven't noticed, I'm a different color, black!" he snapped angrily.

"But if I didn't want you to come with me, then why do you think I asked you in the first place?" I pleaded.

"Yeah, right, what kind of way is it to ask me to go with you and then tell me why I, myself don't want to go? Man, I have a brain. I have a soul. Why don't you just ask me and let me make up my own dam' mind!" was his angry reply. Then my best friend turned his back to me.

He was right, but I didn't see it. Now I do. Willy can make up his own mind. He doesn't need me to tell him what to do. Well, here I am, ashamed of myself again. I know I have to apologize.

"Wilson… you're right, a hundred percent right. I'm sorry. I didn't ask you the right way. And the part about being ashamed, you're right about that too. Except, it's not you I'm ashamed of, it's me. I guess maybe I'm a little scared you might come to shul and some dumb-ass might laugh at me for bringing you. And maybe also I'm a little scared you might laugh at the way we do things there. I mean it's different then what most other people do."

Wilson turned back around and snapped.

"What do you do that's so different man? Don't you pray? What's so different about that? What do you think we do at our church? How come I wasn't worried about you coming with me? What's your problem, boy? You need to check yourself!"

Then he turned his back on me again.

"You're right, you're right!" I repeated stepping around so we were facing one another. "I was just thinking about the way some stuff looked, like the yarmulkes on our heads and the tallis we wrap around our shoulders."

"Yeah, what are those things?" Willy asked curiously. "Do I get to wear them if I come?"

"Do you want to?"

I could see the desire to learn new things in his eyes and then I realized one of the reasons why I liked Wilson so much. He was smart and brave, plus he just wanted to learn anything new about everything. Wilson was just this interesting fun cat! And that's exactly the way I wanted to be. Plus, he was funny too!

"Hell yeah, well, I don't know, do I? Exactly, what are those things?" Wilson finished up eagerly.

"Well, the yarmulke is like a beanie we wear because it's disrespectful to be in God's house with your head uncovered and the tallis is a prayer shawl you receive when become a man. You know, when you get Bar Mitzvahed at thirteen!"

Willy looked thoughtful. Then he said, "You know we take our hats off in church for the same reason that you wear them, to show respect for God. I wonder if there's some kinda connection there? Train, I want to wear the two of them, the yarmulke and tallis, both of them. That is if it's okay with you? I really want to try them out. Now what else you got?"

"There's the reading of the torah…" I mumbled.

"Speak up brother! What's that?"

"That's the living Bible!" I answered emphatically.

"Is that because it's God's words written by hand on sheepskin?"

My mouth dropped open. "How did you know that? You're right!" I asked in surprise.

"See, there you go, startin' that same ol' shit again Mr. Bubblebrain!" But this time he was laughing at me. "Thinkin' 'bout what I'm SUPPOSED to know. Remember how we first met? We were BOTH coming home from the LI--BRAR--Y, Mr. You-think-you-know-it-all! Now by the way, what d'ya' mean 'living' Bible? Can you explain that part please?"

"Our Torah, it has a soul of its own," I stammered, almost afraid to make another mistake. "At least that's what I've been taught."

Wilson replied in a slightly suspicious, but awed voice, "You mean like a living person, like you or me. Was your Torah born? Can it die? Does it have a name, a birthday? How old is your Torah?"

"Shaddup!" I bellowed so loudly everyone else on the other basketball courts turned around.

"Well, okay then, ask me again!" commanded Willy.

"Ask you what again?" I answered puzzled.

"Ask me again, schlemiel!"

Then the light when on in my brain.

"Wilson, 'my brotha' from another motha',' can I have the honor of your company at synagogue on this coming Saturday morning?"

"A Train, my paisan, would you do me the honor of accompanying my family and I to the House of the Lamb's Pure Heart this Sunday?"

We both nodded chin to chest seriously to each other and said "Yes" together. Then we started laughing. We knew this was definitely going to be a weekend to remember.

Amen to that!

Chapter Twenty

Ummm, ummh…

I knew exactly what those sounds coming from Wilson meant.

I was doing my best to keep from making the very same ones!

"Teddy, man, these potato cake things are unbelievable! I can't tell what's happier, my mouth or my stomach!"

"Hey, hey, what's that stuff you're spooning all over yours? Is that applesauce in that saucer? Give it here, my man. Let me try some of that, too?"

"D'yeah, here," was my slurpy answer. It was the best I could do under the circumstances considering my mouth was stuffed up tight with a fresh hot deliciously fried potato latke.

I spoke only after the taste buds in my mouth gave me a break.

"Now try one of these with some sour cream on it," I advised. "If you're really one of us, a Jew disguised as a Negro we're gonna find out right now. By the way, they're not potato cakes. They're called "lat-kas," heathen!"

Willy smiled wolfishly at me like a cat with a mouse filling up its mouth. Then he slowly closed his eyes chewed slowly and finally swallowed blissfully. Opening his "peepers" he looked over at me from under two raised eyebrows and repeated very slowly, "lat-kas." Then he stared over at the saucer of sour cream with a newfound respect, as if he was waiting for it to grow a mouth and say something like, "Hi, I'm sour cream and I AM DELICIOUS!" Finally, he stood up leaned over the table and took in a long deep sniff.

"Hmmm, all this other stuff doesn't smell too shabby either. Kind of like the cream cheese I like on my bagels, only smellier and better. Okay, you convinced me, I'll try another one," he exclaimed eagerly.

This time he carefully covered his latka with a thin layer of sour cream and then took a giant bite. I must have blinked or something because I swear I saw no second bite. All I saw was

Wilson reaching for more latkes and sour cream but now using both hands. Actually, I kind of sympathized with the feeling he was having because I was reaching right along with him for more of everything.

After about ten minutes the munching and grunts of pleasure were suddenly interrupted by a low moan.

"Uuuhh, I feel like my stomach is about to bust if I eat anymore, but I think, maybe…just maybe I might need to have one more…" Wilson mumbled as he fell backwards into his chair one hand on his stomach, the other gamely holding on to a last applesauce covered "belly buster."

He's definitely got to be one of the tribe!

I said that while laughing to myself.

He loves latkes and bagels!

My mother's head popped through the doorway to gauge if there were any "latkes" shortage at the table. Then with a quick nod to herself she turned and disappeared. As I tuned the latke sensitive area of my brain into the next room I could sense Mameh bustling around in her kitchen. I could also hear the accompanying sounds of large spoonfuls of hand-rubbed potatoes mixed with onions and a pinch of garlic being dropped into hot cooking oil.

To make sure I wasn't hallucinating, I jumped up and took a quick peek into the kitchen. There on top of the stove were two large frying pans being worked at the exact same time. It was very clear that there wasn't going to be any latke shortage in our apartment today.

Mameh was cookin' and smokin' in there!

"Man, I ate enough of those honeys to be called Mr. Potato Head," Willy sighed happily rubbing his full stomach with both hands. Now we were stretched out on the living room floor happily watching one of our cartoon heroes, Mighty Mouse, on television. As the Mouse of Steel flew into action his special tune started up.

"Here I come to save the day," sang the muscular rodent.

"Oy vey! He needs to fly straight over here and save me from the belly ache that is on its way," I moaned holding on to my stomach.

"Aw com'on," laughed Wilson, "It's worth the pain! No pain, no gain! What a great day! What a great meal! I'm scared to ask what else your mother has cooked! I can't eat another bite!"

"Oh, by the way, is there gonna be any of that sponge cake for dessert?"

I just turned and looked at him like he needed his head examined as well as his bulging stomach.

Probably both, where in the heck does he put it? How can he still be hungry? There must be another person, maybe even another whole family, living in his hollow leg or somewhere.

I had to laugh out loud at the thought.

"What's so damned funny bud? Wait, I gotta get some milk! I'll be back in a "sec". Want anything?"

Wilson jumped right up and strolled back into the kitchen. The next thing I heard was my mother's delighted laughter. Willy always knew what to say.

He really needs to teach me how to do that stuff.

Then I wouldn't be standing around with my mouth hanging open whenever people asked me things. I made a mental note to myself.

Ask Wilson to help me become more charming!

I sat back thinking of the events that morning. No way had I expected what had happened to happen. To tell you the truth, I started off a little bit nervous. No, actually I had been scared to death. I didn't really know what was going to happen when my dad and I showed up at schul with Willy. I mean this was the same shul that wouldn't let my mother pray alongside my father. That was a "shondeh," a shame. The rule was men and women had to be completely separated when they prayed.

As for bringing a Negro as a guest, I'd never even seen anyone of Wilson's color in our shul.

Were there even any Jewish people who were his color? Hey, what a great question to annoy the Hebrew school rabbi with!

Speaking of the Rebbe, when I asked my Tateh if everything was going to be all right he said he had spoken with him.

"And, what did he say?" I asked cautiously.

"Well," Tateh replied slowly, "when I asked him if it was permitted to bring Wilson, the Rebbe didn't say, yes. He also didn't say, no. The only thing he asked me was if your friend loved God? When I answered him that Wilson attended church every Sunday and that he had invited you to go with him to his own church his answer was simple."

"The Rebbe stated clearly to me, 'If a person loves God, then God's house is the entire world. And it is written that our house is open to all who love God. If there is a problem I will handle it. The world is changing in many ways. Of course, of course, your friend is welcome here!"

I thought my chest would burst with happiness.

I'd been so worried! But if the Rebbe said Wilson was welcome then no one would dare say anything else! It was all going to be okay.

The next morning all of us, including Wilson, arrived at shul on time and dressed in our best suits with yarmulkes perched on top of our heads. Even my Mameh had decided to come.

Strange though, barely anyone is looking in our direction.

My friends from the block didn't even pick up their heads. They stared straight down into their prayer books swaying and praying so hard that heaven itself seemed to be almost within their reach.

I didn't understand what was going on here. My Tateh had spoken to the Rebbe and everything was supposed to be fine. I could see that it wasn't. But Willy didn't seem to notice anything.

I guess that's because he was concentrating on his new surroundings. I turned and looked questioningly into my father's face.

What was going on here? We hadn't gotten even one, "shalom" from a room full of our friends and neighbors. I could see Tateh was upset too, but was trying hard not to show it.

The service continued on in a blur to me. I was angry and embarrassed. I thought I was going to explode soon. But Wilson seemed completely unfazed by my glum attitude or for that matter, by anything around him. He was happy. He seemed to be completely entranced by it all. Willy's joy only succeeded in making me feel worse about the coldness surrounding us.

If these stupid people could only see into his heart and see how good Willy was? If they would only give him a chance!

But in that same instant there came a special moment in the ceremony. Even I had to admit it gave me a chill whenever I saw it. Wilson also could feel something in the air just as we all did. It was now the time when the elders of the synagogue took the Torah out of its special resting place, the Ark.

"It's beautiful." Wilson whispered next to me.

And it was beautiful. The scrolls, the Torah, were covered in a deep blue velvet jacket covered in rich golden embroidery and topped with golden ornaments.

The coverings were very carefully removed and the scrolls were unrolled so that the Rebbe could read from them. As the service went forward the Rebbe called first one elderly man, then another to read from the sacred Torah. You could see from the way each man carried himself forward to read how honored he was to have been chosen.

My father reached over and tugged on my suit's sleeve. I turned towards him and whispered, "What's wrong Tateh?"

"Nothing's wrong, Tevye. But soon it's going to be your turn," he answered me quietly.

"What are you talking about, 'My turn?' 'My turn,' for what?" I asked nervously. A very bad feeling began to swirl in the pit of my stomach.

"You'll see, you'll see! Today, you're going to read from the Torah," he replied excited now, but still gently pulling me along into the aisle.

"But I can't, please. I'm not ready! Come on, Poppa, give me a break, please? Anyway, what about Wilson? I can't leave him standing here alone. That's not the right thing to do! That's not being polite, right?" I continued looking desperately to Willy for some backup.

Wilson had been leaning over and listening intently to everything. He gallantly jumped in and quickly murdered my last defense saying, "Naw, that would be great. I'd really like to hear you read Torah, Teddy. That would be very, very cool."

Can you believe this! He was supposed to be my best friend! Who needed enemies with a friend like this?

I just looked at him hard with stunned amazement for a long few seconds.

"You're supposed to be my pal, my buddy? You're supposed to help me get out of this!" I hissed in his direction knowing I was through.

"I am your buddy, but the only way I get to see the Torah up close is if you go up there. Then I get to go up there with you!"

Then suddenly it all started to add up.

This was all a set–up! Mameh!

She was taking no chances with me converting. She must have spoken to the Rebbe herself about me going to church.

She was going to make me go up and speak directly to God!

As I slowly walked up the steps leading to the Torah I prayed a new prayer. I prayed I wouldn't totally disgrace either myself, or any of my future offspring forever.

And I also prayed that I would also get a chance to get even with Mameh!

The Rebbe positioned me right in front of the open scrolls and motioned to a line of hand lettered Hebrew with his fancy silver yad, his pointer. At first I couldn't make any sense out of what he was pointing to. Then he tapped the line he wanted me to read again. I was hypnotized with fear, but after a second or two the letters came back into focus. And then the line he wanted me to read became even clearer to me. It was a prayer that the Rebbe wanted me to read, only a very simple prayer, the blessing for bread. Someone in my family said it every night at dinnertime before we ate, and that someone was usually me!

The weight of the world lifted right up off my heart. The Rebbe looked into my eyes and smiled. He tapped my fingers one more time with his and asked, "Well young man, are you going to grace us with this prayer?"

"Baruch atau Adonoi…" I sang out loudly with all the happiness I felt filling up my heart. I was singing a prayer in shul!

What a brilliant Mameh I had! And when I finished and glanced behind me I was surprised again. Wilson was standing right there, right alongside my bursting with pride Tateh. Willy told me later my father had pushed him up the steps to the Ark right behind me.

Wilson kept staring right at the scrolls. It was clear to everyone he was fascinated by the Torah. His eyes never left it even as we stepped carefully away and returned to our seats.

Slowly the service was coming to an end. The Torah was carefully rolled together and covered in its rich adornments. The Rebbe then touched his two fingertips to his lips, kissed them and brought them to gently touch the Torah's cover. Then he carefully lifted the Torah onto his shoulder and slowly walked down the Ark's steps into his congregation. He moved carefully through the aisles so that all the people there could reach out and touch their beloved Torah. Everyone crowded towards him being careful to only touch the sacred object but not jostle the Rebbe.

When he eventually came around to our row he stopped. The Rebbe then turned inwards and motioned for me to step over into the aisle with him.

Oh no, not again. What now?

He leaned over to me, blue eyes twinkling and smiled mischievously. I could hear him say out loud to all, "God's words are as wings to a bird. They lift us up joyously."

And with that he handed me the Torah so it lay over my own shoulder like a baby waiting to be burped. I didn't dare move a muscle. If I tripped, what then? I had the living soul of our people in my arms.

This was an honor I definitely didn't deserve. I mean I hardly ever even came to shul!

So DON'T drop it, idiot! Hey, Mr. Butterfingers, just hand it back over now, and do it carefully!

Then as I tried to follow my own good advice and hand it back to him, the Rebbe placed his hands gently over mine and asked, "Don't you think our guest, Wilson, would also like to hold it?"

At that I think every single mouth in the room dropped open. I heard gasps echoing around the room. But not one person dared to move. There was not a single word uttered. Wilson who was standing right behind me didn't make even the slightest movement to get any closer to the Rebbe, or the fabulous Torah. His arms stayed rigid straight down at his sides. Both of us were frozen in our places just like when the lunch whistle blew in the schoolyard.

The Rebbe lifted the sacred Torah from my shoulders back on to his own. But instead of continuing on his journey back to the Ark he stepped directly into the row and moved by me. Standing in front of Willy he laid the scrolls gently down on his shoulders. Wilson's arms slowly rose protectively to embrace the Torah. He held it to himself as if it were a newborn baby, and not just any baby, but one from his own family.

Looking up I saw Willy's eyes were now shut tight and he was rocking from side to side. He opened his eyes and looked straight into the little Rebbe's bright blue eyes. The Rebbe must have seen something special there because he never took the Torah back from Willy. Instead he took him by the arm and gently guided him down the aisle back towards the Ark. Wilson carried the Torah across the length of the synagogue through the crowd that continued to quietly touch and kiss the Torah. He carried our living Covenant right up the steps. It was only when they stopped in front of the Holy Ark that the Rebbe received the Torah from Willy's shoulder and gently laid it back in its place. A moment later Wilson walked proudly across the length of the synagogue and sat back down next to me. Then he turned slowly to me and winked. Leaning across to me I heard the words, "Now that, son, was cool!"

And it truly was. I know it was because as we left the schul it seemed like every person there came up to Willy and me and wished us a, "gut Shabbas."

Now how about those apples?

"Hey Train, would you mind if I take a few of these latke things home for my mom to try?" brought me back from my memories of the events earlier in the day.

Before I could say anything more my Mameh called out from the kitchen, “Don’t worry Wilson, dear, I have a big plate for you to take with you. And you’ll take also with you some applesauce and sour cream in two cups too! How can you enjoy “latkes” without them?”

Wilson walked out the door with his foil wrapped dishes completely filling up both of his hands. He called back over his shoulder, “Now remember, Train, meet me in front of my church at 9:30 tomorrow morning. And remember also that you’re coming to my house after the service. Don’t forget! Bye, bye, Teddy’s Mameh!”

I nodded and closed the door. I could hear the echo of footsteps as they went carefully down the staircase to the front door of the building.

It had been a good day. No, scratch that, it had been a great day!

And tomorrow was going to be an even better one!

Chapter Twenty-One

I was early. That was my first mistake of the day.

And I had no idea of how I'd have to pay for it.

I'd woken up early excitement dancing in my heart and I knew there had to be a matching smile on my face. The early morning sunlight was peeking through the sheer cotton curtains as it did whenever it found the gaps between the building's back alleys. The sun didn't mind my window facing an alley. Most days I barricaded it against the bright light by pulling both the shade and the curtains shut. But this time I wanted to get up so I'd left the window bare and open.

To my right, up against the wall in the bed we shared, was my little brother, David, fast asleep. He was, as usual, deaf to noise, light or anything weaker than the cold water Mameh had to sprinkle on him to get him up. On school days it had become such a regular event my mother had begun shooting us with a water gun. Secretly, I think she enjoyed doing it. She called it watering her "little pishers," her little pissers. Mameh liked making her little jokes.

But today was Sunday, so I tiptoed around the room trying to not make any noise at all. Tateh usually worked five and a half to six days a week so Sunday was his only chance to sleep a little more. Today, I was thinking I had to hurry up so I wouldn't be late. With that in mind I jumped out of the warm bed on to the cool wooden floor. Brrr…but today was still the day I was going to church with Wilson and his family and that made me move a little faster.

Again I thought back happily to the day before, Saturday and how much fun we'd had first at schul and then later at my house.

What an amazing day! And today is going to be even better!

Carefully I started to put on all of my best clothes. I'd laid them out on the dresser and the nearby chair the night before to be ready for this special occasion. I marveled at what a beautiful job my Mameh had done giving everything perfect creases and making it all so spotless! My white shirt gleamed as if it was brand new and my tie was hanging already perfectly knotted. The trousers were neatly pressed and folded extra carefully over the back of a wooden chair. And my shoes were absolutely perfect. They were spit shined to a mirror finish. That was no joke because I saw myself clearly looking back as I inspected them. I knew I could never have gotten them to look like that. My heart swelled from the thought of my father working so hard on them just for my benefit.

I looked at myself again in the mirror after dressing and knew I looked good. I also knew why. Aside from the fact my parents loved me so much they always insisted I had to represent our family with "class."

As I was still complimenting myself on my clothes, I felt someone looking at me. So I ducked down and quickly spun around fingers outstretched six shooters as if I were in a gunfight. And there she was, my Mameh smiling proudly while spritzing a cloud of cologne to envelope me.

"Hey, come on Ma! Stop it!" I cried out in mock anger while playfully shielding my head from the last misty squirt. Done, she turned and hurried back down the narrow hallway towards the kitchen.

As I followed her quick retreat I picked up the aroma of hot oatmeal simmering on the stove. My stomach was ready to rebel at the thought of eating anything just that second. It wasn't that I didn't like oatmeal. It was just that I didn't really want anything at all because I was still stuffed from "latke" bingeing the day before. But then again, things had worked out so well yesterday I didn't have the heart to argue with Mameh about much of anything, especially an "I'm not hungry," argument. Mameh had all ready been more of a good sport than I could've ever hoped for.

"Straighten the tie! Don't embarrass us!" She grumbled beneath her breath as I swallowed down burning spoonfuls of hot cereal then cooling my throat off with large gulps of cold milk.

Slow down, or you'll be in the emergency room instead of at Wilson's church.

Then as I finally stepped out the door into the hallway she called out to me from the kitchen.

"Wait a minute Mr. Sloppy! Where is your watch? Please, try to look like a mensch and not embarrass us! Wait here just a minute mister! I'll get it for you!"

My latest birthday present, a Bulova watch with a shiny silver stretch band, slipped on over my wrist. Now I was ready. The complete picture of sophistication stared back at me from inside the mirror. That image was the one completely shattered in the next second by Mameh's next question.

"Tevye, maybe your Poppa should walk you over to Wilson's neighborhood, heh? What do you think?"

"No, let Daddy sleep a little bit more! It's Sunday and I'm fine, really I am!" I answered horrified by the mental picture of my father walking me down the street.

Wasn't I almost grown? Come on now!

As I took my first step down the staircase she again called out from behind me now in the apartment doorway.

"Tevye, wait a minute! Did you take the two dollars from on top of the dresser for the donation?"

"Yes, Ma," I called back over my shoulder at the same time wondering where on earth she had found out about church collection plates. I guess she must have done her homework with her friends at work.

"Don't forget to put the money into the plate! Don't embarrass us! We're not schnorrers! We're not beggars!" echoed a fading voice above me as I flew down the steps.

"Yes Ma, Don't worry. I'll do it. I'll take care of it! Stop worrying about it, please!" I sing-songed out loud as I continued skipping quickly down the three flights of stairs, all the while congratulating myself on a masterful escape.

A tap dancer couldn't have flashed faster feet than mine flying down these last steps!

That's what I thought smugly to myself shoving open the building's heavy wooden door with a hard shoulder push.

I eagerly stepped out into the crisp air, blue sky and bright sunshine while greedily sucking down a lungful of fresh air.

What a day! When it's right! It's right!

I drew in one more deep breath and could feel the grin on my face getting bigger. No doubt about it, I was happy! And then I could feel that grin growing even bigger and bigger with each and every step I took down the long empty sidewalk. I was on my way to my best friend's church, and a fun day!

Seven blocks later there it was sitting all by itself on the corner of Webster Avenue. As I walked up to the building I read a sign that read, "The Holy Ark of the Disciples of Christ, Baptist Church, Pastor Daniel C. Short".

That's exactly what the sign said in large black and gold hand painted letters. It's funny how you can walk by a place fifty different times but not see the obvious things about it until you stop and really look at it. For example, I never noticed the pastor's name was the Pastor Daniel C. Short.

Hey, wait a minute!

My brain was stung by a strange coincidence.

Short, that's Wilson's last name.

I marveled at the matching last names.

Could this be his father's church?

The thought suddenly stopped me in my tracks. The fact was I had never met Wilson's dad and he'd never mentioned his first name, or anything about what his father did. But then Wilson didn't like to brag about stuff, especially his family.

He always said things like, "Do what you're gonna do, and let everybody else say what they're gonna say."

Willy was pretty cool like that. But was it possible?

Could it really be that Wilson's father was the pastor of this church?

Maybe it was another weird coincidence. As I stood there thinking that over, my eyes wandered to the bottom of the sign. There I saw one last thing that made me forget about what might be and started a warm feeling rising up inside of me. The bottom of the sign said, "ALL ARE WELCOME."

Where is Willy? Maybe I'm too early? What time is it now?

I wondered glancing down for the first time at my wrist. There it was, my pride and joy, a fancy new wristwatch with a shiny silver expansion band. It was my most special present ever. That's because my Mameh had paid away on it for months and she'd finally given it to me on my birthday. I never wore it to school because I didn't want it to seem like I was showing off in front of my friends. And another reason, just as important, was that I really didn't want to attract any attention to myself either.

It sure is a pretty watch though, and it matches my suit and tie perfectly!

"Hmm…almost 9:30 and he told me to meet here at 9:30 sharp," I said out loud to myself.

The service was supposed to begin at 10:30. One of the main reasons I was here so early was because I'd wanted to make a good impression on Wilson's family and friends. After all, Willy was right on time for me yesterday and I wasn't going to let him down by being late.

I turned around and looked down the street in the direction of Wilson's block.

Okay, there he is turning the corner coming up this way.

But no, wait a minute. As the person got to the middle of the block, I could see it wasn't Willy after all. It was actually a boy I recognized and knew a little bit named TJ.

Well, that's okay. No big deal.

I was thinking that cause I knew TJ from the park. In fact, even though he was in high school and a few grades ahead of us he was still one of Willy's best friends.

TJ was usually in the park no matter when we got there after school. He was a good, no a real good basketball player with a lot of "game." But there was this one thing about TJ that made a lot of people, including me, nervous. He had a real mean streak. I mean he was still a great ballplayer and all that. He won lots of games, but still no one liked to play on his side. That's because no matter what happened, win or lose, TJ always had something bad to say about somebody. It wasn't ever enough for him to win and just say "good game." No, he had to rub things in by telling you how bad you messed up and how good he was. I mean if he lost he had to blame everyone on his team and tell them how losing was their fault, not his.

And then even if his team won it was always because he'd carried you.

Believe it or not, that wasn't even the worst part. The worst part was sometimes, and it was a lot, he liked to start stuff with people too. One of his favorites was to bring someone's mother into things during an argument about almost anything. That's when the fights would always start. Sometimes TJ was just a flat out nasty guy. But Wilson seemed to like him and he never messed with me. Maybe, probably, because I always came with Willy.

Anyway, we all seemed to get along, at least most of the time. So I guess it was cool! At least it seemed like it was. Besides TJ never messed with Wilson.

Nobody, I mean nobody at the park wanted any part of Wilson

That always made me smile thinking about how someone so innocent looking could be such a madman.

Whatever, it's still cool to be friends with everyone.

Chapter Twenty-Two

"Hey T! How you doin'?" I called out lamely as he came closer to me on the empty street.

The time for walking away had passed.

"Nuttin' much, my man. What'cha doin' ova' here, babe?" TJ asked checking me out with a quick glance up and down. "You lost or sumpt'in'?"

"Nah," I replied gamely trying to sound schoolyard cool. "I'm goin' to church t'day with Wilson and his folks."

He looked at me with an air of complete surprise, maybe even shock. "Goin' t'church?" He questioned me loudly with the slightest touch of ridicule mixing into his rising voice.

"How you gonna go ta this church? You a white boy, a grey boy, and a Jew Boy on toppa all a dat! What you think you doin' com'in' to this here church? Zactly what're you thinkin' bout. This here's MY church?"

It was clear to me that TJ was getting himself more and more worked up. But what started the icy chill rising from the base of my spine was the growing anger in his voice. Desperately I tried to think of something I could say so he would see me again as Wilson's friend, the baller from the park and not some kind of turf invader.

All I could think of was telling him the truth. So I tried to get it out of my mouth even as TJ slowly closed the distance between us.

"C'mon T, don't be like that, man! Willy invited me to your church today and I said, fine, okay. Y'see what I'm sayin'? What's wrong with that, man? Is this your church too? I didn't know that, man! Do you mind if I drop in today?" I asked hopefully trying to not look too directly into his eyes.

"Naw, Naw, my brother, dat shit ain't happ'nin' here t'day! You can't just be showin' up and steppin' into my church just like it's yours! That ain't comin' at all correct! You bein' a white Jew Boy and all, dat shit ain't gonna fly, not t'day! You wanna come 'round here you gonna need special permission from the past'r!" he insisted reaching over to grab my arm.

This all was becoming more and more confusing and then even more frightening.

"See T, man, I didn't know that! I really didn't know that! But when Willy gets here I'll make sure to ask 'im to get permissi…" I stammered on while trying to pull my arm free from out of his grip.

"Listen here, whitey," TJ interrupted yanking me hard by my arm into a little brick alcove off the street. "If y'really want me to… I can get th' permission you need because, you see, I know the past'r…" He continued on in a lower urgent tone. "But it's gonna cost you somethin'. Y'got any scratch on ya'? Whatcha holdin' in y'pocket?"

The icy coldness that had begun at the start of the conversation was spreading out through my back and gripping me around my heart. TJ's hand felt like a piece of brick wrapped around my upper arm. It was hurting me. Suddenly, I felt another hand patting down my front pants pockets and then my suit jacket pockets.

It was then that I tried my best to yank my arm free, but his grip was too strong.

"Hey, what th'fuck you tryin' t'do?" TJ whispered up close to my ear. That was accompanied by a menacing stare.

"Come on, man! I don't have any money!" I yelled again almost automatically struggling to break away. "Leave me alone, T! Come on man. Leggo-a-me!"

But TJ only used the next split second to shove me harder up against the building's brick wall. Then he stared down at me, but I swear it seemed like he was looking at something right past me. Then he quickly reached around and turned all my pockets inside out.

"Dam'd Jews! Always tellin' lies bout money," he mumbled aloud while yanking the two dollars my Mameh had given me for the collection plate out of my back pocket.

"What's this here, cracker, huh? What d'ya' call this here? I thought y'said y'didn't have no money?" He threw back straight into my face.

"That's my only money. It's to put in the collection plate!" I cried out desperately still trying to pull my arm free.

And then it stopped. I mean everything stopped.

At least that's what it seemed like to me. Because the next thing I knew was that I was stretched out flat on my back on the sidewalk. My brain was spinning, confused, unable to remember how I'd gotten there. All there was, was the deafening loud pounding of my own heartbeat in my ears. My eyes were unfocused. I lay there trying just to remember where I was.

What had happened to me?

I could feel hands roughly pulling on each one of my pockets again turning them inside out to make sure they were empty.

There was also a terrible burning sensation on the right side of my face. I tried to touch the place that hurt but my hands couldn't seem to find the right places. They weren't working right. For a moment, I could feel the individual pebbles on the concrete beneath me right down to the particles of glass that bit into my palms.

Then, as suddenly as they had left, my memories all came rushing back. I knew that I had been sucker punched. I pushed up hard trying to get back up on to my feet, but I still couldn't move. It felt like a tremendous weight was pushing me backwards. Looking up I saw that what was holding me down was a big knee on my chest.

"Stay down Hymie, or y'gonna get some mo'. Y'only thinkin' y'wanna get up! Well then little man, you still so sure you wanna come to MY church? Yeah? Well then muthafucka, here's somethin' else fo' your cracker ass to think about!"

And in one sudden motion, TJ rose up and kicked me in the side as I tried to get up again. I went down, only harder this time, tumbling on to my back while grabbing for the painful explosion in my side with both my hands. As I tried to cover up with my arm I felt my wrist being grabbed, twisted then held up for an instant.

Before I knew what had happened my precious Bulova was gone. The wristwatch had been yanked straight off my arm.

TJ bent down and used his knees to straddle me. He grabbed my throat in both of his big hands. Using his great strength he pulled me up to him so his mouth was right next to my ear. Then he whispered very slowly.

"I betta' never see your ass in this here church, not ev'r! You hearin' me clear, cracker? In fact, I betta' not see you anywhere round here, 'specially not round the courts!"

"And if I do see y'ofay-bitch-ass ag'in I'm gonna mess you up big time! Much worse then anythin' you got t'day! You feelin' me, Train? You do hear what I'm sayin', right Teddy?"

Then he let go and let me fall backwards to the ground. TJ stood up straight and brushed his hands off on his clothes as if he had touched something dirty. After glancing both ways down the empty street for any witnesses he walked quickly away and disappeared silently into the church's front door.

As for me, I lay there on the ground with my eyes shut tight sobbing into my jacket sleeve.

It seemed like a long time, but I'm sure it was only a minute or two. I kept clutching my side and crying hoping nothing was broken.

How am I going to explain this to Mameh and Tateh?

In that moment I dreaded what they were going to say a lot more than the pain I was experiencing.

Could it be that they were right? That I shouldn't have come?

That's when it came to me that I must not be hurt that badly. I was still thinking!

A car door opened, slammed shut and I heard some quick footsteps come running towards me.

"What's wrong young man? Are you all right? Here, let me help you up?" I heard a familiar voice say from close by.

"Oh no, no, Danny! Danny hurry! It's Teddy over here on the ground! Hurry up Danny, Willy, come quick, Teddy's hurt!"

I felt many hands lifting me, trying to get me to stand up, but my legs just wouldn't support me.

"Danny, wait a minute, just wait. Maybe we shouldn't try to move him so quickly? Let's call the police! Oh Teddy, what hurts? Danny, what can we do?"

Again I felt strong hands lifting me upward and someone firmly saying, "Boy, raise your arm around my shoulders for a minute. Lean on me. Wilson, help him from the other side."

"Oh, look! Look, Danny! He has a big lump on the side of his face. What happened to you Teddy? Did someone hit you? Were you robbed? Willy, run into the church and call the police. Oh dear, what's your phone number Teddy? Danny, we have to call his parents right away!" carried on Willy's mom frantically over and over.

Maybe it was all those questions that forced me to focus because when I tried to stand up I found I could do it with only a little bit of help. The strangest part was I could only see clearly out of one eye. The other eye was seeing three of everything in front of it. But as the questions kept coming I realized I could now focus both of my eyes together, if I squinted hard.

"Please don't call my mother. Please, not yet, I'm all right." I heard myself saying to Wilson's mother and father as they looked into my eyes. I saw they were carefully watching me for any sign I was lying about my condition. Both of them were holding onto one of my arms with one of theirs while clutching a Bible in the other.

"I think, no, I know I'm fine, okay, okay…" I repeated several times loudly trying to put them and myself a little more at ease. Actually, I didn't know what kind of shape I was really in exactly, but I did know I didn't want my parents to know what had happened to me. I mean I was embarrassed. Besides, the pain in my back was going away and my face, still burning where I'd been hit, was feeling a little bit better.

"Are you sure you're okay, Teddy? That's going to be a very mean "shiner" you have there. I'm thinking we should take you straight home. What do you think dear?" Pastor Daniel C. Short calmly asked his wife.

"Let's take him inside first and put some ice on his face to hold down the swelling," interrupted Wilson. "Then we can call his mom or whoever."

I glanced gratefully at Wilson. I'm sure he knew what was waiting for me at my house and he was trying to buy me some time to find another way out of this mess. Wilson's mother and father turned away from me and spoke quietly to one another for a moment.

His dad turned back to me and with an absolutely fake, but positive smile announced, "Okay then, we'll see… Let's take a minute and get you cleaned up inside. Then we'll see about what comes next. Come over here boy! Wilson, help your friend! Make sure he doesn't fall out on us!"

I didn't say anything more as they led me through the side entrance of the church.

Strange, I had wanted to see the inside of a church, but not this way.

Inside my head all I could hear was the same thing repeating itself over and over again. It was my Mameh kvetching.

I told you so! I told you not to go, but you never, ever listen to me. Mr. Big Shot, Mr. America needs to have everything his way! Now you see! Now you see what happens when you don't listen!

SEE HOW YOU ARE KILLING ME! SEE HOW YOU'RE TEARING MY HEART OUT OF MY CHEST! YOU'RE KILLING YOUR OWN MAMEH! ARE YOU SATISFIED NOW? ARE YOU SATISFIED? SEE! SEE! SEE!

My poor Tateh!

Chapter Twenty-Three

I was still confused. On the one hand I was angry and upset. I was definitely scared too, very, very scared, and that didn't even include how my heart ached. Plus, my face was still aching where I'd been punched in the face. But even so I couldn't help but be curious about what was going on all around me. First, everyone was looking so damned, oops, excuse me, so darned happy! They were all smiling and greeting us cheerfully as we came walking into the big main room from the side entrance.

Where was the feeling of fearful awe of the Almighty?

"Fear God first, my son," my Tateh always said. "Then love Him!" All these people had happy looks on their faces. It was as if they expected something really, really wonderful to happen. And all the beautiful bright colors they wore! It kind of dazzled me.

Where were the somber grays, blacks, blues and browns I was used to?

The variety of pretty colors rolled gently over me like waves lapping on top of my toes at the beach. It felt like my brain was wading in cool fresh water. Pure whites, bright yellows, hot pinks, pretty blues and all kinds of flowered patterns covered the ladies' hats and dresses. And the men also wore different colors and shades in their suits and ties Some outfits matched, others clashed together but they all blended into a background reminding me of the park in full spring bloom.

Could people be allowed to wear such pretty things when they spoke to God?

But before I could mull that one over, I realized everyone, men, women and children, everyone, was sitting all mixed together.

Now that was definitely something very different for me.

"You sit yourself down right here," whispered Pastor Short to me. "Right here, …right here up front," he repeated once again, "and don't you dare move!"

He quickly walked away after having placed Wilson and I in the middle of the front row, dead center before the raised platform where the speaker was to be.

But when I turned to the left my heart skipped more than a single beat.

And why was that?

It was because sitting right next to me, I found myself staring into the face of the last person in the whole world who I'd ever want to see again.

There looking back at me eyeball to eyeball, absolutely dead straight in my face was TJ. It was also very clear to see that he was even less happy to see me than I was to see him.

As he glared at me he hissed angrily under his breath, "Jus' keep y'big trap shut or y'gonna be real sorry!"

Then he rolled his eyes towards the floor beckoning my eyes to follow his. As mine followed in the direction his took I could see the message waiting for me laying on the seat next to him. It was his very large hand flexing open and shut into a huge fist.

"Jus' remember, what I got waitin' f'you, if you run y'big mouth," is what my ears picked up while my courage was retreating like a chilled prick.

My body shrank away from TJ's. The dread his big body created from being so close was too powerful for me to handle. A spreading tightness began to ache in my lower back. Fear was taking over in spite of the "me" part of my brain shrieking.

Don't show any fear! No matter what happens. If you show fear you are finished, done! SHOW NO FEAR!

Just as suddenly I felt Wilson sitting on my other side moving. He got up from the seat on my left and crossed quickly over to my right. There he pushed himself down roughly right in between TJ and me. Wilson had created his own space for a seat.

Then he leaned over and whispered something urgently in TJ's ear. I barely made it out but it sounded something like. "Why don't you give me some of what you gave Teddy?"

Their eyes locked for a tense few seconds. There was no disguising the shock in TJ's eyes.

But before things could go any further the service had begun.

"Brothers and sisters, family and friends, guests, let us all bow our heads in prayer to thank God Almighty for this truly blessed day ..."

I'm not exactly sure why, but when I heard the pastor's voice say those words some of the tension eased its way out of my body. There was a good solid feeling in me that swore I wasn't going to get beat up anymore this morning. So I crawled back to a comfortable spot in my brain and decided to listen to the minister, the choir and whatever else the congregation here had to offer.

After all, why else was I there?

And then it was like, okay. Nope, it was much better than just okay, it was good, really, really good. Actually, it was interesting and also fun, especially the singing parts. I mean it sounded like God was right here in the room with us, and that He wanted everyone here to be happy and listen to one another. Like I said, it was great! And again I was thinking.

Why is it I liked this music so much? Why did it feel so special and familiar?

Slowly but surely it came to me. There was a haunting familiarity here. It was the same something inside touching me as when the men davined their prayers in togetherness at our shul. It was the same something I felt Sunday mornings from the singing on the Yiddisher radio stations. The music from both places came from someplace deep inside the heart and reminded me of caged birds being set free. There was pain there, and suffering too, but there was great joy also!

And it seemed like it all started with the love you had for God, and the pain you sometimes had to suffer for loving Him. It didn't matter if the music was happy or sad, only the place it came from and the place it was meant to take you to. People in this House were speaking from their hearts. And here He was, answering everyone who was willing to listen.

I was beginning to feel a lot more comfortable here even though I didn't understand everything they were saying about Jesus. But they were still talking a lot about the Bible and that's the same thing I talked about in Hebrew school. Although I have to admit I never heard the name Jesus, mentioned there.

"And now, my brethren, today of all days I have a story that needs to be told, a tale that needs some telling," continued Pastor Short. "It is a story that cries out to be told today because today is a day just like any other, a day that has happiness and sadness found in it."

"It's an old story, one that you've probably heard many times before, but from time to time we sometimes need to be reminded of what's really important in life, the choices we are faced with. Those old biblical tales can show us our way, our path to righteousness. Can I get an "Amen" from the church?"

"Amen," resounded softly from the congregation.

"Yes indeed," continued Pastor Short, "Sometimes we have to be reminded of why we've been placed here on this earth. I say again, sometimes we need to review our life's agenda. But what then is God asking of us? Why are we here?"

"What is it you ask, my friends? Well, this fine day, this beautiful morning I'm going to tell you! We're here, my dear sisters and brothers, the reason we exist on this earth is… to serve. That's right we're here to SERVE God's will! But then what, I say then, WHAT… IS GOD'S WILL for each and every one of us? How do we find our own individual path to serve and follow His will?"

"Amen, amen, brother," echoed throughout the many rows and sections of the congregation. "Preach on! Preach! Speak, speak the Truth!"

The pastor began to tell the old biblical tale of Cain and Abel. Of course, I knew it from Hebrew school and the book of Genesis, but here it sounded different, all new and fresh. Pastor Short painted a vivid portrait in my mind of the two grown sons of Adam and Eve, working together in their fields and with their crops and animals. It was all coming alive anew like a Saturday morning TV program.

"And then one son, Abel, gave up to God the VERY BEST of his produce as the truest sign of his love and devotion, while the other son, Cain, chose to keep the very best for himself, and gave

God his leftovers. After all, Cain reasoned convincingly to himself, "What does Almighty God need with real food? He'll never, ever eat any of it? He's God, and everything he needs he already has! I will save the best for my own table!"

"When God shows his favor to the generous Abel, his foolish brother, Cain, is overcome with hideous jealousy. Cain strikes Abel killing him and then hides his body."

At that point Pastor Short was telling the story so well that everyone began leaning forward hanging on to his every word. That's when the pastor moved to the edge of the stage leaning dangerously forward and looking straight downward towards our own seats placed right in front of him.

Taking a deep breath, the pastor roared, "And then G-O-A-H-H-D… asked Cain again, "Cain, where…is… your… brother? WHERE IS YOUR BROTHER… TEDDY?"

My brain back-flipped. It had to have played a trick on me.

Had the pastor actually just said my name or was this some silly trick my imagination was playing on me?

I nervously peeked over to my side. Wilson was entranced. I leaned farther forward and looked past him. TJ looked like he was carved from stone. There was not a sign anyone had heard what I had.

It's got to be me imagining…"

WHERE, – IS, – YOUR, - BROTHER, _ TEDDY?" Pastor Short thundered again slowly emphasizing each word.

I hadn't imagined it. The pastor had said, "Teddy," not, "Abel."

Then Pastor Short spoke then again in a different voice. This time he assumed a more indifferent voice that represented foolish Cain.

"Why should I know where my brother is? Am I then my brother's keeper?"

And so the minister spun slowly to the left, quickly pointing to a man in the fifth row wearing a beige suit and a flowered tie, "And what say you to that, brother Dylan? ARE YOU… your Brother's keeper?"

"Yes sir, yes pastor, I am. I am!" was Brother Dylan's immediate reply.

Turning quickly around to his right he immediately found a woman dressed completely in pink and white now standing up in the middle of her section with her arms raised towards the ceiling.

"And what about you, Sister Geraldine? ARE YOU, YOU... your brother's keeper?"

"Oh yes, sir, I am truly, I most surely am, PRAISE JESUS! PRAISE HIM! PRAISE HIS HOLY NAME!" was her emphatic reply.

Then again the pastor pointed next back to right, then back to the left, the right, and then the left. The right...and the answers were always the same.

"Yes, Lord! Yes, I am! I am! Thank you, Lord!"

"AMEN, BLESS HIM!"

"Yes, yes, yes!

And so it went on for over a full minute, maybe two until suddenly the Pastor stopped and slowly extended his arm, long pointing forefinger directed towards the very center of the front row. The finger stopped moving only when it was aiming right at the seated TJ.

Pastor Short continued on now quietly asking, "And you, young man, TJ, are you then your brother's keeper?"

TJ sat there stone still and silent for a moment. He was looking directly back up into Pastor Short's deep-set eyes until his chin suddenly dropped straight down on to his chest. The entire church fell silent. Everyone there knew that this was the special moment they'd hoped for when they'd come to church that day. No one could have known what TJ had done, but it didn't matter. This was that precise moment that a soul was going to be saved and somehow they were all ready to rejoice in it.

Pastor Short spread out his arms as if to enfold the entire church between them and said, "Come then, all ye sinners to the Lord God Who loves you all so dearly that He gave up his only Son to save us all!"

I leaned out and again looked across Wilson to TJ. I could see great big tears rolling down TJ's cheeks. His fingers were spread out wide on each leg gripping his knees and he'd begun rocking back and forth slowly as if to the beat of some invisible drummer.

Then came the biggest surprise. Wilson reached over to TJ and took one of his hands in his own. I mean I was stunned by what I saw happening. Willy had been ready to kill TJ only a few minutes ago! And then we all knew Willy's temper was terrible at times, but here he was comforting the one person he was most angry at!

The surprises weren't over yet for anybody.

Wilson took my hand with his own free hand and brought it across to hold TJ's. For me it was like touching a live electrical wire. I was totally shocked.

This is the same hand that beat the crap out of me outside. I fear this hand!

But now it was being offered in a different way. I looked into TJ's face, but I couldn't tell what he was thinking. Maybe it was because my own feelings were all confused. I was still scared. And my eye was still aching. But then I thought I could see some pain in TJ's face too.

But knowing what to do about it, or even what to say next was not me. Luckily, I didn't have to say anything for a while. We sat there, the three of us, our hands wrapped together.

We had become a pretzel.

The service was coming to an end when Pastor Short looked down at us in the front row.

"My sisters and brothers, family, do you really and truly love the Lord with your whole entire hearts? Can I get an, "Amen" from the church?" he asked in an earnest demanding voice.

"Amen," answered the entire congregation in loud unison.

"Then you have to put your trust in Him! You must trust Him as you trusted your own mother's love, your own father's. Because He is a loving God, and He asks that you, you and you," pointing at we three in the front pew, all be "your brother's keepers"... It is our responsibility to learn so very much from Cain's grave mistake and to truly care for one another. For does He not love us all so very, very much that He gave His All for us!"

Now that was a scary picture for me! Young Jesus, the Jewish rabbi being nailed to a cross. Of course I felt really sorry for him, but truth is I couldn't help being really, really glad that it wasn't me up there on the cross. But then I thought to myself.

Suppose Jesus really was God, or even the Son of God? What then?

Before I could think anymore about that my thoughts were interrupted

"Amen, Amen," answered many of the voices around me. I snuck a peek at TJ and saw that he and Willy were looking intently straight up at the pastor.

"Let us pray," said Willy's father, Pastor Short. "God loves you, one and all, and if we can't find it in our hearts to live together in harmony, to forgive one another and strive to find our happiness on this Earth, we then turn our backs on Him and His sacrifice. Let us all bow our heads once again and pray, in Jesus' holy name!"

Every head was now silently bowed, as the minister led us into the final prayer, "Oh Heavenly Father, give us finally, the strength to follow your path of Righteousness and Forgiveness. Let those who have strayed find their way home to You. Give us all the strength to understand your words. And then please also give us the strength to aid those who have asked for your help."

"And O' Lord! Lastly, grant us your greatest gift, the Power of Forgiveness so that your lost children will find true peace inside your embrace. Let them come to know You, O' Lord as did Abraham, Isaac and your own true son, Jesus! In His name, we ask this, O' Lord! Amen."

When TJ's head came up this time, he found himself looking straight into the eyes of his pastor, Reverend Short. For an instant their eyes locked and then TJ immediately looked down at his shoes. I wasn't sure what exactly had happened and I didn't have any time to think about it either. That's because everyone was shaking everyone else's hands all around them and wishing each other, "A Blessed Day!" I let go of TJ's and Wilson's hands and went right along with it shaking one hand after another. It felt really nice.

Without realizing it I'd turned myself completely around my hand stuck out ready to shake the next person's hand. Before I could stop myself there I was face to face with TJ again.

It was another one of those surprises, but I shook his hand wordlessly tongue-tied. He looked back and said what I never thought I'd ever hear from him.

"F'give me, please? I was jealous an' I was wrong."

He pushed some things into my hands, turned and walked away quickly before I could get a word out. Not that it would have mattered anyway because my mouth was now once more hanging wide open. Looking down, I saw my silver Bulova watch and two one-dollar bills.

"Jealous" he had said? What in the world was he talking about?

"Hey man, let's get in the wind now," said Willy some emotion still stuck in his throat. "Come on over to my house and we'll have somethin' to eat. I might even have a surprise or two for you."

"I don't think I can handle too many more surprises right now," I mumbled turning to leave. "But wait, hold on a minute."

I ran over to an older man standing nearby, I think they called him a "deacon." He was still holding out a collection plate over near the exit.

"Here," I mumbled dropping my Mameh's two dollar bills in the plate. The man smiled and nodded thank you.

"Have a Blessed day," he said with a smile.

I turned and walked right past Wilson. "Cookies!" I called back at him. His mom's fresh baked cookies were on my mind! Wilson laughed catching up and walking along next to me.

"You know you didn't have to do that. I mean the money. You're our guest today," he smiled putting his arm on my shoulder as we walked towards his dad's car.

"I know I didn't have to," I answered. "I did it because I wanted to. Besides my mom is always warning me, "Don't be a "schnorrer".

Wilson already was laughing. Finally, he asked, "Okay man, you got me again. I'll bite, Train. What's a, "schnorrer"?

I answered, "That's the guy who wipes his nose on his shirt sleeve because he's too cheap to buy a hanky. A person with absolutely no class!"

Willy was choking now, half bent over laughing.

"What, you chokin' on somethin'? Do you need some water, milk, maybe a cookie?" I asked with a half serious face.

Gasping for his next breath Willy managed to say, "Naw, man, naw, I'm okay, no problem, no problem. Hey, Teddy, my brother, you're definitely not a, 'schnorrer'. Nope, no way, no how, you're a, "schnorrer". But it's pretty obvious to everybody who knows you that you ARE definitely a "schlemiel!"

That's why I liked Willy! He could always make me laugh.

And so away we drove in Pastor Short's car.

Staring out the window I couldn't help thinking things over.

What a day! But bring on those delicious chocolate raison oatmeal cookies! I need something sweet that can definitely ease the pain!

Chapter Twenty-Four

I saw them from all the way down the block.

There they were, frantically pacing back and forth in front of Wilson's house.

I'd hoped against hope that maybe, just maybe, everything crazy was over with when we left the church, but as usual that was just me being stupid again. Deep down inside I knew too much bad stuff had happened and now I would have a lot of explaining to do.

"There they are Danny, pull over to the curb near them," was my next warning.

It was the last calm statement I heard and it was made by Wilson's mom as we turned the corner and drove slowly down the tree-lined street.

"They," of course were my parents, and "they" were already running up the street in a race to reach me.

Here we go…

That's what I was thinking anxiously as the car slowed down and pulled over to the curb. I knew I was in deep trouble because the only way my mother and father could have gotten here so quickly was by taking a cab. And you have to understand my parents never took cabs unless it was a matter of life or death. They were just too expensive in their eyes, an unnecessary luxury.

In fact, I pretty much was taught to believe that anyplace you couldn't reach by subway, bus or on two healthy feet wasn't worth going to, or probably didn't even need to exist.

But there they were and they didn't look happy at all. I was definitely in deep, deep trouble.

Reverend Short had turned his head too as soon as he heard his wife say, "There they are," and with a grim smile on his face he announced to me in a quiet voice, "Teddy, you realize why I had to call your parents. There really wasn't any other choice. I just told them everything that had happened very quickly and then tried to invite them over to the house for lunch."

"I guess I should've known it wasn't going to be that simple when the phone went dead. Come to think of it, I believe your mom hung up on me. But now, I don't want you to worry about it. It will all work out fine. You need to have faith. The Lord works in mysterious ways."

"Danny, can you slow down please! Don't you see them there straight ahead right in front of you?" interrupted Wilson's mom.

Somehow Reverend Short's words didn't seem all that reassuring after seeing my mother's eyes were cranked up to about twice their normal size and she'd begun clicking away on the car door's handle as if it were a cap pistol.

Through the window glass her voice was pleading, "Tevye, Tevye, my baby boy, my baby, my baby, favos? Favos? Vei geist dere? Why do you have to go to these places? Why? Why? Why? Are you trying to kill me? Will you be happier when I am dead?"

And with that latest fragment of guilt buried firmly in my brain for eternity, I lifted the door's handle. Instantly I was yanked out straight into my mother's smothering arms, then engulfed by a flood of kisses while somehow at the same time being scolded for succeeding in being the world's biggest idiot, a complete noodnik. And so it went on for the next minute or two. I didn't try to get a word in. It was useless. But truthfully, it seemed like it went on a lot longer.

My Mameh told me I was everything to her, her baby, her father, her brother, her foolish child, her life and her everlasting source of pain and suffering.

Amazing, I'd every single relative completely covered!

I decided in the end to hug her back and hope for the best.

Who knows? Maybe somehow, I'd get lucky and walk away from this train wreck?

Meanwhile my father had instantly jumped between me, my mother and everyone else he saw around us. There was a strange feverish light in his eyes and it had just a glint of crazy.

I'd seen that look on his face once or twice before. Bad things for everyone around usually happened next.

"Watching? Watching? What kind of watching do you call this? You people promised me Tevye would be safe!" my father bellowed right at Wilson's dad, Pastor Short.

But before Pastor Short could explain, the screen door of Wilson's house burst open crashing against the wooden outside wall. Out stepped a huge angry brown skinned man, barefoot and dressed only in pajama bottoms and a tee shirt. He quickly made his way down the porch steps towards the street. It was Willy's big brother, Stan, and he'd obviously taken the accusation made by my dad the wrong way.

Stan fixed his glare immediately on my Tateh. Willy's brother stood there his eyes narrowed and two knotted fists resting impatiently on his hips.

"Where in th'hell d'you get off sayin' shit like, 'You people,' to my mom and pop? Just 'xactly what's that bullshit suppos'd t'mean? Man, you gotta be outta yo' complete mind, or maybe you was jus' born stupid? You best take that mess back wherever you came from before you have lots mo' than your feelin's hurt out here!" warned Stan angrily.

After a quick backward glance towards my mother and me to assure himself we were okay, my dad chose to ignore Stan and shouted accusingly again at Wilson's father.

"We trusted you with our son, and look, look what he gets? He's beat up and robbed right in front of your church! What kind of people let someone do this to a young boy? He trusted you! We trusted you! You're just, just..." he sputtered on unable to find the words he wanted to say.

"You're just what, what, Mr. Teddy's daddy?" answered back Pastor Short quietly, but with some obvious anger of his own growing in his voice. 'Schvartzes, schvartzes,' am I right?" He repeated twice. "Isn't that the word you have for us? Schvartzes, that's your word for what you really think we are... niggers, right?"

"Is that all we are to you? Here I was thinking you and your wife were different. Can't you see that my son and wife both care deeply for your son? Do you really believe we would ever, ever, let anyone hurt him on purpose? Let me tell you something..."

"Look to his face! Look to it! He has a black eye! Look how upset his mameh is!" roared my father once again, and as if that wasn't enough to make his point, he foolishly took an angry step towards Wilson's dad.

"Hold up right there, mistah Big Mouth! Slow your roll!" threatened Stan stepping out in front of his own father and turning directly to face mine. He raised his hand and pointed a big finger straight down at my Tateh's chest.

"I'm tellin' you this one last time, for your ass's own sake, Mr. Teddy's daddy. Don't be startin' any stuff here, lessin' you lookin' for some to jump back your way," he finished slowly with the threat of what could come made very clear in his voice. Then he pointedly took another step towards my father. They were now only inches apart glaring into each other's faces. I knew it wouldn't take much more before they began swinging away.

My mind was set in a panic once again.

What could I say to stop this nightmare?

My morning's horror was being replayed all over again. Except this time, my Tateh and Wilson's family were going to be the victims instead of me.

Maybe, if I jump in there between them they might stop?

I was pretty sure they wouldn't hurt me if I could only get over there quick enough. But I couldn't!

I was tangled up completely in my Mameh's arms, plus she insisted on crying and holding on to me even tighter. I just couldn't manage to work myself free.

"Please, Tateh, please, please don't Daddy…" was all I could manage as I watched both him and Stan clenching their fists as they eyeballed one another. Their hands were now tightly knotted up, and both of them had fearfully bulging eyes packed full of menace.

A cold shock of fear jolted my body as I realized then that something terrible was about to happen and that Willy and I'd never be able to be the same friends again. That's when, thank God, something good finally, finally happened.

"Wait! Wait! WAIT A MINUTE, STOP! You can't fight each other. I won't let it! This can't happen!"

And then there came Wilson to the rescue! It was like a scene from a Superman comic. Willy jumped between Stan and my dad with his head bent down and his arms stretched wide apart. He held the two big men apart from each other like Samson holding up two falling pillars. Each of his arms ended in a clenched fistful of their shirts and it was clear he wasn't going to let go of either of them.

"Sweets, little man, leggo-a-me! Get out of th'way. This motha' is beggin' fo' a serious ass whippin'!" snapped Stan angrily.

Willy lifted his head up looking back into his big brother's eyes and said, "Nah, no way that's gonna happen here today. You hear me, Stan! Nuthin' like that is goin' down here, not today, and not between you two, not ever, NEVER!"

Surprised, Stan stopped pushing. He looked like he couldn't believe his own ears, and to tell you the truth, neither could I. I mean, Willy himself, sometimes couldn't control his own anger. He was always the first one to get angry. Then he'd explode losing his cool altogether. Now here he was being the complete opposite! Wilson was being the peacemaker, Superman, the Man of Peace to the rescue! Man, oh Man-ishevitz, a wave of relief swept over me. My body was tingling with joy.

"Blessed are the peacemakers," from the Bible is all I could think of at the moment! Thank you God! I still had a best friend. Oh, and a Tateh still in one piece.

Luckily, by then my Mameh had seen enough of my father's crazy antics to let go of me and grab him! She pulled the foolish man away.

"Leib, Leib, what are you doing? Gevalt, have you gone crazy? Meshuganeh, Tevye is gut. It was an accident, an accident, accidents can happen!"

"Kimahere, Leib! Come! Right now! Madman! Idiot! Noodnik! Let's go home right NOW! Gevalt, gevalt," she continued, "all of sudden a suit presser is a prizefighter!"

Pastor Short also used the same opportunity to wisely step behind his son, Stan and take hold of his arm to make sure his son was finished. But Stan wasn't quite ready to let this thing end quietly.

"Why you holdin' on to me Dad? Why shouldn't I bust this disrespectful Jew's ass? We ain't nobody's "schvartzahs"! He best believe that!"

And with that he once again halfheartedly tried to step around Wilson's still outstretched arm.

"Com' on now, Sweetie? You heard how th' Jew man talked about Mom and Pop? Lemme go!" but Willy, the pastor and now his wife too, also had hold of Stan and they wouldn't let go. They all held on to him. Wilson totally frustrated by all Stan's anger grabbed his brother's shoulders with both of his hands and shook him hard.

"Listen to me Stan! Listen for Christ sakes, dumbass! Damn, man, will you just stop actin' stupid for a second and just listen? Look at their arms Stan! Look at Teddy's mom and pop's arms!" Wilson shouted into his brother's face. "Look at those blue numbers tattooed on their arms! Damn it Stan, you blind or what? Can't you see! Don't you know what those things are?"

Everything stopped. It was like a scene from a movie where time stops and you wait for the unknown to happen. We didn't have long to wait because everyone's eyes were now focused on the bare forearms of my Mameh and Tateh.

Of course, for me those terrible blue numbers were nothing new. They were an everyday part of my life. Actually, truthfully, sometimes I was ashamed of the tattoos because they marked my parents as "greenhorns." In our neighborhood "greenhorn" was one more ugly name we were sometimes called. Only it was our own Jewish neighbors, the mean ones, who used it daily.

They might not of thought so but it always hurt. It meant you were new to America, kind of like fresh off the boat and stupid to boot. Stupid because your family didn't escape Hitler fast enough like their families did. Even some of my good friends snickered and smirked whenever the topic of "greenhorns" popped up.

I'd learned to never ask my Mameh and Tateh about their numbers because they wouldn't speak about them anyway. But I knew the answers were far too terrible for them to talk about with anyone but their closest friends. Those who'd been there locked away in the "lagers" and concentration camps, with them. But all we kids who had parents with those tattooed numbers, and there were a lot of us spread out around the neighborhood, had found out enough in our own ways. We all shared that living terror in common, the one that came along with those precise little numbers.

"Are those…are they what you were telling us about?" Stan said looking first at Wilson and then back at my parent's arms. Willy turned and looked sadly at me. Then he turned back and nodded at Stan, "Yes."

I looked at Wilson now standing there looking shamefacedly at me. Then I glanced over at the glum faces of his family and had to ask them, "How do you all know what those numbers mean?"

That immediately snapped Willy's head back with an irritated expression.

"There you go again Teddy, thinking you're the only one who knows how to use the library," he answered with a sad smile.

"But when, and why?" I persisted.

"Because we're friends, man! That's why I had to know! You remember the first time I was at your house? That's when I saw those numbers on your mom's arm and it bothered me right away. Why would people have numbers on their arms like dog license's? I mean I liked your parents right away and figured maybe if I knew a little more I could help out somehow. But I was too embarrassed to ask you, so I went to the library the next day and asked about it over there."

"The librarian steered me towards some books and then I did something maybe I shouldn't have. One night a few weeks ago, I told my family about the concentration camps and what the numbers meant. I know that stuff is real personal, but they like you so much I thought it was important for them to understand why you're the way you are. I hope you don't mind what I did. I guess I should have asked you first, but…" his voice trailed off.

"No, not me," I answered unsure of what I was saying, "I don't really mind, but…just what do you mean by, "The way you are?"

"Damn, Teddy, man, sometimes I think you might be afraid of the whole wide world! Sometimes, I don't think you're completely right in your heart. Honestly, a lot of times you remind me of a puppy somebody kicked around a lot! You're so afraid of too many things, way too many! And you don't…"

"Don't what?" I said afraid of the answer before it came out.

"You don't smile as much as you should."

I couldn't say a word back to defend myself. Someway, somehow Willy had seen into the most secret part of me. Sure he was right. But how had he known? And more important to me, did everyone else see the same things too?

I turned and looked over my shoulder at my folks. I knew they didn't like to talk about their bad times during the war. But they seemed to have calmed down along with Stan who was transfixed by their numbered forearms. Everyone else was staring at Wilson and me.

"Dad," asked Wilson, turning around to speak to his father, "can we go inside and show them the lock? I'd really like for them to see it. Is that okay with you, Ma?"

Pastor Short shot a questioning glance over to his wife. She looked at us and immediately nodded back her own approval.

"Stan, Stanley, son?" called out Pastor Short. Stan jerked himself out of the trance brought on by the tattoos he was still staring at. "Stan, go up to our bedroom and in the bottom of the big chest at the foot of our bed you'll find the lock. It's wrapped up in a small blanket. Could you bring it down into the living room? Thank you, son," finished Pastor Short.

"Yes sir," was Stan's meek reply turning his large frame around and trotting quickly back up the porch steps.

As Stan left, Wilson's mom stepped past me to reach out and take my Mameh's hands in hers.

"Mrs. Teddy's mom," she began speaking quietly.

"Please, please, my name is Raizle, Rose," interrupted my Mameh softly while gently covering the other woman's hands with one of her own.

"And mine is Carol. You have to know we really love your son!" Wilson's mom said clearly close to tears.

"I know. We both know," answered my mom, casting a quick look towards where my Tateh stood now head down, ashamed. "We love Wilson also. What a brilliant boy he is! He has such a beautiful soul! And so handsome too! My Tevye says he learns so much from him! It's a blessing to have a son with a good heart like his."

Wilson's mom continued on urgently, "This bad thing that happened. It was such a terrible, terrible mistake. I am so sorry that it upset you and your husband so. Please, won't you come inside and have something to eat with us? Maybe something cool to drink? We have lots to talk about. Please, won't you come inside?"

My Mameh has such a pretty smile.

That's what I thought whenever I saw it. All of her friends say she lights up a room with her cheerfulness. Flashing that smile she walked straight over to where Willy and I were standing.

First she took my hand in hers, and then she took Willy's hand also. Then Mameh took both our hands and clasped them together. Holding them tightly she sadly looked into both of our faces and said. "Friendship is a zisser, zisser gift. It must be nurtured and protected, even from a distance. Kenahoreh!"

And with that she turned around letting go of our hands and taking up my Tateh's. Without a backwards glance, they climbed the steps together and walked inside the house.

"Kenahoreh?" Wilson asked with a raised eyebrow.

"God's blessing on you," I replied to his question.

"That's beautiful Train, Kenahoreh! Sounds African? Hmmm, what do you think?"

"I think I'm hungry!" I said suddenly feeling a lot better.

"Kena-hurry!" Willy laughed, "Yeah, man, let's get a bite! And what does, "zisser" mean?"

"It means sweet..."

"Sweet like my name, Sweetie?"

"That's it!"

"You mean sweet like my jump shot?"

"Exactly."

“Very cool, then my game is…zisser?”
“No, just “ziss”, sweet!”
“Very cool, call me, “ziss”! That’s me, man, Sweet!”

Chapter Twenty-Five

What's next?

That's what I dared to think walking up those steps.

Maybe my luck is turning? After all what else could go wrong?

"Oh God," I sighed aloud without thinking. That single word got an instant response.

"Teddy, son, please don't ever use God's name in vain," asked Wilson's dad of me right away. Hearing that my Mameh turned her head around and shot Pastor Short an approving look.

"Please, please, everyone, please sit down! Sit, sit, and, make yourself at home," Wilson's mom urged.

Wilson's home had a long dining room with a table and several chairs sitting at its center. There were eight simply carved wooden chairs, so there was plenty of room for everyone to sit down. The room was decorated comfortably with the pictures of many family members hanging on the walls. And it also smelled very clean. I knew that piney smell because my mom scrubbed our wooden floors every weekend and it smelled the exact same way. I recognized the furniture polish smell too. That was my job along with my brother. The entire room was sparkling clean.

I breathed a sigh of relief because my mother never would have sat down if she didn't feel comfortable. And the thing that made her feel comfortable the most was cleanliness. So I knew Willy's immaculate house had already impressed her.

Good, one more point for my team!

I wasn't sure how this was all going to turn out but I knew my friendship with Willy was still on the line here. I looked over at him eager for some kind of sign, you know, a wink or thumb, anything.

I needed some sort of hope.

But he wouldn't turn his head to meet my eyes. Instead I could see he was concentrating only on my Mameh, trying to catch her eyes with his. Then it suddenly all became clear to me. He knew Mameh was the key. Willy knew exactly what he was doing.

He understood if he could somehow get my Mameh on his side, my father would have no choice but to follow.

Man, what a genius! I need to watch him more and learn! Here is a master at work!

"Please Rose, won't you let me get you something to drink? What can I get you?"

"No thank you, Missus," Mameh said quietly looking quickly to my Tateh to make sure he wasn't doing anything embarrassing to the family.

"Well then, maybe something in a moment, but won't you please sit down anyway. We'd like so much to explain what happened to Teddy. It truly was an accident and should never have happened," insisted Wilson's mom, Mrs. Short.

"You know the boys are such good friends and we love Teddy like he's our own. Isn't that right, Danny?" she said also with a sideways glance to her husband.

"He's a good boy," echoed Wilson's dad immediately.

"Missus Wilson's mameh, I already knew you cared deeply for my son, even before we came here. He talks all day long about nothing but Willy said this, and Willy did that. It's all day and all night! I have come to have much respect and affection for you and your family too. And that's even though we have never even met."

"Oh, the stories we have heard about all of you! They're wonderful stories about very good people. In fact, Tevye never would have been allowed to come here if that was not so. But you have to understand the way you and I feel is not the problem here. Tevye just doesn't belong here with you. That's why he was almost hurt so badly. This is not about you or your son. We love Willy deeply also. My heart tells me your son has the soul of a tsadik. My father, for whom my son is named, was a tsadik, a very learned man with a righteous soul, and I see that clearly in your son. He is a special person and will one day be a great man."

"So you see it's not him or you, it is only because we are so different…and only trouble will come from their close friendship. It has to end. For the good of both of them, they must stop being such close friends. I'm so sorry to say this, but I feel strongly that I must."

I felt crushed inside.

My chest hurt as if someone had punched me right in my heart. I couldn't think of any words that could save this moment. They had all been said. My Mameh had said what was in her heart and I had no answer for her.

It became terribly, terribly quiet in the room. Then Mameh reached out her hands to either side where my father and I sat alongside of her. She took our hands up in hers and stood. Then addressing the Short family she spoke.

"Come, it is time for us to go home. And thank you once again, Missus and Mister, for all your guthartsikayt, your kindness and good hearts."

With that we slowly pushed away from the table and moved towards the door.

"But then what about the numbers on your arms?" Wilson suddenly called out after them breaking the stillness that had followed my Mameh's goodbye. "Have you forgotten what they mean?"

And with that he quickly stepped over to my mom and gently took her hand from out of mine and into his own. Then one hand slowly rose until its fingers reached those terrible blue numbers.

There my friend stood, looking directly into my Mameh's eyes gently rubbing her forearm with his fingers, as if he could magically erase that foulness there with his efforts.

After what seemed like a full moment had passed with not a single word uttered from anyone, my Mameh finally looked from his hand on her forearm into his eyes, the eyes that searched her own.

She asked him in what seemed almost a whisper, "What do you really know of such things, zisser kinde? Why do you ask me to explain this terrible pain, this misery?"

"Please Mameh, please sit back down with us for just a minute," Willy quietly asked, naming my mother as if she were his own, and then leading her back towards the table.

I could feel my eyes filling up with tears from hearing him use that one word.

"Please Mameh, please listen! We, me and my family, know only a little bit about your hurt, but we'd like to show you something that will explain a lot more than just words. Stan, Stan, did you bring it? Do you have Great Grandpa's lock from upstairs?"

Stan walked slowly over to the table carrying a large bundle wrapped up loosely in a rough piece of burlap. Even though he tried to place it down gently in front of my Mameh its weight made the heavy thunking sound that iron does as it touched the wooden tabletop.

"Vas is dos?" My mother asked tentatively reverting automatically back to her native Yiddish. Her hands remained folded in her lap as if they knew there could be no pleasant outcome from touching the covered object on the table.

And as those words came out of her mouth everyone else in the room slowly approached the table until we were all either sitting or standing around it staring curiously at the roughly covered parcel.

Wilson, who was sitting alongside of Mameh now, reached across and gently uncovered the object that had been wrapped so carefully within the folds of what now appeared to be not a blanket at all, but an old sack. There it was, now sitting uncovered. It was an old cast iron lock. That's all I saw, just an old lock.

Maybe it's a family antique?

"You can touch it if you like," said Willy softly. "It won't bite you."

With a look of uncertainty cast towards first me, and then my Tateh, Mameh reached over and picked it up. She had to use both of her hands because of its weight. She slowly turned it over and examined it carefully.

Then Mameh said, "It is old, very old…and handmade, but I have seen others like it. Farmers where we came from in the old country would lock up their animal pens with these to keep the beasts from running away."

Then she passed it over to my Tateh who had been apprenticed to a blacksmith as a boy.

"This was a good lock, handmade, a strong lock, a farmer's lock," he agreed turning it over in his strong hands and then laying it down on the table. Still puzzled, they turned towards Wilson.

He picked up the lock and stared at it. Then he laid it back down in front of Mameh and said, "This lock is our mark, our family's mark, just like the numbers on your arms is yours."

Tears appeared in the corners of his eyes. "This lock didn't chain up farm animals, it chained up the people of my family."

A strange fear immediately covered my Mameh's facial expression as she seemed to visibly shrink within herself.

Suddenly, she tried to violently push herself away from the table. Somehow, someway she had come to fear that lock. We could all see it and I could even feel her fear.

IT MADE MY SKIN CRAWL!

Inside my heart that old familiar feeling was stirring.

Whatever it was about that lock, I knew that I feared it too!

Wilson's mom continued in an even voice, "That lock was used to chain my great grandfather to a wall every night of his adult life so that he would stop trying to escape his life as a slave. His master would've probably killed him as an example to all the other slaves, but he was too valuable. You see he, himself, was the master blacksmith who had been taught to make all the locks and chains that guarded his master's property."

For a moment there was only a terrible deep silence in the room.

I guess for me it was the shock of hearing something so evil!

Then suddenly there came a sound unlike anything I'd ever heard in my life. As I turned away from the lock I saw it was no one else but my own Mameh screaming!

There was one shriek of terrible pain followed by another, and another coming from a face so contorted it was almost unrecognizable! I sat there frozen by the moment, unable to even move. And then finally, she collapsed on the table in convulsive sobs. My poor Mameh had covered her face entirely away from the sight of the old lock burying her head deep into the folds of her crossed arms. Her body shuddered from the powerful sobs that wracked her small body. My Tateh jumped up from his seat and gathered her up into his arms trying to protect her from any danger.

"Raizeleh! Raizeleh! What is it? What is it?"

But there wasn't any physical thing for anyone to protect her from. Whatever was threatening her was buried someplace deep down inside of herself.

What do you do when the strongest person in your life is helplessly in pain right in front of you?

I found out that day.

You stand there and cry.

We were all helpless. Willy was crying, I was crying, Stan was getting ready to cry and everyone else was stunned in some kind of frustrated silence.

That is except for Wilson's mom. She reached over my Tateh's arms and took my mother's hands gently in her own. I could see their fingers slowly intertwining with each other's until they seemed to be linked in a delicate brown and white chain.

"It will be all right, Rose, it's gonna be all right. Just trust Him. I'm here with you, too! We all are. Don't be afraid. It will be just fine," cooed Wilson's mom.

What should I do? What had just happened?

I'd never, ever seen my mother like this. It was absolutely, completely terrifying.

How could touching an old lock create such fear?

But I had to help somehow. So I did the only thing I could think of. Stepping around my Tateh I put my arms around my mother's shoulders and hugged her as hard as I could.

"Mameh? Mameh? Are you all right? Answer me please, Mameh? Please say something to me? It's me, Mameh!"

Slowly, so slowly, she raised her head from Tateh's shoulders and I could see she'd grasped both of Wilson's mom's hands even harder. The two women's eyes met and then they were hanging on to each other both crying.

Wilson's dad, Pastor Short looked over to my father and said, "Why don't we leave the ladies alone for a little while? Let's go into the kitchen with the boys. They might like some freshly baked cookies? What do you say Leib, or is it Moses, your middle name you prefer? That is Moishe in Yiddish, am I correct, my brother? I think the ladies may need another few minutes by themselves."

My pop, stunned into silence by what he'd just seen, didn't say another word. He didn't have to. But it was good to see him nod his head as if to say, "Okay". Yeah, he was confused too, but then again, we all were.

I guess the fact I was still hungry was probably a good sign.

Chapter Twenty-Six

"One tea, one coffee, and three milks, do I have it right fellas?" asked Pastor Short in response to his previous, "Cookies or cake, what are you gentlemen going to have?"

We were seated around a table in a spacious kitchen. It was nothing like the cramped kitchen my family of four barely fit in. At my house we ate dinner in shifts of two to make life easier.

"Stan, could you get the milk and the sugar bowl please? Oh, and Stan, look in the upper cabinet on your right and get the box of sugar cubes out for Leib. See, Leib, you didn't even have to ask. I'm ready for you," the pastor chuckled. "Actually, I have tea with a group of rabbis and ministers once every month, so I know all about the sugar cubes. Kosher cookies, anyone?"

Pastor Short stepped over to the oven, opened it, and slid out two large pans covered in aluminum foil. My mouth began to water in anticipation of the oatmeal raison and chocolate chip heaven ahead.

Yippee!!

I was hungry.

But before the pastor could take a step towards the table with his treasure there was a knock on the kitchen door. Stan walked over and opened it.

"What up, Cuz?" Stan asked as the visitor stepped inside. Guess who was the one that was most surprised? Right, it was me again because there in the doorway stood TJ.

"How was church, T?" Stan asked absently. Stan obviously wasn't up on the news of the day. Still, something must have given away my surprise. Maybe I flinched or something because my Tateh immediately noticed and put one and one together.

He was no fool.

"Is that him, Tevye? Is this one the thief who struck you?" My father asked in Yiddish rising ominously from his seat. I said nothing. I was too afraid of what was going to happen next. Everyone in our family knew his quick temper.

"Leib, don't! Teddy, tell your father to respect our house!" interrupted Pastor Short. The tray of cookies in his hands didn't stop him from putting his body between TJ and my poppa.

"What the fu…why are here TJ? Don't you have any sense at all? WHAT THE HELL IS WRONG WITH YOU?" yelled Wilson putting a hand on TJ's chest and pushing him back towards the door he'd came through. TJ tried to hold his ground, but it was hard without picking up his hands to push back. His hands stayed down.

"I have sumthin' t'say and y'gotta listen to me! I tried t'go home, I really did. But I couldn't do it. I had t'come here t'say what I have t'say."

Wilson jumped in, "It's way too late for excuses, man. Why don't you get…"

"No, let him talk," I heard my own voice interrupt.

I'm not sure why I said it, but I did.

"It's okay, man. Say what you got to say."

TJ tilted his head a little to the left and gave me a questioning look. He turned outwards a little so that he was facing all of us and began all over.

"I'm jealous. I'm sorry, but I need for y'all t'forgive me for that. Please…"

Everyone stood there stunned.

Stan spoke out loudly, "Jealous, jealous of what? Who you jealous of? Lord, help me please, Jesus? I'm seein' people ready to fight, arguments in the street, women cryin' and now you sayin' you' jealous? What you jealous of? Jealous of who? Who here's gonna' tell me what's up here? Anyone? Cause I ain't got a damn clue?"

I turned to see my father lowering himself back down into the seat he'd jumped out of. His face was still red with anger, but there was something else there too. It looked like he all of a sudden felt sad about something.

TJ, face slanted to the floor continued on slowly, "I kinda knew it was all wrong when it was happenin', but it became real clear to me when Pastor Danny spoke on the jealousy between those brothers, Cain and Abel. I didn't want that to be Wilson and me. See Train, Willy is my cousin, really more like my brother, and every Sunday after service it's me who comes over here, not you! Willy and me, we eat, talk, laugh…"

"But not today, man. Today, you're here, insteada me."

"Come on TJ, man, you know it's not like that, not ever!" jumped in Wilson. "You know you never need an invitation to come over here, ever. Be for real, brother! It's not like that at all, We're family!"

"Yeah, what are you talkin' about? We're blood always, my man, and bloods way thicker than mud. You should know what that means," added Stan. "I can't believe what I'm hearin' from you. Exactly what'd you do?"

Ignoring Stan's question for a moment TJ continued, "It's not jus' bout the Sunday thing. Seeing Teddy in front of our church jus' put it out front fo' me. Sweets, before you two got tight, it was you and me. We was th'ones hangin' t'gether. We was tight like brothers, not like cousins. Remember how we'd go to the park every day after school and ball? We'd serve up whoever showed, then later jus' chill on out. And if there was a probl'm I had yo' back and you had mine. Yeah, we was tight."

"But Cuz, once you changed schools and started hangin' wit' him everything changed! Then it was you an' him, goin' to the libary afta' school, and even when you did come to the park, it was you and him, you and him who were down togetha', not you and me anymore!"

And with that a tear rolled down his cheek. Turning and talking into the closets nearest towards the kitchen door TJ said, "I'm sorry for messin' up everythin'."

He stepped towards the back door.

"Wait, wait up a minute T. You can't leave!" Wilson said firmly. "We can fix this. I didn't know it was like that. Come on TJ, you know you're my main man always. Hey, like Stan says, "blood's thicker than mud", right?"

"But people got to grow some too, that's part of living also. Am I right? But I hear what you sayin'. Maybe we need to spend some more time together, maybe even, like all three of us. How's that sound to you, Teddy?" Willy went on enthusiastically giving me a hopeful look.

"That's fine with me, great," I jumped back in. "I mean sure, that's cool with me… "

"But you guys spend too much time in th' libary! I don't like that place. It ain't me."

Wilson gave me a little nod no one else could see. Then he went on, "It could be a whole lot more interestin' if you could read a little better."

TJ's face began to flush a deep red.

"How you know I can't read jus' as good as you can?"

"How long we been cousins, T, forever right? Remember, I'm the one who reads you all the directions when you build those model planes you love so much. Come on now? This is me, Sweetie! Be for real, man!"

"Model airplanes?" I heard myself asking. "I build model airplanes too!"

"Oh yeah, like what kind?"

"Well, I'm working on a British Spitfire right now. I'm building it out of an Aurora balsa wood kit. What about you?"

"Mustang, P-41, Mine's balsa too. I got the wings all pinned up and ready for dopin'."

"Sounds very cool. I'd love to check it out. Maybe…"

"I don't know if," TJ said slowly.

"We know," said Carol, Wilson's mom loudly from the doorway where both our moms were standing. "That's more than enough pain and suffering for one afternoon. It's not a contest, right Rosy? The Lord wants us to be happy!"

My Mameh smiled happily.

"So Sweety, go get Teddy, Stan and TJ to help you set the dining room table. Use the good china and silverware from the sideboard. Let's get to it now, people! Everyone is hungry!"

"Amen, to that momma!" said Stan a cookie held high in one hand as he headed for the dining room. But not before he swiped another cookie for the other hand.

"Come on, y'all. Good as this cookie is I need to eat!"

Chapter Twenty-Seven

We're getting back to normal… I think. At least I hope so! Things are much better than they were. My Mameh and Wilson's mom are getting real close after what they went through together. They even go shopping together. Turns out, Wilson's mom loves to buy those sew-it-yourself Simplicity and Butterick patterns for the latest dress styles and so does my mom.

Small world, right?

And it also happens my Mameh is a great seamstress. So now it turns out they've got more in common than ever! So far it's worked out super!

Wilson's mom has gotten a ton of compliments on the dresses my mother has helped her sew and Mameh has built up a little dressmaking and alterations business on the side. The ladies from church are calling her up all the time! So I guess nice things are working out for nice people.

Other things have been working out for us too. Oh yeah, and don't let me forget TJ either. We're now the newest version of, "the Three Musketeers." It turns out T.J. never gave the library much of a chance, but once he hung in there its worked out a lot better than we ever expected. We're all supposed to meet there every day after school.

You know it's got to be better there than where I am now. This classroom is boring, boring, boring. I hate learning grammar!

At this exact minute my pointy yellow pencil is pretending to be the atomic submarine Nautilus and I'm Captain Nemo sailing her deep under the North Pole.

Look out! Look out! Holy crap, it's a giant squid attacking from the port side! The Kraken lives! Dive! Dive! Dive! Take immediate evasive action!

Down sinks my pencil point seeking safer shelter inside the inky darkness of my desk.

It's not that I'm a bad student, I'm really pretty good. Usually, I'm interested in whatever the teacher has to say. But a good daydream brought on by total boredom is not such a bad thing. I listen carefully to Mrs. Stein because I need to. I've been having a lot of trouble seeing the blackboard clearly.

At home I don't see the TV too well either!

But in the house it isn't such a big deal. All I do to fix that problem is put my face about two feet in front of the TV screen.

Then I can see everything just fine.

My bigger problem is in school. I sit in the "outfield", the way back of the room. I guess it's because I'm tall. So now I end up squinting hard a lot and sometimes even worse, I have to ask my neighbors what's written on the board. It's getting worse day by day. I mean I can't see the board at all like I want to. But I think I'm still doing okay. I just need to get to summer vacation and maybe my eyes will get better.

Today is gonna be different.

This is the last big math test of the year before report cards and final grades. I know I need to ace this one, but then this test is going to be on the entire fraction, decimal and percent unit and I also know I am ready!

I have that stuff down cold.

In fact, Wilson and me studied and studied together for this test yesterday and we are both sure we're going to murder this test.

Bring it on ba-by!

"All books off your desks, please!" ordered Mrs. Stein "Today's math test will be your last chance to raise your year's final math grade. And that final grade is the one you'll see written on your report card. I want you to try to do your very, very best and I'll try to have your tests graded and ready to be returned to you by Friday, the last regular school day before the end of school. Monday is a half day and that's when you'll receive your final report cards at exactly 12 PM, no exceptions. In addition, and I'm sure you all know this already," she continued speaking brightly, "you'll all be receiving your new class placements, and that includes all S.P. assignments, at the very same time."

"Pencils ready everyone?" Mrs. Stein's voice rose with a musical lilt. "You'll have exactly thirty minutes and not a second more to finish. I also suggest you check your work over carefully and if you finish early, recheck it. Remember, this is absolutely your last chance to raise your math grade," she added pointedly.

"Are there any questions? No? Ready? Then begin!"

After a final rustle of papers and a few noisy creaks from bodies shifting around on ancient wooden seats we all set to work as fast as we could. I threw one last glance in Willy's direction, three rows away. He'd lost no time becoming engrossed in his work.

Well, let me get busy here.

I carefully copied the first example off the blackboard. My eyes squinted powerfully to make sure I saw the numbers perfectly.

Not bad, not bad at all!

I congratulated myself on completing the first example with no difficulty at all.

You can do this!

A magical voice in my head began exulting. I quickly copied down the next example and ran through it.

Yippee-Ki-Yo-Ki-Yay, baby! I mean this is exactly what Willy and I studied. We're hitting a home run baby, a grand slam on this one!

"I got this one right too," I mumbled happily under my breath to myself. "I definitely got this one right!"

When I was completely finished with everything written on the board I carefully double checked all my work and leaned back slowly to take a deep breath.

What a relief to be released from being hunched over. This grade just might do the trick for me!

That was the only thought that passed excitedly across my mind. I knew I was borderline in math for the prestigious SP class. And getting into that class was exactly what I'd secretly been aiming at all year long.

You see, in our neighborhood it was the greatest honor of all to be selected for this wonderful class that worked so hard it completed three years of schoolwork in only two. That was what the SP, or Special Progress class was all about. But honestly and truly, I didn't care much about the school part, the three years in two.

Truth is I never wanted to work that hard.

See, I'd figured out if I got into the SP's I wouldn't have enough time to play basketball or read my library books, my two most favorite things in the whole wide world.

But I still wanted to make that class badly. Even more than badly, I wanted it desperately. I wanted it to happen for my parents, especially for my Mameh. It would be a great honor for the family and would also give her the right to hold her head sky high among her friends.

The SP mothers on our block all walked up and down the block like queens. They got special respect from all the other ladies. When they sat outside in front of the buildings in their metal folding chairs they were royalty. When the mothers gabbed about their kids, the SP parents' words on school were always the final ones.

Then there was also the never ending bragging about whose kid was going to be a big shot doctor or lawyer. Everyone knew SP kids were only a few steps away from success. I wanted my Mameh to be able to hold her head up among the highest. She needed to be up there as high as all of the ones who liked to look down on us "greenhorns."

Maybe they didn't know how much those names hurt! We didn't deserve them just because we were the newcomers to the block, the latecomers to America.

They laugh and call us "greenhorns"? Aren't we all Jews?

Mameh deserved this honor after everything she'd gone through. And if it was in my power, I wanted to get it for her.

I knew my grades were pretty good. And I knew why. It was only one thing. It was because I loved to read so much. In a lot of ways it was all I had. My teacher, Mrs. Stein had told my mother on Open School Night that I was far ahead of my class in my reading level, maybe even as much as three or four years. In fact, it was probably how I'd ruined my eyes. I loved to read so much I finished four or five books every week. Often, I read those books in poor light.

How was I supposed to know I was straining my eyes?

But I'm not sorry I hurt my eyes. I guess it was the books that helped me escape from my very small life and I needed that. Those books magically carried me all over the world and became as important to me as my best friends.

Before I met Willy, I had some good friends, but I never had a true best friend. My books were always my best friends. They made me feel special, important, and were never too busy to be with me. They let me dream about going to fantastic places and being somebody who mattered. We always mattered to each other.

Oh, how I loved my books!

But my math test scores were another story. They were just not as good as my reading ones. Don't get me wrong now they were good enough. But they were not years ahead of grade level. They weren't special grades. I knew I had to pick them up but now there was time for only this one last chance.

"I don't give a rat's ass about getting into the SP's," remarked Wilson casually at lunch later the same day.

"That's easy for you to say, man. You got grades, not me," I answered. "I need them! You know you're lying anyway. Getting into that SP class would make your mom really happy too. Don't give me that, 'She don't care BS! I ain't buying it."

"My mom says she's already proud of me, and that's twenty-four, seven, all the time, in school and out!" he insisted. "Besides she says I should take my time and make sure I learned everything the right way. She said I wasn't in any kinda' learnin' race, and that learnin' isn't a contest, and that college and everythin' else would still be there whenever I get to it."

Whoa, Trigger! That idea sure is something different! Lemme stop and think about that one. Whadda-you-mean it's not a race?

I asked myself that because the idea of taking your time to be thoughtful was so foreign to what we were all taught it actually shocked me into silence.

Work hard, be the best, graduate on time or faster, get to college, be a doctor, be a lawyer, be an engineer, get married, be successful and do it all as fast as you possibly can.

Yeah, for shit-sure it was a race, and the faster you ran it, the smarter you were!

Now Wilson's mom was saying it wasn't a race. That was an interesting idea from an interesting lady, but it couldn't be true. My Mameh always knew best.

"Besides," continued Wilson, "once you get out of college you have to work for real the rest of your life! That's a long time. So what's the big hurry?"

Willy's logic was powerful.

Maybe I have things wrong? But then again, Mameh was rarely wrong and everyone else in my class was trying his or her very best to get into this SP class. So just who was I to say anything different?

Switching subjects, I asked Wilson, "Going to the library after school today?"

"Yup," he answered. "I'm meeting TJ there and we're going to pick out another book to read. We just finished reading, "Man child in the Promised Land." And you know what? T.J. has gotten to be a much better reader, and, he's done it double-time quick. He's come a long way in a few months."

"Yeah, I saw that last weekend when he came over my house to work on my new Red Baron Fokker model. He read me all the directions for putting on the decals. You're right! He's gotten pretty good. How did he manage to get better so fast?"

Wilson looked up from the Superman doodle he'd been sketching on his brown paper bag and said, "You know, I didn't help all that much. What I did was I just kept reading out loud with him, you know, like taking turns and showing him little rules and stuff. We picked out a few books at the library my father suggested. Like this book by Claude Brown, Manchild in the Promised Land, it's really interesting to TJ. He says it reminds him of stuff going on around him. I mean, I started helping him with a few letter sounds and stuff, and boom, we were thirty pages into it before we even knew what happened."

"What's the book about?" I asked curiously.

"It's actually pretty cool. It's all about a Black kid growing up in a tough neighborhood like ours," he said with a twisted little smile.

"Sound like it could be good. Can I read with you guys at the library today?" I asked without even thinking.

Wilson hesitated for a moment. Then he continued on slowly, "You know, let me ask TJ first. I think right now he sees this reading time as kind of a 'me and him' special 'us' thing. Maybe he still needs that to feel better about himself. What do you think Train?"

"Yeah, sure, that's okay, I mean it's cool with me", I said feeling a little hurt. I mean the thought crossing my mind said something completely different.

You're supposed to be MY best friend, Willy!

A feeling of dejection sank through my mind.

"Okay then man, I'll see you tomorrow morning, right?" I continued lightly turning to walk towards my block instead of straight ahead to the library.

"You got it, hombre, tomorrow morning, as usual. Maybe I'll drop a dime on you later," sailed back through the air at me.

Then another thought invaded my mind.

Maybe this was the way TJ was feeling every day before he and Wilson mended their friendship? It doesn't feel good. In fact, I feel all messed up inside.

It was a long walk home.

Chapter Twenty-Eight

I keep getting these weird chills.

They were playing tag up and down my spine all the way to school today. The kids going down the street were just blabbering away. I guess they were excited by today's possibilities. I think, no, I know I was the exception. We're all of us in the "two" class, that's the second from the top best class. Mrs. Stein has told us that many times, and everyone knows we have a good chance to go to an SP class. Fact is, almost everyone in the "two" class every year usually gets into the SP class and we all know it. So today should really be more of a celebration than a contest.

So why then am I so nervous?

I know I don't have the super confidence in my own self so many of my classmates seem to have been born with, but, hey!

All I have to do is jump a little bit on my math grade and I know I'm in.

Walking down the street next to Wilson I could see he was his usual confident self. He was the only one out of a sidewalk full of kids who seemed to be totally cool with all the whispers and gossiping. That made me smile. Wilson was telling me about the latest Robert Heinlein sci-fi book he'd finished, *The Door In To Summer*. Mr. Cool was literally on a completely different planet than the rest of us. But that's why I like him. He's always himself, genuine real-deal Willy with absolutely no shame in his game. The book sounded great too. I made a mental note to take it out on my next trip to the library.

"Have you ever thought about traveling to other planets and dimensions Teddy?" Wilson asked me his eyes shining with a bright look.

Only every single day!

I was dying to say it out loud, but I held back the thought while we entered the silent schoolyard. The whistle had just been blown so now everyone was running quietly to his or her class line.

Okay, here we are lined up! So then, let's get this day started.

Forward marched the paired up straight lines right up the wide concrete steps into the old building. Then they stamped quickly up the metal switchbacks of stairs to the top floor. There was some familiar comfort from the overpowering smells of damp mopped floors and tomato soup. School was a second home to us all and that peculiar acrid smell from the cafeteria always announced that we'd arrived. Then it was a short walk down the hallway to the classroom door. Our two straight lines never wavered, one boy's and one girl's, until we arrived with a final step one, two at our classroom's door. There we'd waited patiently for the enter signal from our general, Mrs. Stein.

"I'd like all of you to put your things away in the clothing closet, and then sit quietly at your seat for some announcements before we begin our day," she ordered in her smooth confident teacher's voice.

But then before she could utter another word a sudden blare for attention came from the hallway's loudspeaker. The deep voice of our principal told us to stand quietly by our seats and recite along with him the Pledge of Allegiance. We all hurried to rise besides our seats, place our hands over our hearts and fervently promise, "With Liberty and Justice for all!" I especially liked that part because it reminded me of Wilson's favorite hero, Superman. He was always fighting for, "Truth Justice and the American way!" Superman was big, strong, fearless and American. Nobody could beat him, except Batman on a really good day, and we all wanted to be just like him. I was yanked out of my, "What if I could be Superman?" daydream by my teacher's continuing loud announcement.

"Well class, today is a big day for us! So we'll want to use our time as wisely as possible. Later today I will be giving you back your class folders, the ones containing all your work and tests. They're yours to keep forever! Please take them home to share with your parents at the end of the school day. I'll also be giving back to you the very last thing you'll be putting into them and that would be your final math test. I'm sure you all know your report cards are ready and that your very last chance to lift your math grade was that final test!"

"While we are on the subject of report cards, let me just say they will be given out on Monday, along with your next year's class assignment. That will happen no earlier than five minutes to twelve. Is that understood? Are there any questions about that?"

We all stared around and over our shoulders searching for anyone who had the nerve to ask a question.

"What, no questions?" the Mrs. Stein asked slyly. "Well then, folder monitors, please pass out the folders."

The large brown manila envelopes that held all our essays and tests were far too large to keep inside the small rectangular space inside our desks. Also, they were stored in the supply closets located in the back of our room. Whenever we needed them they were passed out by the teacher's chosen few pets. The pets were the same goody-two shoes monitors who were picked by Mrs. Stein for everything.

Boy, did I want to be one of those monitors who gave out those crappy folders!

There it sat on my desk finally in front of me. It was the giant envelope that held my "golden ticket" to the SP's. If my math test score were good enough, it would lift me to grand new heights in my Mameh's eyes. Sweat was beading on the back of my neck. I could barely sit still, but I worked to control my excitement. I quickly twirled the locking string in a counter clockwise direction, flipped open the cover and reached inside to pull out the paper clip bound pile of tests that would trumpet my future. My latest test should be the one on the very top.

Yes, here it is!

That's exactly when my mind went blank for I'm not sure how long. Maybe it was a few seconds, maybe a few minutes, I'm not sure.

I just don't damn know!

What I do know is I felt cold, very, very cold. I was an icicle from the hair on my head to the nails on the tips of my toes. I couldn't see too clearly either. My vision was blurred. It might have been from the surge of tears welling up in my eyes, or maybe it was the dizziness of the shock. That numbness came from what I was looking right at.

I'd gotten a grade of twenty-eight percent on my fraction-percent test.

How was this possible? How could this be? There had to be a mistake!

That thought thundered through my mind over and over again. I'd studied so hard. Plus, I knew I was ready. And I'd checked and rechecked my work over and over again too!

What had just happened to me?

Around me the air was bursting with busy, happy sounds. Kids were excited, laughing, waving their test papers and comparing their almost perfect or perfect grades. It could've been Santa's workshop with all the happy elves bouncing off the walls, windows and ceiling. But me, I was hunched over staring vacantly at that math paper that refused to change no matter how hard I wished it. There were no mixed emotions here either, only the one.

I hated myself.

I sat there alone with my stupid self, waiting impatiently for the gates of Hell to clang open wide and take me. Believe me, I was ready to go!

"What's shakin', Teddy bear? You're lookin' a little down over here, my brother," said Willy sliding into the empty seat in front of my desk. Turning around completely so as to face me, he asked, "So, what's good?"

"I, I don't know. I just don't know…"

That's about all that would come out. I guess I sounded like a broken 45, one with a tear starting to roll down its vinyl cheek.

"I mean, I studied so dam' hard for this! And I failed! I messed up this test so bad!" I sobbed into my arms crossed over on the desk.

Wilson stared down at me first with amazement and then at the crushed paper in my hand. He said nothing more. He slowly pulled the paper ball out of my hand.

"Lemme see that!" He whispered in my ear while smoothing out the crumpled paper on the wooden desk with the palm of his hand.

"Wait a good god-darned minute! Hold on! Lemme get my paper. I just need to check something out here! Don't move!"

Funny guy! How was I going to explain this mess-up to Mameh?

I'd wanted to give her some joy but instead here I was about to shame her.

Some "precious jewel" of a son I was.

"Like I thought!" Wilson said excitedly. "You did every single example exactly right, but you copied eight examples down with the wrong numbers! What's wrong with you?"

At first it made no sense.

Why was Willy yelling at me? That was cruel. I wouldn't do it to him if things were turned around.

I stared up at him as if he were a Martian in *The Red Planet*.

"So, I'm stupid. And you think that's funny...." I started.

"No fool, don't you see? It's that you CAN'T see! You're blind as a bat! Sorry, man, but it's true," he continued on patiently.

"We have to tell the teacher! She'll understand. You copied everything wrong from the board, but all your work is right! Come on man, let's go speak to her. Come on, get up!"

I couldn't speak.

Could it be? Would she give me another chance?

I felt a surge of hope deep down, but at the same time I was still very embarrassed.

How stupid could I be?

And suppose I did get up and go to her desk wouldn't everyone in the class stare? Then they'd laugh and call me blind man's butt. Willy's my friend and he just called me blind.

Maybe it'd just be better to sit here quietly and pretend nothing was wrong. I can do that easily. I'll just sit here with a fake smile on my face and pretend I am as happy as everyone else to get a great math mark. Then I can go home, shut the door of my room and cry into my covers so no one will hear my disappointment. But at least then nobody will know how I'd messed up.

Yeah, maybe that's what I'll do.

"Get up man! Get up, Teddy!" Willy hissed into my ear.

"Leave me alone Willy, just leave me alone. I'll talk to the teacher during lunch," I whispered back fiercely looking around desperately to see if anyone had heard us.

"I said I'll do it later man. You know for sure I will!" I finished weakly. "C'mon man, give me a break. Somebody's gonna hear you?"

"Teddy, man, cut the crap! You got to do it now. Get up man! Let's just go talk to the teacher. I'm telling you she'll understand! It'll be fine! She's a cool lady!"

"No, they'll all laugh at me! She will too!" finally burst out of my mouth as I stared shamefacedly down at the scarred wooden desk in front of me. I read the names that had been carved into the old wood as if that would make them appear to protect me from my friend's gaze. I mean I couldn't even look my best buddy in the eye.

Wilson moved a little bit closer and whispered in my ear. "What did you just say? Did you say what I think you said?"

I refused to answer. Finally, I turned my face away from him and stared blankly at the wall of wooden clothing closets.

"Yeah, I said it," he repeated, "and I'll say it again. YOU"RE DOING THAT SAME SHIT AGAIN!"

"Doing what, doing what again?" I spun around defensively and continued. "Whaddaya really know about me? You only think you know me. You don't know me!"

Unmoved Wilson just continued to toss his words in my face. "You're acting like you don't belong here again, like you're not good enough, like you deserve all the bad things that happen to you! Like somehow you've earned them and you've got to accept the punishment that goes with them. But that's not the real you man! I know the real you!"

Then in a flash it all zoomed back to me. "That day at your house, you told me I acted like a whipped puppy..."

Wilson looked straight in my eyes and continued, "The first time I saw you, you were getting your ass kicked, but you still tried to fight back. The same thing happened the second time when I saw you stand up to that ass wipe, Miles."

"You sure don't look like much and you can't fight for shit, but there's something real inside of you."

"And do you remember the day you jumped in when Big Steve had me? I knew right then you had heart man. I knew right then we were going to be friends because you cared."

"It ain't easy to fight your fears. Believe me, it ain't about the fightin' man, it's all about the livin'. I see what's inside you man! I know you! You want to see it all, do all kinds of stuff and enjoy it all. And Jesus help me please, so do I. That's what makes us the same, and that's why we're always gonna be tight!"

Wilson looked down at his hands on the desk after his speech and continued on in almost a whisper.

"Train, man, since we became friends, books, ball, school, food, everything's been better. Don't you go quittin' on me now!"

I was ashamed of myself. It was simple to see what was wrong. I keep looking at our friendship like it is always about me.

What was I getting out of it? What in it for me? How good did it make me feel? I never really thought that maybe it was just as important to Willy?

"So what you're tellin' me is I'm more than your little Jewish scrub. I'm more than just Tonto?"

"That's a whole 'nother thing I like about you, man, you're funny. You got jokes. So tell me Teddy Bear, whatch'you gonna do? You gonna talk to the teacher or you gonna go out like a punk? I know you think you're the smart guy, but y'see, that's part of your problem? Deep down inside you think you know it all. But, here it is, you can't see what's standin' there right in front of you."

"You know, no, I guess you don't know, lots of people 'round here like you, but you never give them a chance to get to know you. You're behind a wall on lock down, baby! But remember, man, when you lock people out, you lock yourself in."

"Teddy, bro', we're down, buddies, do or die. We share stuff, and buds are always there for each other. That's it. That's the end of my speech! That's all I got to say and that's all there is to it! Now, whatchyugonnado, brotha'?"

I felt tingly like someone dumped a pot of cold water over my stupid head. Sometimes you don't want to wake up even though you know you have to. My heart was echoing every single word Willy was saying. It swore it was so.

What was I thinking about?

I'd never, ever had a friend like him.

Why wasn't I listening with my heart and brains instead of hearing sounds with only my ears?

We might look different on the outside, but we were the same on the inside.

What a complete jerk I am. Here my man Wilson is looking out for me and all I can do is find weak little excuses to hide behind.

"Let's go see the teacher man. Thanks for the pick-me-up and that really long-assed speech!"

Willy flashed me a warm smile and a shrug, "What goes around, comes around, Train…"

Then he grabbed a handful of my shirt and gave me a little shove towards the front of the room.

"Just in case baby! Just in case!"

Head held straight up, test paper in hand, I walked up the aisle towards the teacher's desk.

Chapter Twenty-Nine

"Four Eyes!"

That's my new name. It's not so easy walking around with these coke bottle glasses sliding around on a big nose. It's expensive too. I busted one pair right away on Saturday, my very first day with them. I was dumb enough to wear them to shoot some hoops.

Did I realize I wasn't supposed to wear them to play ball? Nope, I thought my new and improved eyes would make me deadly from the outside. That part was a good idea, and it worked great in practice but one good crack in the head jumping for a rebound changed my mind.

Mameh wasn't as mad about that as I'd expected her to be. Luckily she'd bought me an extra pair when she got the first ones. It helped that the second pair was way cheaper because if you bought two…

Well, on the good side I can now see the blackboard a lot better. The eye doctor said I was, "myopic." I don't know why he was so surprised when I answered his question about, "Do you know what that means?"

After all he asked me didn't he?

I mean I'd read all about why people need glasses so I gave him a short explanation of nearsightedness. It wasn't any big deal but he sure thought it was. Like I said, I read a lot. Anyway, he said I need to wear my new glasses all the time, but I don't really think he meant to include shooting hoops.

His advice to always wear them doesn't make me happy. It means everyone who made fun of me before now has even more ammo. Thanks to my new brown horn rimmed glasses, I'm no longer just a Jew Boy, now I'm a blind four-eyed Jew boy. But again, honestly it doesn't bother me much. I see the whole thing more as a fair trade. On the good side I get to see a world that looks even more interesting than it did before. The bad side is that a few morons get to add some new ranks to the already long list they try to terrorize me with.

Fair is fair, I guess.

Today, Monday, on the way to our last day of school, Wilson showed me something way cool. He reached down into his pants pocket and pulled out a small hard leather case. When he opened it I had to laugh because he took out a pair of silver wire rimmed glasses. He slipped them on and asked me, "Whatcha think about these "specs"? Pretty cool, huh?"

I started laughing and followed up with, "Where'd you get those binoculars? Are you joining the bird watchers club after school today?"

Willy thought that one was pretty funny.

Wilson couldn't stop laughing either when he saw the two geeks looking back at us in the store windows.

Maybe seeing better was going to be tougher on our images than I thought. We did kind of look like two professors who'd escaped from the library.

"You know it's funny how stuff happens," began Willy. "I'm tellin' my mom about what happen'd in class with you Friday afternoon, you know about seeing the board and stuff, and she gives me the "look". Then she reminds me I've been complainin' about my eyes hurtin' a little bit when I get in after school. So she calls up your mom to ask her where you're going to get your eyes checked. Then next day she takes me down there and, bingo, here I am buddy, with you guessed it, reading glasses."

I was puzzled, "So then how come you're not pissed off about having to wear those things? I know I am!"

"Attitude my man, attitude, I mean, you know I'm lookin' fine with these spec's on. These here give me that worldly Mr. Peeper's look, you know polished, like I have "savoir flair, mon ami". Now the chicks will dig me even more than before."

Before I could jump in with a rank disputing that Wilson coolly went on, "Besides, like my mom says, I'm doing better in school now than I've ever done before. I even think I have a great shot at getting into that SP class with you. So, I figure why take any chances! If these specs can help me, I'm down with that!"

That thought brought me falling straight back down to planet Earth.

That's right, today is the day.

Yeah, the day we're going to be getting our report cards and our new classes, hopefully SP classes. The teacher's being super nice to me. And since I got my new glasses my answers this morning have been excellent.

I've gotten nothing but smiles from her. Can't I hope I'm going to make it? And why shouldn't I believe?

After all, I'm in a really good class, the "two" class where almost everyone goes on to the SP's.

Maybe, just maybe, the teacher knows how important it is for my Mameh to be able to hold her head up high?

"You'll see, Train," Wilson's voice brought me back to reality again. "We'll be together again next year, and we'll be kickin' butt there too! Superman and his dog, Krypto, leave Smallville. Your ass can be Krypto, he was white with a little black in him too!" Willy laughed. "Watch out world, we're a comin'!"

I couldn't twist my fingers into a Jewish star for luck so I crossed them and prayed for the best to happen.

Now it's a quarter to twelve and the tension in the classroom is thick enough to raise goose bumps. Mine were coming and going along with large drops of cold sweat running down my back! Up at her desk her head bent down writing something the teacher seemed to be calm, cool and collected.

Yeah sure, it's easy for her. She's getting left back for who knows, the umpteenth time. So, it figures she's used to it. It's her job.

Strangely enough the only other person in the room who seemed unfazed by the report card count down was Wilson.

He looked relaxed and strangely at ease.

Maybe he knows something? Nah, can't be, Wilson would have told me.

I slowly turned the idea over in my mind. He wasn't that good at keeping secrets.

Yeah, there he is, relaxed as can be. In fact, all morning long he'd been raising his hand to answer every question and then smiling at everyone just like he was running for mayor. You know the look the crooks have on their faces when they're running for office and the fix is in. Willy has it right now.

Finally, finally, it was time, 11:50 A.M.

The teacher rose from her desk. She began speaking in her best "teacherese" voice.

"I want everyone to know this was a truly grand year and you've been a truly great class. You've all worked very hard and deserve to have great success in your futures. I'd like to take a minute right now to make sure you understand an important idea about our learning process."

There was an audible group deep groan anticipating her next words of wisdom.

"Everyone's learning does not progress at the exact same pace. Everybody here is an excellent student and I'm sure you will all have tremendous academic successes in the future. That means each and every one of you. I believe in you all."

There was stunned disbelief and awe following that statement.

"And now when I call your name please come up to the desk and get your report card. I'm hoping you'll keep your excitement and your new class assignments to yourselves until after you are all outside the school building."

There wasn't even the sound of the smallest exhaled breath now. It was like we'd all sworn off breathing until we could get our turn to go up to the desk. And with that mystical silence Mrs. Stein began calling us up, one by one, in strict alphabetical order of course. As she handed each person a report card she also pointed to a place on a paper sitting on the desk in front of her. That place indicated their new class for next year.

It was about then that the tension translated into joyous excitement. This was, of course, only after each person's quick return to their seat from the front of the room. Time and again there was an excited yelp or happy sigh, or maybe only hands jumping over a mouth so as to not give away happiness from a hypnotized audience.

Honestly, I can't blame the winners for the excited jumps and screams. They'd earned them. I can't blame anyone for his or her success.

I just wanted to share the same feeling!

"I believe! I believe," I kept mumbled to myself in quiet prayer. If I could will this thing to be it was going to happen.

This is gonna happen for me, like it's happening for everybody else! I'll be good! I'll be better than good. Just let me have this one thing!

Now I was bargaining with God.

I'll be the best son, the best student ever! I'll even go to shul!

Chapter Thirty

Every single person who'd been called up so far, that's more than half the class, had returned to their seat with "the glow" surrounding them. It was kinda' like that circle of light, you know, like the halo you saw shining around the head of a saint in a religious picture had been transferred into our room. My classmates all seemed to have become, "blessed" up at the teacher's desk.

You know I wanted that feeling desperately.

Wilson's name was called and he, being the only black boy among us, got the immediate microscope treatment. But, as he strolled up there wasn't the slightest hint in his step of any pressure at all. Extremely calm, Willy walked slowly up to the teacher's desk. Without a blink of emotion other than a polite smile and the slightest up and down nod of his head to Mrs. Stein, he gave away nothing to the rest of the class. Then he walked calmly back to his seat without any clue dropped for the satisfaction of his puzzled classmates.

But I knew Wilson way too well by now to be fooled. The little things told the story. I could see my answer in the slightest tilt of his body as he moved. Even the swing of his arms told me everything I needed to know.

Holy Crap, he'd done it! I know he's made it. He's in the SP class!

Willy might be able to fool the others, but I could feel his confidence bubbling up and over his nonchalant attitude. He'd done it, and now he was enjoying holding it back from all the nosy bodies who were dying for a chance to look down on him. Wilson looked over at me and stared blankly, just stared me down, dead in the eye! Then very slowly, slowly he winked.

There, there it was! That was it! I knew it! I knew it! Willy was in the SP's!

It was at that exact moment I could tell for sure we were best friends. Because when I checked inside myself the only thing I could find was how happy I felt for him. Sure, I wanted the same thing badly for myself too, but that had nothing to do with Willy making it. My friend, Wilson, had gone and done it, and to me it felt better than hitting a jump shot to win a big game. Maybe something inside of me was saying that this would last a lot longer than a few minutes. In my heart I knew his mom, just like mine, wanted nothing but for him to do well in school. And here was Wilson moving on along with the sons and daughters of doctors and lawyers.

He'd captured the dream, my man, Wilson!

But my dream was still on hold. After what now seemed like forever my name was finally called. Honestly, I didn't even hear it. It was a surprise because I had lulled myself into a daydream where I ran home happily screaming and showing my Mameh the report card with SP boldly written on it in royal blue ink from out of the teacher's fancy fountain pen.

Mameh was so happy she cried!

A rough push from the boy who sat behind me woke me.

"Wake up, stoopid! The teacher's callin' you!"

Then I heard my name called a second time.

This is embarrassing.

I got up so quickly I ended up tripping when my foot got caught up in my own chair. After getting my balance back I looked around and realized only a few people were paying any attention to me. Most of the order in the classroom was long gone. All I could hear was loud excited voices and lots of noise. Everyone was up on their feet either packing their books or busy showing their report cards to each other, despite what the teacher had asked for.

"Oh no, I can't believe it! We're going to be in the same SP class together! We're going to be together again! Can you believe it? We've been in the same class from kindergarten! My mommy and daddy are going to be so happy. I have to call them as soon as I get outside! I'll call you later." And so on.

I approached the teacher's desk timidly and shyly raised my eyes to meet hers. In that instant I knew my dream wasn't going to be coming true today.

It was gone and I had failed.

She had a look of sadness mixed together with deep sympathy etched on her face, but hardest of all to bear was the pity. I could see the teacher was in a lot of pain from this also.

So I knew what I had to do.

I liked my teacher a lot, in a not so strange way I loved her. She was like my second, "Mameh", except only in school.

I was not exactly sure why but I knew I had to try and make this easier for her.

So I made myself smile while my eyes followed her pencil down to that new class designation. There was no SP written there. I kept smiling and even nodded obligingly at the right times to whatever nice things she was saying to me. It didn't matter what it was because I couldn't hear the words where I was hiding now.

Listen! Don't be impolite and embarrass anyone any further. Everything is bad enough just the way it is.

"I'm so sorry Teddy," I heard her murmur from what seemed like a great distance. "It's still a very good class. It's the best of all the regular classes on the next grade."

"Thank you m'am," I barely heard myself whisper in someone else's voice. Then I turned around quickly and went back to my desk. I was trying very hard to keep my head up and my eyes empty of the tears I could feel behind them. I didn't have Wilson's gift of coolness.

"Everyone line up! Time to go!" shouted our once never frazzled teacher. It was clear to everyone the year was over. The only thing left for her to do was manage the most peaceful exit from the building possible. Then the school term would be officially over and done with.

With my hastily assembled book bag in my arms I stumbled over to my size place at the very back of the line. My head was down, my eyes were wet, and I was completely unable to face anyone. The dull pain in my heart made me ignore everyone's questions about next year by turning my face when they asked. Suddenly they seemed to realize something was wrong. It was like my classmates realized I had a terrible disease.

Almost immediately a space opened up around me and I was an outsider. My year had ended with a whimper.

Chapter Thirty-One

"Class forward," called out the exasperated teacher from her doorway position at the head of line.

The two lines of excited boys and girls surged forward. Mrs. Stein made only the slightest token attempt to "shush" this year's group of "graduates." She knew it was an impossible task and it no longer matter at all. The year was over, dead and about to be buried, and everyone on that line knew it. Summer vacation, theirs and her own, would begin unofficially at 12 P.M. sharp.

So what if it starts a few minutes early with a noisy line-up. Who cares?

I knew those idle thoughts were probably doing laps in the teacher's brain.

But me, I was still rooted to the same spot I'd taken on the line. I had tried to make my legs move but they wouldn't.

Walk!

I ordered my feet to move in my head. But I couldn't help it. They refused to go. It was as if they had their own mind. There was absolutely nothing I could do then but try to fight back my burning tears. I stood there quietly alone now and sobbed to myself like a big baby. The salty drops overpowered my eyes so quickly I couldn't see anything but the vague outline of my Converse sneakers. They seemed so far away and lonely. Kind of like me feeling sorry for myself all alone now in this empty classroom.

I'd slowed down to just sniffling and wiping away the tracks of my tears. At last I felt like I was ready to try and take the long walk to the doorway when I felt a hand on my shoulder. I knew immediately it was Willy's. A hot flush swept over me. I knew I'd been standing there in one spot crying for a couple of minutes and that meant that Wilson must have witnessed my weakness through it all.

What a sissy he must think I am!

Sadly, and fearfully one other thought raced across my mind.

I've probably just lost my best friend.

But without a hint of judgment in his face, Wilson looked at me and said simply, "It's gonna be all right. Trust me, man. It's gonna work out fine."

I wasn't sure of what that meant, so I decided to just try and trust my heart. It was the only thing that had worked for me before.

If Willy really thinks it will be okay, maybe things aren't as bad as I thought. Maybe, what I really, truly need is to be more positive and trust the people who care about me?

That idea raced through my head as I sat my worthless fat behind down into the nearest empty desk's seat.

With a lump in my throat, I said a little too loudly, "Man! That one really hurt. But you know what? I didn't expect to see you here. Why did you stay? I figured you'd be long gone with all the others, you know with all the other winners."

"You didn't have to stay, Willy. You should be home telling your mom and dad the good news right now. So why don't you just go on and beat it!"

Ignoring everything that had just came out of my mouth, Wilson answered, "Train, man, I know this ain't easy. You're hurtin' deep inside. I could see it all from the second you went up to the desk. Don't you think we know each other a little bit by now? That look on your face, it was like she told you someone in your family died. The weirdest part of this is that the teacher looked almost as bad as you! She really likes you man. You could tell this whole thing really hurt her too, 'specially since you might be the smartest guy in the class 'cept, of course, for me! And yeah, let's not leave out whacky ol' Braverman. But then he's probably a geeky alien computer only disguised as a human kid anyhow. But then except for Brainiac Braverman you read more books and know more interesting stuff than any other dude in the whole class!"

"But I didn't make the SP's, Willy! You did, Braverman did, they all did, everybody did except me!" I yelped in frustration.

"Everyone is going on, but me! I'm the only dipshit who didn't make it! Hey, wait a minute, what about Big Steve? Don't tell me he made it too?"

"Where's my violin? Listen to you whine, y'big crybaby! Show me your broken leg? Where's the blood? Come on man, it's time to toughen up," teased my partner bringing his make believe baby face close to mine. "No, the sky isn't fallin' and Big Steve didn't make the SP's, big surprise right? But he's movin' on and he's happy!"

"Man, I can't believe you don't see the real big picture here. Let me spell it out for you because it's obvious you're not a very good at it. You not smellin' the roses here at all! You're special because you stupid, YOU are interesting! AND because YOU ARE SPECIAL, not because you're in a class that says you're special!"

"You, pardna', are legit, the real deal! You hear what I'm sayin? Some of these guys may be doctors and lawyers one day, but if they don't wake up out of their comas, they'll never be curious about anything besides the lint in their bellybuttons for their entire lives."

"Braverman is their hero and he'll probably end up being an assiologist, you know a butt hole doctor. What other career is a better fit for an A-hole?"

He had me laughing by then.

Wilson was too funny.

Here I was giggling at the hilarious picture of Mr. I-have-my-hand-up-so-please-call-on-me-to-answer-everything examining butts for a living.

"Spread wide and fart, please!"

Man, I hope I can be there for Wilson one day like he's being here for me today.

And I also added another heartfelt silent prayer that it would not be my butt that Braverman got to play with.

Chapter Thirty-Two

Just then Mrs. Stein walked back into the room and with only a glance at the two of us realized something was not right.

"Are you all right, Teddy? I wondered where you were? I wanted to pull you aside at dismissal and ask you to come back upstairs so we could discuss your situation. But when I looked for you, you were already gone. I was wondering where you were?"

"That's okay, teacher. Everything is all right, really it is," I said hurriedly scooping up my stuff and taking a quick step towards the door. "I have to be going now. My mother is waiting for me at home. Thank you for everything I learned. Wilson, you coming, or what?"

"Wait a minute man! Hold up a minute, Teddy!" shot back Wilson impatiently. Turning towards the teacher he asked, "S'cuse me teacher, I think my mom called you yesterday afternoon to ask you about somethin'?"

He looked at her hopefully. I didn't say anything. I was puzzled by the strangeness of the conversation.

What was up here?

"Well, yes, actually Wilson she did call me at home. We had a long talk," responded the teacher cautiously. "But are you sure that's what you and your family really want to do? Did you discuss this very carefully? After all, this is a decision that could make a big difference in your life. You know you're giving up something everyone else in the class is trying to get, don't you? Are you completely certain about this because there is no going back once it's done?"

"It's okay," replied Wilson easily. "I've talked it over and over with my mom, dad, uncle, brother and cousin. Everyone is fine with my decision. Actually, we're all one hundred percent with it! We think it's going to make a big difference in my life. I mean it already has!"

"What decision? What are you all fine with? What's going on with all this? Does this have anything to do with me?" I asked with my voice rising.

Yeah I could see it was about me. I could tell from the looks on their faces.

Mrs. Stein turned around to face me and then placed both of her hands on my shoulders. She looked first at Wilson, who was smiling happily, and then straight back into my eyes. Then she quietly said, "You know what you guys have is a very, very special gift. True friendship is a blessing and you need to try to treasure it!"

"But now, to the business at hand. Teddy, Wilson, with the approval of his family, has asked me to have his class changed from the SP's to the same one as yours. As I said before to you, that class is the best class on the next grade in your new school!"

I guess I must have looked pretty stupid with my jaw hanging down against my chest. It took a moment for the facts to sink in. Then I exploded at Willy.

"You can't do that! That's crazy and stupid! I won't let you do it!" I sputtered angrily thinking of the sacrifice Willy would be making for me. "That class is way too important! Are you nuts or something? No way! No way you're doin' anything that dumb! Case closed!"

"It's done, Teddy, right teacher? Tell motor mouth over here the facts of life," he said looking me in the eye while tossing a confident glance towards our Mrs. Stein.

The teacher shrugged her shoulders and nodded it was so.

I can't let Wilson do this. My problem is my problem, and I can't let him make this kind of a sacrifice for me.

"But that's everything you worked so hard for all year. What about your mom?" I threw out desperately playing my last big card. "She'll be totally pissed-off! And, she'll bust your ass!" I blurted out unthinkingly.

Wilson walked over to where I'd sat down again and said, "Move your big heinie over so somebody else can sit down too."

"Now, try to listen carefully. Try wrapping your big, "I Know It All," brain around this. You're confusin' what YOU worked so hard all year for with what it is I want. Let me tell you what I want and we'll see how different it is from what you want."

"See, I just want to learn about stuff that's interesting to me and maybe find out what I want to do with my life, and, oh yeah, please, also stay out of trouble in school."

"When I first talked to my mom about all this she said, "You know Sweetie, this is the best year you've ever had in school. You've learned the most, gotten the best grades and, also pretty important too, fought the least! It's been the happiest year ever for you. Now baby, why do you think that is?"

"Now you tell me Mr. Smart Ass, why do you think that is, Train?"

I was arguing with a lunatic. That much was clear to me!

Wilson was totally confused. Even more upset by what was going on I asked him, "Did someone hit you in the head with a brick? What's wrong with you? This ain't a game we're playing here. This is the real thing, your real life. It's the SP's we're talking about here! It's not about feeling good or bad for me."

"Just take it! Opportunities like this are once in a lifetime! Why is it so important to be in a regular class with me? We can still be friends, I promise! What else can I say? We'll just meet after school, like we do now." I finished up lamely.

Willy stared at me for a long few seconds and then said with a disgusted shrug of his shoulders, "You still don't get it, do you, man? It's you and me together that makes it work, chump! It's US! It's our friendship that's made the difference for BOTH OF US! WE BOTH NEED EACH OTHER, at least for right now we sure do!"

"Wake your silly ass up and smell the gunpowder! Don't you see the reason you're not happy a lot of the time is because you feel like you don't belong anywhere? Same exact thing is true for me too. Don't you feel it? Don't you understand the truth? Can't you see when we're hanging out together our friendship is a perfect fit! And when we're happy we can handle the whole wide world! Why do you want to mess that up, YOU DUMB SCHMUCK?"

Then he continued, "Why would I want to be unhappy all by myself again next year, even if it's in the SP's? Think about it, if things were turned around, and it was your choice, what would you do?" Wilson said ending his speech in a question.

I thought about it for a moment. I mean I reached right down into that deepest dark place where I could feel the little kid in me who was always afraid hiding out. When he looked back at me he made me shake like a leaf, but still I had to ask him what to do.

"Willy, I don't know if I could do the same thing for you that you're doing for me. I mean, giving up that SP spot. I don't think I could do it," I found myself saying almost as if I were a ghost standing next to myself, listening. I stood there failing my friend.

Suddenly, the teacher interrupted, "Well then Teddy, do you want Wilson's placement? You're next on the list and there seems to be a newly available opening. You're next now if you want to be in the SP class. What is it going to be Teddy? Do you want Willy's seat? You have to tell me right now so I can go down to the office and do the paperwork."

I looked down at the laces of my "Cons." I was so ashamed of the thoughts running through my mind that I had to hide my face. In the darkness created by my fingers I could see my Mameh's face in front of me so clearly. She was smiling proudly at me.

"Mameh, what should I do?" I asked her already sure of her answer.

When I finally looked up, I could see Willy smiling at me.

"Hell no, teacher! You can keep it!" I burst out my pulse pounding in my ears. "Mrs. Stein, I just figured out that I'm just exactly where I want to be right now, and thank you very much for helping me to see that!"

I continued hurriedly scooping up my book bag. Mrs. Stein smiled and gave me a tired nod.

"I had a feeling about how it would work out for you two. Bye boys, and have a great summer," was her final words of advice.

When I turned around it was to find Willy waiting in the doorway half bent over holding on to his stomach. He just couldn't stop laughing at me.

"What's the damned joke, Mr. Funnyman?" I demanded throwing a short jab that caught him flush on his shoulder.

Falling back a step he grabbed his shoulder in mock pain, and croaked, "It's just, it's just, it's just that we all knew you couldn't do it! We all knew you couldn't take my spot!"

Mystified, I warily asked, "Just who's the, "We" you're talking about?"

"Who do you think "we" is, smartass? It's my mom and your "Mameh". Howdya like those apples son?" he said while snake-quickly administering a painful right cross to my left shoulder. I was so surprised to have been so completely played like a piano that I barely felt the shot.

My surprise also helped to let Wilson get off to a good head-start running down the hall towards the "down" staircase. But before he disappeared through the door to the staircase, he leaned his head back around the corner and called out to me.

"C'mon, A Train! Race is to my house. My mom baked sponge cake, yeah, your mom's recipe! Last one to the kitchen is a stone schlemiel!"

"Oh yeah, first one there is a bigger… a bigger shlemozel!" I countered weakly.

Then I ran as fast as my two feet could carry me to catch up to my friend.

Epilogue

There hasn't been much time yet to miss Wilson. He just left yesterday for his mom's and uncle's hometown, a place called Leeds in Alabama. He's gonna be spending the summer there with his grandparents. I guess I'm kind of jealous about that, maybe it's because I've never had any grandparents, uncles, aunts or even cousins. The concentration camps took care of all that.

We still had a pretty great last day together doing all kinds of stuff. Actually we spent most of it at the library picking out summer reading books. The library is pretty cool about that. They let you borrow ten books at a time and then stamp them for eight weeks so if you're going away on vacation you can take them with you. Wilson and I both decided to take out some of the same books, like Isaac Asimov's "Foundation and Empire" and "Second Foundation." Those books look fantastic. We both loved his first book, "Foundation" and reading the next two over the summer will give us something great to share when we get back together.

I'm hoping the time passes quickly. It's sounds crazy to wish it was time to go back to school, but we're both looking forward to a new school and new stuff to do. Later in the afternoon we went back to Wilson's house, listened to music and ate, you guessed it, fresh baked sponge cake and, of course, fresh baked chocolate chip cookies.

Meanwhile, today I'm still situated right here in the Bronx. Right now, as usual, I'm out of breath from running the three long blocks to the basketball courts at Taft. I'm here right now leaning up against the heavy wire fence looking in. That's right! Here's exactly where I was headed when this story began. It's a strange thing but I love this schoolyard. I can't forget about the library either. These are the two special places in my life that I care about more than any other ones on the whole planet.

You askin' me why?

It's because shooting hoops and reading books are the two things that make me feel free. Inside both these places, the schoolyard and the PL, I feel equal to everyone else. When I'm there I'm a real American because in there everyone is treated the same. I love them both.

From the schoolyard gate to the courts it's so far that it's still almost impossible for me to make out faces clearly, all I can see is that all of the guys shooting around on the far court are Black. I'm thinking one of the big guys with his back turned towards me could be TJ, but I'm not sure.

Besides, I thought he was supposed to be going down south with Willy?

So it's probably not him. But now it's time for me to choose again. I can still turn around and go home.

That is if that's what I want to do.

Even after everything that's happened that would still probably be Mameh's advice.

Don't take chances, be careful, be safe, stay away from strangers, and go home!

I can hear her voice in my brain speaking out loud to me. And you know, I can't really blame her for that advice, even after everything that's happened. In her mind she's only trying to protect me, and that's what she's always going to do.

Or I can step through this open gate to the schoolyard and take my chances. Either way I'll get to play or get shafted. But to tell the truth, honestly, it's not really a choice for me because I want to play.

"Next!" I call out trying to look as cool as possible while jogging slowly across the blacktopped field towards the courts. All of the shooters spread around the basket's foul line turn to see who the sixth man is gong to be. That's the guy they need to complete the two three-on-three teams.

As usual I see some eyes rolling in dark faces I've never seen before. I know now I might need to brace myself for some of the usual put-downs, "White boy, Grey boy, Jew Boy, this boy, that boy, yada, yada, yada," and so on. That just comes with the territory. But one thing I've learned is you can't get too excited about every single thing you hear.

Not if you want to play ball in the BX!

You've got to develop some thicker skin, or you're

gonna spend all your time nursin' those hurt feelin's.

Suddenly I hear something called out that thrills the mess out of me.

"Yeah, bo'! I got m'man, Teddy down with me! That's right, A-Trains on my side! We got our three, y'all. Our squad got the rock out behind the line, baby! C'mon A, let's show these country boys what's up in the big bad B-X, right baby?"

TJ slaps me five, and bounce passes the ball casually behind his back to me to start the game up. I take the ball, grip it tight between my two hands, bend my knees and hold it for an instant feeling the seams speak to my fingertips. A quick inside pass to TJ and a slight head fake to the left throws my defensive man off balance. His feet cross as he tries to recover from his too wide defensive stance. I make a sharp cut the opposite way to the right sliding quickly towards the basket. TJ ball fakes a shot up and then drops another perfect bounce pass to the spot where I'm gonna be in a split second. I catch the ball stretched out in full stride pushing off my left foot and stretching my right arm out as far as it allows me to. The ball kisses off the backboard and falls sweetly through the hoop.

"Yup, yup, yup, that's what I'm talkin' bout! Way t'get t' th' rack, Train," calls TJ slippin' me a pound.

"Way to move the rock, T."

We played on until the streetlights were shining their strange messages against the empty walls of the schoolyard. With one last farewell between the players we all headed for home.

Yeah, I guess today was a pretty decent day in the B-X. Now just how would Stan put it down?

Lil' man, we solid? We tight? We good?

Yeah, Stan, Willy, TJ, we are good!

We all good, in fac' t'day it's all exactly one hundred!

"Yo! Yo! My man, you got next? Can we get down next w'ich you?"

Yeah, f'sure, t'day it's all good in the B-X!

The author, Ted Mieszczanski is still a retired New York City public school teacher.

Acknowledgments

The author would like to again thank the NYC Public Library for giving a poor refugee kid the keys to his kingdom, his imagination. Oh, and a second big "shout out!" to the Bronx UFT's Si Beagle Retired Teacher's Center's Writing Class, led by Ms. Carmen Mason. I'm honored that you all listened!
Carmen, congratulations on getting better!
Kudos also to the Kingsbridge Library Writers' Group for their unflinching support. Thank you all!
Ron Trenkler, a special, "Thank you" for sharing your skills.
Thank you, Ms. Joyce Hansen for the encouragement and advice. I look forward to your next book! I'm sure it is worth the wait!
Thank you Liz and Hector for the unflinching support!
Thank you Miss Charlotte, Miss Constance, Miss Marilyn, Paula, Lucy, Dianne and especially, Henry T. and Terry for your friendship and support in my growth as a writer.
Thank you Miss Eleanor S. for your beautiful inspirational cards. It is only possible with the help of a village.
Thank you Vilma, Joe, Kacie, Brian, Judy, John, Margaret and your sweet departed moms for letting me be part of your family.
Thank you Linda, Larry, Beverly, and Curtis for another wonderful summer of friendship. Thanks for listening to another season's ramblings. Once again, they became this book.

What could be better then another summer and another book? And thank you, Martha's Vineyard, our special home away from home. I'm sure there are many others that feel that same way. But I must say, we, all of us, love you!
And once again another shout out to my other support group, the ROMEOs*, Lew, Rob and Joe, see you guys Thursday!

* Retire Old Men Eating Out.